The Majestic Columbia River Gorge

The Drums of War

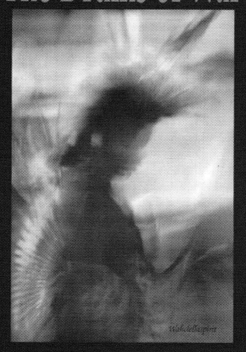

Wah-della-spirit

Volume III

A Journey Treasured Throughout Time

A Cooley Cultus Potlatch Kopa Hyas Ahnkuttie

The Majestic Columbia River Gorge

The Drums of War

Volume III

A Fictional Writing and Photographic Guide Through the Valley of the Eagle and Into the Lands of Wah Within the Columbia River Gorge In Oregon and Washington

Author and Photographer
Wahclellaspirit

To order additional copies of this book, contact:
Xlibris
1-888-795-4274
www.Xlibris.com
Orders@Xlibris.com
764015

Table of Contents

Steven Warnstaff

Preface

The Drums of War

Change has begun to enter into the lives of many of our people. From the villages of the Haida and Makah of the north, to those of the Nez Perce, the Klickitat, Yakima, Shoshone, Paiute, Walla Walla, Umatilla, and to all those whom prosper beside the waters of En che Wauna and along the long beaches of the sea belonging to the Chinook Nation, we are all now beginning to question why many Suyapee come and do not return to their villages?

Suyapee has come to stand before us from great ships and tell they have journeyed many suns from where he first rises above these lands.

Today, they offer trade for the warm furs of (Eena), Beaver, and (Nawamucks), Sea Otter to many of the villages of our great Nation, and trade is good between us.

There is much wealth collected by the chiefs of many villages who sit near where the big ships wait for their shelves to become full with furs.

Now, as we have taken many Eena and Otter from the rivers and streams, those spirits we have listened to their needs have become fewer and many of the lakes have begun to turn to meadow as we have taken much more of the Eena than what we had first been told to choose under the authority of our Hyas Tahmahnawis.

Sadly, there are few remaining of the Eena's lodges where today we can sit and learn of them as they take sticks from the forest's edge to build their villages.

Much complaint is heard spoken by the High Spirit as he demands answer for what we have chosen to take from his lands without first giving thought to what may not return upon the lands of Wah. As he looks out beside Naha over the creation they have both honored our people from the peak of Walowahoof, they are saddened by the greed we have now allowed to enter our hearts.

Those animals who had once walked the same trails, and those whom have swam in the same waters as we, for those that have survived our traps, they have now left the lands beside those of En che Wauna and journeyed to the kingdoms of Wy-East, Pahto, and Lawala Clough where we cannot share in their toils.

The Good Spirits had first brought prosperity to fill our lives each season. But today, we are fearful we have become like Suyapee as we remember we had once honored all the land's spirits with our hearts and felt their gift before us with our souls before we made decision to take their spirits from upon the Illahee, (Earth).

We have forgotten the High Spirit has given each of the kingdom's animals and birds air to breath and feather and legs to live upon his lands, just as he has honored our peoples with feet to walk as we journey across all his kingdoms.

We have heard Hyas Tahmahnawis become angered through the great storms that have fallen across the lands from the heavens. We have allowed the greed of our own spirit to be freed from our souls to fall upon those gifts he has placed upon his lands.

We have not only failed our Hyas Tahmahnawis, we too have failed our own people.

Now we have left little that will bring warmth to our souls and bring smiles upon our faces as we walk lonely upon the trails of our fathers.

Dark clouds have begun to drop upon us from the heaven as storm comes upon us with great vengeance. We are soon to stand alone as our souls freeze beneath the great snows of many winter's storm.

When the big ships come to our lands, those that choose to sit in council with our peoples speak with their eyes as they are drawn to study the (Chak Chak) Eagle and (Moolack) Elk, the (Pish), fish, and (Ehkolie), whale, whose spirits are alive within us as we honor their spirits upon the face of our canoes. These spirits who we honor are too painted upon the cliffs along the shore of En che Wauna where they cannot be seen as they watch over those that come upon us with question.

Upon totems carved from Red Cedar of the Hyas Eagle, the Raven, White Bear, and the Whale can be seen in the villages of our brother of the north. Suyapee asks to make trade for these when there are few furs to take back to their villages, and it is then I have become promised to believe Suyapee will not stop taking from our lands what has brought us great honor before those others who come to sit and smoke from the long pipe that offers only peace between our peoples.

Soon, Indian and Suyapee's purses will lie bare from the gifts we had once been chosen to reach from the lands of our Creator.

Suyapee offers clothes to our peoples like those worn of the men who come with the big ships. They wish to make our peoples believe we all are brothers upon these lands as we both follow the lead of the same Hyas Tahmanawis Tyee in the sky of our heaven.

Suyapee bring buttons of many colors and beads of many sizes. Our women weave them both together to make necklaces proving of their village's great wealth before those others they share potlatch.

Suyapee have brought copper kettles to warm our water and they bring the musket and powder so we can hunt without first hearing the voice of those spirits we take from upon the lands of our villages.

We have learned of knives made from metal, and Suyapee offers stone that makes sharp edge upon the blade of the long knives so we may take from the Eena their warm coats.

As we have made trade for many seasons without thought of our tomorrows, I have stood before my brothers and have asked them to answer only to themselves; "Why do you need more than what Hyas Tahmahnawis has first given our peoples as we have lived for many seasons with less?"

As the new seasons come and the snows of winter fall upon us, we see there are many new boats that bring Suyapee to look upon our lands with keen eyes.

When I have sat at the village at Knope and watched our people offer the Hyas Eena to trade for the musket and powder, I have become concerned. I have begun to fear Suyapee will quickly number as many as the sticks of our forests and our lands will be no more as they have been for all days.

Those captains that come to our lands in ships are called Gray and Skellie, Meship, Mackey and Balch. Our favorite that brings many gifts is called Haley. There are many captains that promise to return in the new season. It is told, as each new moon arrives above us, waiting along the shores of the Great Waters, many tall ships wait to sit along En che Wauna to be filled with the warm furs.

These tall ships come from lands named Spain and Russia, and others speak of England and France, and now, there are many that come from America who they tell is now called; "All Our Great Nation."

Without first thought of our peoples, Suyapee are able take from us whatever they wish as we become blinded by their trick, as does Great Coyote upon those she wishes to pry from their souls their spirit that offers them hope throughout the days of their lives.

There are those Suyapee that come only to hunt elk to feed their peoples. Others come to take from the great forests tall sticks where large skins blow in wind upon the long sticks raised upon their ships.

What brings worry to my heart are those that come upon us with wide eyes and choose to journey far into our lands and see and hear nothing of our people's ways. Those people who hide within their souls, those who go out and search the lands without telling what they seek, we must walk amongst them with watchful eyes.

Many seasons past, before my grandfather stood as chief to our village, grave warning was first shared by many shamons who had visions of people from distant lands coming to the kingdoms of our people. Much that they had seen offered only the gravest of concern and frightened them greatly as they peered into our tomorrows through the looking glass as they had seen what those tomorrows would be promised to bring before our peoples and to all the kingdoms of our peoples.

There were visions of our peoples ravaged by disease as many ships came to the shores of the Big Water. Today, our visionaries speak they see only death and disease spread upon us from the purse of Suyapee as they march upon us and cross our lands with the greatest of hurry.

It was seen in the dreams of the Great Medicine Men that many villages would soon lie emptied as our brothers, our sisters, and many of their children, would be seen lain lifeless upon the banks of En che Wauna.

Many more of our people that live upon the shores of the rivers that go where they meet the Big Waters as Sun rests at night would too prove it is by Suyapee's disease they shall perish.

Slowly, those of our people who will lay wasted by disease will be taken from their spirits and will lie forever silenced to their pleading for forgiveness upon Wind's travels without hope of one day sitting beside the chairs of their fathers in the great village of our heaven.

There will be no one left to raise them from upon the mat. Now, they will lie dead for all days and shall not be offered to their father's keep upon the Big Island.

The same islands of En che Wauna where their spirits can be chosen to ride upon the (Tkope Kuitans), White Stallions that cross our heaven at night when their spirits go to their fathers and sit with them before the eternal fires of Heaven's village.

Many days have passed since we had journeyed to stand before Suyapee at Knope and speak of trade. Many braves of villages we are surrounded have gathered before the warmth of our fires.

From the long prairie word is brought to our potlatch by a
messenger of the Nez Perce that has heard story coming from a
village of the Black feet that strange men have begun to make the
long journey across Indian lands. They were last seen to walk
from the villages of the Mandan many days ago and now they
come across the long prairies and will soon touch the high peaks,
far from where is told their own villages stand.

It is told a man named Lewis, who sits at the right of Clark had
asked question of each stream and to each river that would lead
them to the big waters where Sun rests each night.

Word has begun to spread amongst all the villages of the north,
message of men they have called Lewis and Clark, and those
of their army who follow them. They now have passed beyond
the lands of the high plains from the shores of Big River, the
Missouri.

It has been spoken they have been seen to take the bird, the furs
of many Coyote, Antelope, and from the Golden Bear. They place
into their purse many roots, and the tall grass that has always
swept free in the breaths of Wind upon the long prairie. What
they have taken from the lands of our spirits they hide from our
eyes as they know it is not good to steal from the purse of the
Great Creator.

We sit and listen to the message that comes before us this night,
the message bears warning of what is soon to appear as Sun
rises. We now see through all the visions that have come to our
fathers and to their fathers before them, there will be many men
we will not know of their spirits or of their souls who will march
hurriedly into our lands.

These men will come from lands beyond where the buffalo run
free upon the great plains where grass grows tall like tree. They

have told others of our nations they have begun to make journey to search for the Big Waters like those of En che Wauna that will lead them to stand upon the shores at Knope.

It is told they wish to reach the sands of our shores, where our kingdoms were first bore from the Big Waters, and there, they hope to look out over the villages of the Ehkolie and see a great ship that will come to return them before the chair of their Chief.

It is said they will return to their villages and sit at the foot of who they say is all our Big Chief in Washington, and they will speak to their people of our lands, and of our peoples.

As message of this comes from the villages of the Black feet, we sit with wide eyes to what we hear is soon to approach.

We now see through the visions shared from our fathers our lives may soon be placed in great jeopardy.

Our worry is now cast out upon our peoples we will quickly become surrounded and we will not know of the truth to those spirits Suyapee may hide.

We know through our father's visions those we have been told who will sit before us will not know of the gift of being honored to walk the same trails and breathe the same air as those of our people's spirits.

It has been told by our fathers we must not fear those who are promised to walk from us and not choose to know the good spirit of our peoples, but we must be alerted to the change they will bring upon us.

Our fathers tell through their vision they will not choose to hear our voice!

I question if my peoples will then choose not to share our fires, or not welcome those who will come with opened arms to make trade?

As I close my eyes to the coming storm that cries of Red Cloud, from within the purse of the bad spirit, I hear the moans of our brothers and sisters souls as they become attached to their endless journeys upon the breaths of Wind and spread word of what has been seen to soon approach our peoples.

Our brother's cries for help fall heavily before our feet with much warning for what they have witnessed, and it is not good.

Their hearts lie anxious for their tomorrows, and as quiet comes again through the long arms of the sticks of our forests, their cries will soon fall silent for all days.

As we walk upon those trails where we have followed our father's lead for many seasons, those voices of our brothers whom are lost to us shall be turned towards us in great mourning. Their wails will rise up to the heaven and touch the feet of our Hyas Tumtum from the closed ties that bind them within the bad spirit's purse.

Their cries shall share warning to the most courageous of our people's braves as many of our warriors will then take up their bows, and carry with them their truest arrows to pierce the hearts of those that come in much hurry and do not choose to understand the value of our principles.

We, Indian, are too honored to prosper upon the lands of the High Spirits kingdoms as we whom have stood before the Wall at Wahclella bring understanding to the needs of the lands and to the life that shares the air we each breath.

We honor always each day as Sun rises and Moon falls from the heavens.

Through the lessons of all our fathers whom we have followed for many seasons, we have heard the wisdom of our Hyas Tumtum as he has spoken of compassion and of preserving the gifts we have been honored to share upon these lands from upon the Great Wall at Wahclella.

Through the words spoken by all our father's who stand strong upon the Walls of Wahclella, our peoples have prospered and have been offered much as we have chosen to sit and learn of our great leader's understanding to the relevance of living with respect and in tolerance for each species upon this (Illahee), Earth.

I ask; "When we walk through the Valley of the Eagle, as we look up towards the long arms of the tallest firs, can we not hear the Hyas Chakchak cry out with happiness as we both share of these lands with others that come to gather beside each of our kind?

"When we journey to stand beneath the calling of Elowah, or from beside the banks of Great Multnomah from where the daughter of the Great Chief had mercifully offered her life to save her peoples, I ask you all, can we not hear of their kind words even though they have suffered much?

"Can we not understand or accept the wisdom they have come to inherit that has made them honorable for many more seasons beyond those our names will be heard called out by others?"

"I ask Father, must I believe the visions we have now begun to see before us from behind the forewarning of Red Cloud that offers only favor in bringing despair before the doors of our *lodges, are these the same visions once spoken by your father and his father before him?*

I ask; "Through the hearts of Suyapee shall all our days rise in the darkness and unknowing of tomorrow through the bad spirit's most heedless dance?"

I too must think these peoples will never hear of our own people's story after we have journeyed far from where our villages had once stood.

Stories of our peoples have always rose up to meet the purest of clouds in the heaven as they have been spoken as truths from our hearts to those that have come in peace to our villages.

Stories that have promised to keep both our hearts and our minds pure before the eyes of the Great Creator.

Stories that offer integrity to who we are and give answer to the questions of why we were first led and chosen to live upon these Majestic Lands of Wah.

We have told this land is a land where Pish leap pleasingly into our nets as they too give us purpose for our commitment before the High Spirit to honor both the land and life that runs and swims free within it.

We have told many others who have sat before our fires; "This is a generous land that brings all our peoples together as we must honor the spirits that bring Pish to return before us each season as they offer their own souls before our tables so we may live in each of our tomorrows."

We tell them these lands are lands where elk and deer lie down before us and accept the sacrifice of their souls so we may survive the long winters that come upon us without warning.

We must ask; "Why do these peoples wish to take from within their hearts what leads their souls upon us with the gravest promise of error?"

"Do they not see with their eyes and feel with their hearts?"

"Will they not know the lands were first formed by the Hyas Tumtum for all our peoples to live and to prosper as one peoples to this earth?"

"We each must remember we must hunt and fish to survive.

"We are no different than one another. We walk the same trails, we see the same mountains, and we breathe the same air. Does this not make both our peoples coming from the same Good Spirit?"

"Father, do we not all wish to lie upon our mats each night at rest without worry or complaint from the other?"

I find my heart sullen as I am forced to ask questions before the chair of our Great Father.

"My Hyas Tahmahnawis, where will we go to hide and escape the long arms of those that wish to take us from our lands, and why are we to be taken from all that you have offered our peoples from the beginning when you had first led our peoples to live and prosper upon these lands?"

I too must ask; "Why must our peoples suffer before the feet of others when it is our people that have first stepped upon these lands and have proven of our worthiness before the High Spirit and to the preservation of all the Great Creator has given our peoples?"

I too ask; "Have we not offered Suyapee food from our tables and mats with which to sleep within the warmth and safety of our lodge?"

"My Father, have we not walked amongst the spirits of our lands and accepted the lessons they have willed upon our peoples so we too may better understand all that it is to live beneath the promise of the heaven's sky, and from beneath the waters of En che Wauna where comes Pish each season to feed the many?"

"My Father, we do not understand why we will be forced to walk from the lands we were first bore?

"I ask you, have we not labored for many seasons, and have we not been welcomed into your opened arms from the beginning of our promise before your commands?

"Father, this kingdom is all we know as it is here where our greatest shamons had first heard you call out their names as they followed the trails you had led them and our peoples for many seasons before they first rested beneath Che che Optin and to these Lands of Wah."

"My Father, I plead with you. Take from upon our lives the Red Cloud that is soon to begin swarming like bees from the hive upon our lands with pestilence and disease. Protect our people with the kindness and warmth of your soul.

"Father, only then may we once again walk with great vision amongst the shadows of our lands without turning in fear to question what is to follow in our footprints."

Sun and Moon has not been seen to rise and fall for many days, and as I sit here this night, beneath where the fires that never dim now lie darkened before my eyes high up upon the big meadow,

I have not heard the howl of Great Coyote call out from the meadows or from the peaks of our mountains.

From distant hills we once could hear chorus of Coyote's song, but as the fires of our fathers are not seen through the cover of cloud that brings darkness to the heaven, with much sadness, tonight only rises in the memory of Coyote's songs upon the passing of Wind's trails across all the lands.

Wind too has begun to change before us as it howls with great force through the sticks of our forests. As it travels swiftly along the shores of our rivers and passes across our lands, the cries of all our peoples that have yet taken of the Journey of the Living Dead can be heard mourning in great despair knowing their souls will one day soon fall lonely upon lost trails.

With much sadness, I know they shall not be ready for their final journey to kneel before the chair of the High Spirit, and they will not find rest at the sides of their fathers.

Even though the threat of Red Cloud nears our peoples from each corner of our kingdom, we must choose to hold strong to our faith that change will too be placed within Suyapee's souls.

Our prayers cry out that Suyapee and Indian will walk as one upon the soils of all our kingdoms in peace and in the understanding that life is only a gift we each must cherish. We must each believe all life is to be honored so our children will too stand upon the shores of En che Wauna and watch pish come to their nets.

"Hear me Father, hear my prayer!"

There have been many nights where I have sat alone in our village as my thoughts welcomed all the good spirits to invest their souls within my own.

I have been honored to have seen (Hyas Talupus), Great Coyote once walk out from within the heart of Great Cedar's brother.

As my brothers and I sit this night before the warmth of the great fire, and as we look to the heaven for word from our fathers, Coyote again appears before our circle as she walks in amongst where our thoughts are joined.

My peoples do not see Coyote.

She walks silently, circling where we each sit.

Coyote looks deep into each of our eyes as she lays challenge within our souls to be witness if our spirits are good and will all days walk upon the trails our fathers have chosen for us to follow.

It has been told for many seasons as our fathers have sat beside the fires of heaven, Coyote searches for those whose spirits are weak to take them from those of who's spirits are strong.

From the weak, she steals what is left of their spirit from within their souls.

They were not promised by the Hyas Tahmahnawis to see the light of tomorrow through visions that brings hope from faith.

It is the darkness of night their eyes will only see as the light of tomorrow will not be granted before their vision to what tomorrow's days have been promised.

Otelagh's smile is lost deep within their souls in each of the dawns of all their tomorrows, and they will spend their lives walking upon the lonely trails my father had not long ago spoken that has neither good beginnings nor better endings.

As Coyote walks amongst us, and as she steps before those she is soon to take, we hear the weeping of many of our brother's souls coming from deep within Coyote's belly.

Suddenly, Coyote cries out with much mourning as she raises her head towards Moon, and from her heart, she passes the spirit of one of our people who she has stolen from the purse of Tsiatko from within her belly. Upon the side of the trail it comes as stone to offer our peoples and to Coyote protection from what may wait to pounce upon us from the evil darkness yields.

It is there, where she stands alone, unseen, where the mystic spirit of our kingdoms casts spell upon all the lands. Coyote's howl promises to the High Spirit the powers she has been honored will for all days keep safe the trails where he chooses for us each to make journey.

Great Coyote takes both the spirits of dog and man and casts them from within her as she cries out to Moon.

Those of our brothers whose spirits who were first born weak of spirit are now raised upon the soils into those pillars we see standing beside the trails of our lands.

It has been told they will guard over the trails Coyote leads her people through her bond with Hyas Tahmahnawis.

This is what Hyas Tumtum and Otelagh have agreed as they had one day long ago sat together before the table of our father's great meadow above.

There, as the first day's Sun rose upon the lands, and tree and animal first came from the waters of the sea, and as our peoples began to come down upon the lands from atop Wallawahoof where Hyas Naha's nest now lies emptied of her children, they chose to keep strong the spirits that stand along the trails that lead across the lands of all our kingdoms.

This is the way of Great Coyote...

With much hope to see our peoples safe beneath the swarm of Red Cloud is what I must too plead of Moon.

I pray she too shares that vision offering promise to our tomorrows upon the lands of our kingdoms as does our Hyas Tumtum towards the spirit of Coyote.

I ask our Great Fathers that Suyapee will choose to see deep within our hearts to what makes our spirits strong.

With much hope, they will take with them not only the furs of our animals, but too, the bounty that comes from within our souls and of our spirits to share with their peoples.

As Suyapee leave our lands and return to their villages, I plead loudly to Moon so we will be again set free to walk below the wide smile of Otelagh as we care for the lands beneath his longing gaze.

Then, we will be free to walk without worry of one another, and life will rise up before us in honor to what we have chosen to be right under the leadership of our fathers.

As I stand and look over this mighty kingdom of Wah, I have learned to respect and find honor in all that she offers.

From high above in the trails of the sky, it is the cry of Red Tail that first beckons warning as she too sees beyond today into the darkness of tomorrow where our lives are promised to be lain with much question.

"Hear me plead my father, hear me plead!"

Suyapee has begun to build villages along the waters of En che Wauna to keep safe the coats of those animals we bring to their tables.

The furs of the land's spirits are stored high up from the damp floor in the cover of darkness as they wait for the return of the big ships to be taken to lands we do not know.

We are not welcome into their village, and we must question what spirits they keep hidden that are not of those we have known to share of our lands?

They do not trust our peoples as they choose fire and smoke to come from cannon to warn us when we choose to sit with the big chief at their village.

This is not good…

Suyapee have begun to claim much of the lands of our kingdom for their own people as they build villages along the shores of En che Wauna. We fear, soon, they will take all the lands from beneath our feet, and we will be left with nothing but long trails swept distant from our villages by the coarseness of Wind's mightiest and most disheartening breaths.

Many chiefs and shamans whom have led our peoples safely through the storms of many snows have stood before the Walls of Wahclella.

From there, they have listened closely to our great leader's speak. It is to those same visions that are now apparent today where we find ourselves laying caution to where we place our every step.

Suyapee must not follow the same trails that lead to where we gather strength from the soul of the Hyas Tahmahnawis Tyee high above our villages in the mountains of the highest of our Spirits!

I remember, one day, long ago, when my father spoke to me of my thoughts to accepting my journey upon the trails we have been taught not to place our step.

I was not pleased to what my father told me in my wanting to find battle against the peoples of the Snake.

He told me the fight was not mine to wish. He told me if I wished to find battle I would discover myself mourning deeply as my actions towards those that had taken my brother's spirits would not bring my soul honor, and I would forever walk with my head held in much sorrow for the lives I took from their villages, and from before all the peoples of our Earth.

My grandfather told me one day he too had chose battle over the teachings of our High Spirit.

My grandfather told the Hyas Tahmahnawis was heard to tell our peoples to always keep peace between others.

Grandfather shared the Good Spirit spoke to him, and he was directed to stand beneath the heavens upon the highest hill as I do this day.

My grandfather told me that night, as the first snow fell before his feet, he was told to listen to the truths as they rose up from within his heart.

He explained from within the calm and silence of winter's first storm, his thoughts had easily come to his soul without obstacle as they had journeyed quickly and with much clarity to the righteous path our peoples would then need to accept.

Through all hardships we may encounter, we must be promised to the leadership of all our fathers so we awaken in the morning and lay witness to the Great Spirit's promise of our tomorrows.

Grandfather too told me, once he had felt the lessons his heart was reacquainted, the darkness corruption yields within us had fled far from his soul, and his spirit was then set free to share before all the people.

Through the truths that had spoken to him, his thinking did not from that moment hold his soul captive to the wantings of the mesahchie Tahmahnawis again.

He did not find himself willing to accept the deeds of Tsiatko (Bad Spirit), again within his soul.

My grandfather told me from that day forward, he has kept his heart clean and his soul free from the evil ways of the bad spirit.

I have stood high above my village upon the peak of Great Larch many times. It has been from there the Good Spirit has led me to look over the kingdom of Wah from where once breathed fire and where too spewed thick smoke from within its much angred throat.

As I stood upon the Hyas Larch and peered out across the mighty kingdom of Wah, the Hyas Tumtum offered my eyes a vision I shall not forget.

I have seen many of our peoples taken from our lands. Many of their voices will soon be forever silenced before the ears of *their brothers who will still stand in wait for the High Spirit's commands.*

It has been spoken, one day when Pish choose to not return to En che Wauna in great numbers, those who had once taken us from along the shores of the Great River will call out our names and seek answer in what they must do to prove to Pish all our peoples are worthy of their catch.

It will be many snows before Suyapee kneels before us to ask, but through the vision I was witnessed, that day will come as our people will be welcomed within their villages as we sit before their tables which through talk, will unite all those of our people to understand and accept the ways of the Great Creator.

It will be a day when Otelagh smiles down upon the Earth when Suyapee is heard to cry out that Pish do not swim in the waters of En che Wauna so they may place them upon their tables for the long winters.

We, Indian, shall listen to the pleas of Suyapee from lands far away where they have led us, and that day, we will each again stand side by side, and peace and understanding will come to both our peoples as we accept to battle together in saving the gift of Salmon the High Spirit had first given to all our peoples many, many seasons before we came to these lands.

I have seen through the looking glass to all the visions our great chiefs have spoken. As I look back to that lesson my grandfather shared, it is through that single teaching that keeps my heart promised to walk with the Good Spirit and not want to find battle with those whose fight is within their own misguided souls.

It is not our people's right to take from others their final breath if we disagree to how they think, or to what they believe to be the only truth they have been taught to believe.

As Suyapee comes to our lands with many, and as our peoples are then few as we fall from their disease, it is wise we walk with silenced breaths and wait until the Good Spirit leads us to once again guard over his peoples and to the lands he once chose for us to honor with understanding the gift which life is promised.

It is not our way to run before others and wield the spear or arrow in our hands, but as Suyapee has been promised to come, there is much warning of battles rising up from the lands of our peoples as the scent of war crosses the lands through the messages cast out upon Wind.

I am assured when Moon rises, and the sky becomes red with threat, smoke will soon bellow up from the plains and rise far into the heavens.

The cadence of our drums will then rise up and join those others upon the travels of Wind as they announce the final days of our people.

When our drums have announced the beginning of our people's endings upon the lands of our kingdoms, a great prophet will appear and stand before the fires of our villages.

He will speak of Earth Mother.

He will tell we should not take from the purse of Earth Mother more than what she offers to harvest from her lands.

If we are to find prosperity through her offerings, it shall only be through our choice to accept in her exacting and most demanded decisions we will be seen to survive and live into our tomorrows.

Smohalla will tell we must not follow the ways of the whites that choose to force us from our lands. He will give warning they will carve from Earth Mother's soul with sharp knives and steal the tears that fall from the cheeks of the Great Spirit.

Those same tears that have all days brought new life to rise up from beneath the soils of our lands will not be the same again.

When the lands become deserts, and we cannot find roots to keep our hearts strong, and once the day pish shall not be seen to swim in our rivers, he will ask; "What have you done?"

It is Smohalla that is told sees into the days of all our tomorrows. He shall tell our people one day soon the Earth Mother will shake the land as she cautions to the choices we may choose to follow as Suyapee comes.

With grave warning, Earth Mother shall denounce the changes Suyapee chooses to reinforce upon her lands.

Those choices will neither be good for her or for her peoples.

Smohalla shall stand before us and speak as a prophet to all our nations.

It shall be from where the golden grasses of the plains where buffalo and antelope run free, and from the great peaks where Tkope Moolack peers down upon our people as he sees beyond today into the dark days when our peoples shall not be seen nor heard again for many more, we will hear grave warning cast out across all the lands upon Wind's labored breaths.

Smohalla's message will be shared to all those that hear the Great Earth Mother's call for them to feel of her own soul's crying pleas.

Her pleas share before her children we must not lie down unmoving before Suyapee's quick march upon us, but we must stand before them and speak of the truths that have been heard spoken by our greatest leaders upon the Wall of Wahclella to the price of Suyapee's most grievous of errors.

Suyapee has named our beliefs to be nothing but a religion in bringing honor to Earth Mother, and they have named our peoples who believe in the Earth only as Dreamers.

Though Suyapee have yet to believe we are all born to the soul of the same Earth, when this day comes, when they do not understand to follow in the choices of Earth Mother, they too will kneel before the High Spirit and wail before his feet in their most grievous of error.

One day I must stand before Suyapee and ask; "Do you not too dream of all the days beyond tomorrow?"

"Do not your spirits lead you across these same trails, and do you not see the same lands, smell the same flower, and take from En che Wauna the same pish to eat?"

I shall ask them; "Are your peoples spirit's stronger and wiser than our own when it is your people that first point the musket toward us as you bring war between our peoples when we wish for peace?"

As I sit here tonight upon the peak of the Great Larch, my eyes are sadly drawn towards the lands where Sun first rises as I remember the words wisely spoken by my father, Bright Wolf, son of Nenamooks.

It was his father, my grandfather, that first spoke these words as he lay upon his mat and spoke proudly until his final breath was drawn.

My grandfather's final wish for his peoples was to know there is always hope for tomorrow once we follow in the *Hyas Saghalie Tahmahnawis'* teachings as our own spirits have been promised to join those of our fathers in the great village above.

"My Brothers, to you that share with me in spirit, hear this as it was first spoken by a great leader that was stricken to lie upon his bed as he awaited his return to the side of his father before the fires of the *Great Village* many moons ago;

"As the warmth of today's sun has fallen from the heavens, and the cold of night approaches, my life has now passed through the avenues of all the suns and moons that have stained the heavens above you.

"My mortal spirit shall be soon routed unto the clutches of the *Hyas Saghalie Tyee* as I shall then be aligned with all my brothers that have chaired before our people's council.

"My spirit shall be taken upon the *Hyas Chinook*'s breaths as has many a fallen leaf that had sailed across the great river and had begun to take seed upon the distant shore

"My tutoring before the *Hyas Spirits*, and my address before my brothers with whom I had crossed paths has begun a change in their awakening towards all charges from those that are not blessed by the gift of our dominion.

"The *Hyas Saghalie Tyee* had appointed my path upon earth to save the entirety of all forms of life who have been bore upon the

Great Illahee from the beginning our brothers have been blessed to share in its great wealth.

"Upon my reception before the spirits of these grounds, my teachings have led my peoples, you my brothers, to find the answer of your worth before the Great Spirits.

"My belief in the Hyas Spirit's philosophies has permitted my obedience to be lain before their feet without fault or question.

"As I have accepted their wisdom and have spread their words upon the paths I have chosen before all those whom have stood before me, my beliefs, all which have allowed me to soar above our land's domains.

"To those which have permitted my individuality to rise up from within me and become independent from mankind's most burdensome disputes, I am forever thankful!

"If you too believe as I do today, we, together, will then be the same as the Hyas Chak-Chaks', (Great Eagles,) as they are seen to soar freely beneath the heaven's gateways as they peer down upon the soils that are spread magnificently beneath them.

"As each seed brings life upon our lands from all the earth's species, you, the caretakers of our Illahee must not portend that one species is of less importance to the continuation of all life our Earth supports upon the Hyas Saghalie Tyee's, (Great Spirit's) kingdom.

"Our brothers must survive with all other species upon Earth's face.

"Through your acceptance of their standing, life shall thrive throughout all the suns and moons that pass above your blessing upon the shorelines of En che Wauna, (Columbia River).

"Mankind must be determined to overcome all differences that are sorely placed before them by those tainted toward the wishes of our Hyas Saghalie Tyee!

"We must be ready to attach our triumph to the gifts that stand magnificently before us all!

"Toward these same tracings, we must be concerted given our symphony to the treasures our Earth is blessedly adorned.

"We, as humanity, must not be found wandered upon our lands as are the fallen meteors of our heavens!

"We must be taken by our invitation upon this great Earth as we discover the sacred grounds we encounter!

"We must not be led astray from the gravity of their burnished and most honorable paths!

"I ask you my brothers, upon my passing to the land of our High Spirits, choose your souls to be as dynamic as my own, and you shall be lodged in spirit alongside all our fathers.

"As you are joined in your labors to follow in our vision, we shall all be remembered through the legends that are decided by our traces permitted upon our Illahee.

"Do not let pass our vision.

"As you emerge before the peoples that choose their stance upon our majestic lands, may their lessons be compellingly influenced by the truths you profoundly speak!

"We Shall Honor the Earth and the Heavens!

"We Shall Honor Mankind!

"We Shall Honor the Spirits Bore to the Earth's Trails!

"If your spirit stands proud and wise before the Hyas Saghalie Tyee's inspirations upon the paths you follow throughout the travels of your life, you may one day be promised to be observed crossing the heavens as do the Hyas ChakChak!

"Your spirit on that unparalleled day shall then be seen proudly stationed upon the Saghalie Tyee's chosen star as it glistens with your ascension before the gates of the High Spirit's castle, and as you rise above your brothers, you too shall be accepted by the Hyas Saghalie Tyee, To Have Seen the Sun of Tomorrow's Day...

"I must ask you; if it were not for our dreams, could we not witness to the rising of Sun upon the heaven's trails before tomorrow's day?

"I leave you to discover the worth of your soul as you reflect towards the answer to this question that may permit you one day to rise up and be firmly set beside your fathers at the foot of the eternal fire within the safety of the High Spirit's village...

"Klahowya......

"Welcome to the kingdoms of Great Spirits.

"May you see through the eyes of Hyas Tslallagal, and may you feel from her heart as she walks hidden before you."

"Welcome to the lands of our fathers, and of those fathers before them.

"May we all walk in peace and in the understanding to all we are surrounded.

"May our souls become one with our spirit, and allow all the peoples of this Earth to walk upon this Earth as one body, and with one mind.

"May we each protect all we have been gifted that has been bore through the hands of those spirits that walk beside us each day upon the treasure of this land."

As I stand here today, under clear skies, my thoughts are too clear as my vision into our tomorrows observes our sacrifice will allow our peoples to awaken each morning as Sun rises and Moon rests.

Our acceptance of Hyas Tumtum's wishes too brings honor before him to our names for all days.

We must compliment the Great Spirit and Earth Mother for our lands are plentiful with pish and game, with reeds and Great Cedar.

From these, our people shall survive always upon these, The Majestic Lands of Wah..."

Steven Warnstaff

Steven Warnstaff

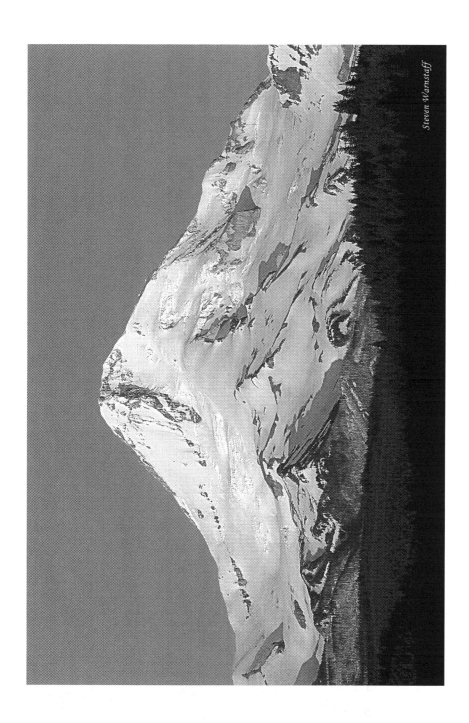

Steven Warnstaff

Chapter 1

Hyas Saghalie Tahmahnawis Tyee Speaks

I, Raven, who has been named for the spirit of the wise bird that covets over our lands, today, speaks with my son, Ikt Klaksta Hyak Cooley Ticky Kuitan, (One Who Runs Fast Like Horse). As we sit at the side of En che Wauna and look over to the Valley of the Eagle, I tell him;

"Though many seasons have passed behind me with good favor poured from the High Spirit's hands, there have been many challenges placed before me that had brought great pause to each of those days passing with clear heart and opened mind.

"My son, I have been honored to have climbed upon many peaks of those mountains we are surrounded, and as I journeyed through these lands and looked down upon our peoples, admiring what the Great Spirit has placed upon these lands for our peoples, great visions began to form messages I have to this day kept close to my heart.

"Many of these visions shared of trials that would be set harshly upon each of our villages. As each season passes there have been many times I have found weakness within myself as I searched my soul for answers to what troubled me. I struggled to grasp the spirit of the Raven that would bring understanding and direction before all my peoples.

"I prayed for our Great Spirit to lead me safely upon those trails I could not see lain before my feet. I prayed for Sun and Moon to guide my steps as I journeyed through each stage of my life, and once I learned to honor their decisions, I was rewarded to venture further into all the lands of our kingdoms as they saw hope in my leadership through the strength of my faith.

"Each day life brings challenge before me and our peoples, and through my faith in the words spoken by the Hyas Tahmahnawis, I have been honored through his directives to have chosen the right trails to lead our brothers and sisters from those whom are surrendered before the wanting of the bad spirit's drum."

"One Who Runs Fast Like Horse, as we look across the Big Waters, there, at the foot of Che che Optin, (Woot-Lat,) (Beacon Rock,) where our fathers first built the longhouses of our village, those who return from the river and from upon the mountaintops find comfort as Raven and Coyote look down upon them with favorable eyes.

"Many days, Raven and Coyote have been heard to call out to us to follow where their spirits have been told to lead our peoples. Their spirits are good. They have not led us before where awaits the long arms of peril.

"Those that walk the many trails that lead from the village of the Multnomah to the Valley of the Eagle will soon hear our chant.

Our prayers shall be spread across the trails of Wind to the great village above where looking down upon our peoples sits the Hyas Tahmahnawis.

We must plead for his consideration towards our people's safety in the days that may soon bring question upon our hearts."

I remind myself, as I stand up and face the heaven, I must raise my arms to reach out to their spirit in all respect for if it were not for what they give to our peoples we would have nothing to offer others in return.

I must ask them to lead us safely across our lands as Red Cloud has again begun to cast darkness across the lands of our kingdoms and upon our lives.

Hyas Tumtum had first placed his step upon the trails we have followed from the beginning, and in those steps, we have found safety from the evil the mesachie tahmahnawis wills upon our villages.

I plead they will look down upon us with much favor, and will guide our peoples so we might survive the approaching change from those that are soon to walk blindly upon us.

I have chosen to take with me One Who Runs Fast Like Horse as I have been called to climb to the peak of Multnomah where we will stand above the great tumwata and look out over the lands of Wah.

As we stand where once the daughter of Multnomah offered her life to save her people, we will call out to the Good Spirit together.

Through the acceptance of their mighty powers our prayers will be cast out before the ears of our Hyas Tumtum, and they will listen to all we speak knowing we are bound by their will.

Our great chiefs will sit proudly before the fires of heaven as they look down upon us with pride. They will see we follow in their lead without first jurying their decisions.

One Who Runs and I have stood here, upon Multnomah's mighty tower above En che Wauna for many days. We have awaited word from Moon to accept our pleas as we pray she will lend our peoples her support through the long nights of our lives and keep us safe from what we cannot see.

Far in the distance, where the mountains lead to the waters of the Great Sea, new storm's rise and are soon to fall upon our villages. This storm is not like those we have seen in past days. This angered sky of our heaven promises storm to strike quickly upon all our kingdoms with great fury.

We too ask Moon to keep us distant from the long arm of disease as we have tired of bearing our eyes towards many of our neighbor's villages that are lain in ruin as their people lie dying upon the tainted soils.

One Who Runs Fast Like Horse and I stand together with hands raised to the heaven. We each call out to Moon with great faith she will welcome all our peoples to stand safely beneath Sun as the new season comes fast upon us.

We ask she allow our people to walk out from beneath cover of our lodge without fear to what we have seen come before many of those villages that speak no more upon Wind's most longing breaths.

We ask for our peoples to be set free from the grasp of the bad spirit's long arms that only offers despair and sadness to fill our people's hearts as it darkens our souls from what was once bright with hope.

This disease that has come upon us from the purse of Tsiatko which Suyapee carries hidden spreads quickly across our lands. In

4

its wake, it has proven to offer nothing but the bleakness of death to enter within many of our opened doors.

When we approached villages we had for many seasons shared potlatch, we found their spirit stolen from their souls as they were seen lying upon the land and cast beside the fast waters of streams and rivers.

I grieve their loss as their voices are now forever silenced to the summits of our people.

When my son and I approached the entrance to their villages, with weak voice, we heard many calling out to the Great Spirit for forgiveness for what they could not understand.

We heard them in great agony crying out to the Great Spirit as they each asked; "What have we done?"

They know not why he has allowed disease and death to spread amongst them, or to the peoples of those villages they had first witnessed stolen by the depravity of the bad spirit's wanting which were freed from within White Man's purse.

Each night as Sun passes beyond the tower of Woutoulat, (Rooster Rock), the cry of Great Coyote rises up from deep within the long valley.

Throughout each of the passing nights we hear Coyote cry out to Moon as she draws nearer to the peak of Multnomah where we reach out to the Great Spirit.

Through light cast out from Moon we see her shadow swiftly cross the trails below. Confidently walking in and out from behind the trunks of trees.

She comes nearer each night, and through the cold of each night we wait.

We wait anxiously, knowing she will lead us from the peril we today pray.

Tonight she climbs higher to touch the heaven upon the high peaks of our kingdom so she may reach out to the gates of the Hyas Tumtum's village.

It is from below the tallest Fir where we see her head raised to the heavens, and it is there she too praises the Great Spirit for the gift of freedom her spirit yearns.

As Runs Fast Like Horse and I listen to her call, we each grasp hope that through her mighty powers she will lead us into those tomorrows we have not yet walked.

Through the long nights my son and I stand accepting the unknowiness of our tomorrows.

We have each spoken to Otelagh as he rose up into the heaven, just as we have called out to Moon as she too has risen above us. It is not our decision, so we must wait patiently for answer from Sun and Moon, and pray they do not choose to pass over where we are seen pleading beneath the heavens where they pass.

Then, as night fell across the valleys, the mountain's shadows grew dim, quiet fell gently upon all those who then slept.

Wind did not bellow harshly from the breaths of heaven or from upon the wave of En che Wauna.

Life rested peacefully under the watchful eyes of Owl.

A new day dawned as Sun rose hidden by cloud into the heaven, warning that storm had come to the lands.

We had again called out to Sun as he rose up from his bed, and as we waited and hoped for answer, the ground began to shake beneath our feet with great suffering.

We struggled mightily to regain our stance beside the waters rushing from Multnomah's stream so we might not fall from above the cliff of Multnomah which we had promised to stay until we had been awarded answer.

All the lands of Wah appeared to sway from each side of the mountain peaks before our eyes.

Trees danced without song first sung by Wind.

The lands of our kingdom rose and fell many times, as if to bow before the powers of the Great Creator.

Trees again performed in dance to the cadence of the missing drum, each bending side to side as if influenced by every breath the Hyas Spirit drew into his mighty chest.

Deer and elk ran from meadow to meadow behind great clouds of dust until we could not see them hidden beneath the darkest of veil.

Birds flew across the shorelines of En che Wauna as dark clouds formed where they gathered that took light from the sky. With swift wing, they journeyed across the heavens to join upon lands distant beyond our own.

Without warning, Wind began to descend harshly upon us from above. Each breath grew stronger until we could not tell from where it came or to where it had journeyed.

Wind did not spare the lands from its mightiest complaint.

One Who Runs Fast Like Horse and I looked to one another as we too danced to the silent drums of the ghost spirits.

Unknowing to the sudden threat we were challenged, we stood, each shaken, each questioning, why?

My heart was suddenly filled with the fear of not knowing.

Helpless...

Weakened by my own questioning of what answer we were lent...

I felt I was peering through closed and clouded eyes as I attempted to cross upon a towering cliff that fell from the heaven.

Fear, a fear I had never known before this day swept hurriedly through my soul.

Our souls were each frozen.

As we each questioned of our next step, lay the question of why the cold of winter had invested itself fully within our souls.

Calm was taken from within the soul of Multnomah upon which we stood as the power of wind crashed against us from below its great cliff.

We too bent upon the ground from side to side as if we were like the sticks of the forest.

To and fro we each bowed to keep from being swept from upon the crown of the cliff and thrown helplessly to the rocks below.

As the lands kept rising and falling the storm quickly swallowed the calm we had for many days became acquainted.

Storm thundered many times across the heaven. Its voice promised of anger as it rose up with greater force as it came nearer where we stood.

My son and I waivered in our decision if we were meant to survive, unsure, we were held firmly within the throes of our fears.

We stand together.

Each bewildered.

Each shaken.

We did not know why Wind had suddenly challenged us to surrender our souls to the waters of Multnomah from the high peak?

We did not know why storm had come, or if it were to be lent beyond te lands of our kingdom?

Storm did not move through the heaven as the breaths of Wind came hard from above…

The spirits of many trees in the forest now lay broken upon the soils where the seeds of their mothers first fell before they had grown strong and rose up to touch the edge of heaven. Thunder again roared through the Lands of Wah. Its journey echoed throughout all the valleys from above us as long spears were cast down onto the lands.

The Hyas Tahmahnawis' Great Drum began to send message of war between himself and his foe. To which he chose to battle we did not yet know.

Cloud swarmed across the land as they rose quickly before us from the base of Multnomah's cliff.

As suddenly they had shone their angered face below us, they were lent as hurriedly to the heights of the heavens above.

The light of day quickly turned to darkness. We feared the evil spirits that walk upon the lost trails of our people's souls would strike without first hearing my son and I plead for our lives.

The land below us appeared as if a great herd of Antelope had run quickly across the flat plains as dust of the earth had fallen from upon their swift hooves in their escape from those that had come to hunt.

I asked in my own uncertainty; "Are we not now the hunted?"

We could not see beyond the first line of trees that stood before us as they, with swiftness of feet, bowed to their brothers that too waivered upon their sides.

They, as we, were begging for the end of Wind's mightily drawn complaint upon us.

I knew my people were standing with much question, not knowing what would appear next to wreak havoc into their lives.

They too must be speechless as the cold of winter invades their souls and as the unknowing of darkness marches into our lands, where then could they flee to survive?

Their lone question must ask to what life may offer them tomorrow?

My son and I stand strong and unwavered before the power of Wind as our faith offers us strength to live through this trial we are now surrendered.

We fought Wind fiercely.

Each breath promised to take us from high up upon Multnomah's cliff.

If our people could see One Who Runs Fast Like Horse and myself combat what has come hard against us, they too would know their strengths lie within their souls, and if they were to follow our example, they too would not question of their survival as we did in the beginning.

My son and I know, even though we struggle much against the complaints of Wind, we would return before those of our village. Our spirits would be stronger and our minds quicker to react to the obstacles we are to be faced before this trial.

My son certainly understands now life as a test of his survival upon these lands. I know as he stands before the face of danger and shows he fears not what he cannot see, he will go far under the guidance of the Great Spirit through the faith instilled within his soul.

It was not long after storm ceased to bring warning to the lands when message was spoken from the High Spirit as it was cast down upon us and warned we must listen with clarity to the message he had now chosen to covet upon those living upon the lands he had created.

With certainty, I knew his message could not bring good from his heart as he brought storm to fall heavily upon us.

Great sorrow began to enter my heart as I became overwhelmed through the shadows of my own sadness.

Our Hyas Tahmahnawis Tyee had brought judgment upon all our peoples.

I felt great distress as he cried out in disappointment throughout all the lands as we heard his message thundered through the valleys along the course of En che Wauna, and throughout all the Lands of Wah.

From across the heavens he proved without doubt he was angered against our people's decisions. His children, for who he had hoped would understand his judgments given all the animals he had too promised life, but as they had now begun to be sacrificed through the greed of our souls, their spirits, now lost.

His sorrow had brought him to call out those of our people who choose to follow the ways of Suyapee, those who do not share the same convictions upon that life we each pass.

I ask; "Where if we, who had first been chosen of these lands, did not adhere to his way, would we too soon be like those Otter and Beaver who do not swim in our waters today, but lie helpless and without spirit upon one's shelf?"

Sadly, the lands he had chosen for his people were not the same lands as were first offered as a gift where we, who lived and breathed upon them, could learn of honor and of trust.

From the beginning when the Great Spirit drew breath upon the first bush and tree, to the bird and to the elk, to all life that shared Sun's rise from the labors of his grandest dream, they each were now challenged to survive all that has changed in the thinking of our people and of those others who have now come to take from the lands what the Good Spirit had first offered to each and all of our peoples.

We have together, failed our Great Spirit.

We have culled many of the kingdom's spirits and had not first thought of what would be left in all our tomorrows.

We have taken many spirits from not only all our lands, but from before the eyes of all the peoples who will one day make journey to stand in these lands where the Great Creator first drew breath to all that lives today.

Though we have strived to follow in the teachings of our Hyas Tahmahnawis Tyee, he told us not to find fault with those that come to stand upon our lands.

We had accepted his words, and have without complaint, lent them to become infused deeply within our hearts. But yet, today, many have lain their souls blindly before the Great Spirit's table and choose not to see what he has offered to sustain all our peoples.

We, today, still choose to take the lives of animals who had walked favorably and peacefully amongst us in trade for what we have not known to ask before today.

We deny the wisdom of the Great Spirit as we choose the musket to take game, and the bead to prove of our wealth before each of our brother's villages.

We are held in great shame before the Great Father!

Our peoples have quickly surrendered our feet from following upon the sacred trails our Great Fathers had led us for many, many, seasons before our own lives began.

Our hearts, now swollen with greed, have become hardened through the gifts we have traded for what we once held honorable within our now weakened souls.

I find it saddening we choose to walk away from the honor our lives had been chosen to follow without offering thought to how prosperous our lives were spent before Suyapee came and offered our peoples our souls served upon our own tables!

I ask; "How can we return to the life we believe to be honorable beneath the clouds of our heaven?"

We have traded our lives for gifts we have not earned as we steal from the lands of the Hyas Tumtum.

"How"; I ask; "Can we return to where we were once allowed to live without living in fear by our own fraud?"

Our greed has allowed our peoples to become forgetful to the ways of our fathers as we search out those that bring the shiniest bead and the sharpest knife.

These gifts, who the bad spirit hides, which Suyapee offers makes our people to believe the bead and musket, and the long knife each bring us honor before the Great Creator.

It is now evident they only have made our people as ravenous as the spirit of Klale Lolo.

Suyapee too craves for our souls as does the bad spirit, and we have these passing days proven we first think to take the Eena and Otter from our waters as we allow ourselves to sit before

Black Bear without first offering caution to what may lie in the darkness of his den.

As I hear the message our High Spirit speaks towards all our peoples, I understand we must not allow ourselves to sacrifice from the land what is not our own to take.

We must believe our survival depends solely upon those gifts the Great Creator has offered for our use. Our father tells us it will be through the combination of all the gifts he has offered that our peoples will survive through all the many adversities we shall be faced.

The camas, the sweet berry, wapato, pish, deer, elk, bear, the duck, and goose will each allow our peoples to live gainfully through all our tomorrows as they freely offer their lives to be placed upon our tables each season with honor.

Their coats shall keep us warm, and their bones shall permit our women to sew our clamons and make quivers to carry our arrows.

Soon, there shall be no more beaver in our rivers or otter in the big waters who will bring smiles upon our faces.

Only then will we understand the anger of Hyas Tahgmahnawis as the dark clouds of despair shall fall heavily upon us all as we walk alone and desperate in our own disrepute.

We, our peoples, will not walk proudly across the lands as free men, but we will walk alone without spirit and our souls will lie emptied.

Each brother's soul shall be darkened with great shame as we realize we are no longer brothers to the Spirits of the Earth who first breathed life into our lungs.

The Earth has begun to settle once again in storm as it rises with grave warning from upon Wah's lowest of valleys.

From high above in the clouds of Wy-East cries out the voice of Great Spirit through all the lands of his kingdoms.

As I stand in disbelief to what I hear, Great Spirit speaks my name. I am told the time in my life has arrived to join my spirit upon the soils of the Earth.

Hyas Tahmahnawis tells me I will soon walk with him as he leads me safely upon the many trails I have yet to place my mark.

My Great Spirit too asks I prepare my heart for a long and arduous journey. A journey I will be led to one day stand upon the high slope of Wy-East and look outover the kingdom of Wah at the side of Hyas Tkope Moolack.

Suddenly, a cold breeze crosses over me.

My heart's rhythm is drawn short.

My soul wanders from within me as I can only listen to the Great Spirit's words as I question of why, today, and not tomorrow, am I summoned to journey from the side of my son and from my people?

I began to mourn for the days when I would not return to my village.

In the Great Spirit's message I hear his words, I feel his heart, yet I stand uncertain to why it is me he today calls?

Though today's calling has allowed my heart to become unsettled as I have walked far in my life beside the Great Creator, I know as the Great Spirit warrants my presence presented before Tkope Moolack, I must not question why it is I, he today calls?

The honor of my standing with Tkope Moolack shall be added to the legend of my name before all those that will come to live upon these lands.

I sit with great esteem for what I have been honored to share to all those of my people who I will soon stand and peer down upon their villages.

If it were not for my family, my wife, my sons, and my daughter, I, today, would not have walked knowing of faith in the presence of hope for all our peoples so they too can see in all their tomorrows.

Though I know I will all days be with them, and look over them as they journey through their lives, in the pity now strewn from my heart, I fear my breaths will quickly become labored and one day soon fall silent upon the ears of my son.

The Great Spirit again spoke with much clarity to what he had chosen for my final trial;

"Walk with me my son and I will lead you safely upon the slopes of Wy-East where your soul will join that of your heart, and your spirit will then become brothers with that of Hyas Tkope Moolack.

"You will then walk at the side of the Great White Elk and go to where no man had been chosen to walk in all days of our people.

"All those of our peoples who have ever lived in the kingdom beneath Wy-East, and who are attached upon the Walls of Wahclella, have known many seasons of your journey.

"Today, as I look upon them as they are gathered beside the great fire of our village, and where they have awaited for many seasons for your name to be called, they too know it is time for your soul to rest.

"You must call out through the heart of your spirit and share with your son that our peoples must make change to what brings them honor before others. If they do not, only the darkness of our sadness will be spread before the tables of others as the rhythm of our drums cast out the call to war amongst those who will soon come to join the bad spirits of Suyapee who willingly await them.

"There, where the Winds of the Chinook blow hard in winter, you will see all the lands of our kingdoms through the eyes of Tkope Moolack.

"Tkope Moolack has great vision, and he knows what will be remaining of all our tomorrows if our people do not return upon the paths of those principles your fathers had too been promised to lead."

At that moment I knew I must speak to my son and share with him what I now believe was my purpose in leading our peoples through all the trials we have encountered.

I have walked knowing the teachings of the High Spirits, and I have been led through much adversity without falling in disgrace below the soles of their feet.

Soon, I will look through the eyes of White Elk, and as his eyes peer beyond what lies before us today, he and I will look into the looking glass of all our people's tomorrows and will then know what we must do to sit at the side of our village's fires without fear and sorrow entering into the hearts of the many.

My heart was laden in great pain as I too shared with my son that I was quickly growing feint with each passing day. I believed the Great Spirit would soon look seriously into the goodness I had grasped tightly within my soul, and would choose to send his White Stallion to ride into the heaven to the village where my father sits and awaits me.

"All I could ask," I told my son; "Was for our fathers to not only feel what is right within my soul as I stand before their judgment, but that our fathers would too see your own spirit was lent to their mightiest decisions."

"My Son, you must walk in honor always each day for what the Good Spirit has awarded our peoples. The value of that honor will arise before you through all good and all bad. It shall be through those trials you will become stronger and see beyond what is evident today."

"Through the visions of tomorrow which shall be shared before you, you will know where to lead your peoples so they too may walk with the High Spirit and be saved from the darkness of life's uncertainty.

Then, as you become stronger in the counsel of the Hyas Tahmahnawis Tyee, you will be favored to rise up and sit beside our greatest leaders in the heaven at the side of your father, as I too will soon be with my father.

From there, you will smile down upon our peoples knowing they shall always be survived by their children, and our peoples will forever be known to have settled upon the Lands of Wah with much favor from the Great Creator."

My time was near as the Hyas Tahmahnawis would call upon me one final moment to submit myself before the fathers of our people.

I spoke of this to my son, and he looked upon me with great sorrow.

I knew of his pain as I had carried these feelings within my heart as Sun crossed the heavens as they too reminded me to the day when my father was led into his own Journey of the Dead.

I bowed my head, and as I stood at the side of my son, I raised my head to the heavens and cried out to the High Spirit and prayed for him to keep my son strong in his faith as he followed in their lead.

I slowly turned and walked from where my son and I stood. It was there, at the side of En che Wauna where we had spent many seasons together, we shared the final moment of our lives...

I had walked only a few steps from his side, and I knew I must turn towards him and bring proof to fall before his ears how his heart has affected my own as he has brought much pride to my life. He did not bring much in challenge to what I had shared with him in those days long past, and it was good.

I knew my son would be called upon to kneel before the Great Wall at Wahclella and be led to his own understanding to what trails he must follow to lead our brothers and sisters through each coming day by our Hyas Fathers.

This too brought great pride to overwhelm me as I knew my son would lead our people through all evil that may stand before them as they stand committed to the principles of our Great Creator.

This was always my dream that my son would follow in my footsteps and prove himself worthy of leading our people along those trails that first were kept from the light of promise.

I knew One Who Runs Fast Like Horse would become the great messenger we had witnessed rising from the floor of the Earth through the visions of many of our fathers.

My son was to become a great chief.

My son would become the greatest chief and shaman to our village at Wahclella as he would bring back to these lands our people from where they one day will go far from the waters of En che Wauna and sit upon the barren peaks of mountains where only the eyes of passing Moolack will look down upon them.

He would stand before the Spirits as they directed him to reach out and lead our peoples upon trails that would keep their hearts pure and forever bind their souls to what is spoken as righteous and forthcoming before all others that walk through our lands.

One Who Runs Fast Like Horse would bring honor before our peoples to those who will come to settle upon these lands.

Yet, I wish my son would lead our people once again to the womb of our mother, Naha, where she awaits upon the peak of Walowahoof for our people to again settle beside her.

From there, all our peoples would again welcome safety from the storm of Suyapee as we would then lie hidden above the promise Red Cloud has been sworn to be drawn.

Then, one day, when Suyapee had crossed our lands and could not take treasures again from our kingdoms, we would climb down upon the lands of Wah once more and earn back all that has been lost from our purse.

We would again walk amongst all our spirits without fearing of our own ruin at the hands of those who do not believe in the ways of the Great Spirit.

"My son, I know many suns will rise and fall before the new season returns to our lands. The cold season will bring much storm to fall upon you, and you will not go out upon the shore of En che Wauna for many days.

But as storms begin to end threat upon the lands, and snow falls into the waters of rivers, good fortune is promised to return to your people.

The sky will be cleared of cloud, and warmth will rise up from the soils, and your misery will be lifted from your souls.

Your spirits will too rise up to reach out to the heavens in the greatest of happiness, and life will become renewed as in all seasons long ago.

"Hyas Tahmahnawis Tyee tells En che Wauna's waters will quickly be filled again with color. Pish will suddenly appear, and they shall willingly jump into your nets and their spirits will be quickly placed within the shelters where they will lie drying as the sweet aroma of Alder will lie heavy upon the air.

"Life will be pleasing to all those that walk in from the trails of Wah and come to your village's fire as your peoples shall prepare feast and speak of good catch.

"As those Suyapee you have yet to meet come and shout out from En che Wauna, you must welcome them into your village as we have promised to always find honor in others as they sit before the fire of our council.

"You will smoke from the long pipe, you shall make trade, not for the furs of those spirits who walk beside us all days, but to offer Suyapee hope in the faith their souls will too share understanding to the gifts Naha has offered from the sticks of her nest.

"Life then will be good between our peoples. Though we have been told of Red Cloud forming upon the lands once more, through our efforts in understanding the ways of Suyapee, and hoping they one day will too understand our people, life will never be questioned again between us.

Then, all our tomorrows will rise and fall as Sun and Moon smiles down upon all their creation.

"You must remember the teachings of the High Spirit as he has taught us, as cold returns to the lands and leaves begin to fall from the long arms of trees, warning must be shared to all our peoples to again gather to make ready for winter before the braves of your village join those of distant villages and ride off to bring meat to our tables from the great hunting grounds.

"Each season, when Otelagh has fallen low to the heaven we have always begun to make ready to celebrate for the season's final hunt. In every task we had accepted, we knew we must be ready before the first snows of winter offer nothing that proves of Sun's promise above us again for many more days.

"Remember first, you must gather wood to keep your family warm as you await the return of Sun. Then, you must take the canoes from the banks of the Big River and lash them to the trunks of Cedar at the sides of our lodge as the Big River will rise up as season again changes and brings the Big Waters to rise up upon its shores.

"There is much work for all to share as you each are important to the existence of your family. Life would become hard if you do not work together as one people.

"If you do not make ready for the return of the snows of winter, life will quickly be as bitter as is the green berry first grown upon the vine we picked as young children before our mothers told us to wait until the end of summer to taste of its sweet nectar.

"Your wife and children will first gather and store upon the shelves of your lodges the food you will need to survive the cold storms that are certain to come with great fury upon you.

"They too must gather the rush and vine to make baskets, and as the celebration of the hunt nears, they will be asked to gather the great robes of Moolack and Mowitch you will wear across your broad shoulders as each of your hunters shall rise up before those that sit before the dance of the Moolack and Mowitch Spirits as you bring honor to them.

"I can remember when my brothers and myself circled the night's fire and rose up from upon the soil as did the Ghost Spirits, and as the horns upon our head raked the heaven, and as our feet stomped the ground, we danced as the Deer Spirits across the stage before our peoples.

We became like deer and elk as our own spirits were once again reunited, and we became one with one another.

"The best hunters from the villages that join in the hunt pretended to place their mark with arrows upon the hearts of those deer and elk who were chosen to be sacrificed. Then, as we turned from those that sat before the warmth of the fire, the great horns of those elk and deer we had taken from the great meadow would rise up and appear upon our heads as we called out to the High Spirit.

"Through the beat of our drums we prayed the Great Spirit would allow us to succeed in our hunt, and he would permit each of our brothers to return safe to their villages with meat for winter.

"The Great Spirit must know of your respect as you ask him to choose of those deer and elk who will fill your shelves so you do not take the strongest from his herd who will one day offer many more of their brothers and sisters to lie down before you.

"Through the long night, we have always danced below the full moon to bring good fortune to our hunt as we gathered before the big fire.

"Our souls had become one with our hearts.

"We danced with much spirit.

"You will know as we knew, our village would be spared hunger through our praise offered towards the High Spirit for all he offers through each of the new season's passing.

"Soon, the lands will lie frozen beneath your feet, and game will not be seen again standing in wait to be taken, but through your dance, you will appear from your winter's lodge and walk out into the light of Otelagh that offers life to all those he has chosen to receive the gifts from his creation.

"One day, as sun rises, you will look out along the shore of En che Wauna, and you will see there are many hunters, fathers with their sons, many who will soon join in the first hunt of their lives.

"From distant villages, they will begin to gather as they promise themselves towards the long ride beneath clouds that wait to drop from the peak of Wy-East and loom heavy with threat of winter's approach.

"Those that choose to hunt shall ride upon their horse for many days as they approach the trails that lead into the high desert.

"It will be from beneath the shoulders of Wy-East that your brothers will emerge from behind the pine forest and look out over the big meadow.

"This place, a land spread open and wide below the broad shoulders of Wy-East is where I first discovered great herds of Moolack and Mowitch awaiting for our peoples to come.

"When the storms of winter come and swallow grasses and bush below the frozen depths to await the return of new season, it is there you will find those who have chosen to rest and eat the long grass along the rocky shores of White River.

"My Son, long ago, before the great mountains fell into Wy-East, my grandfather told he too had first joined the hunt when he was a young boy with his father, just as you had first sat beside me upon our first hunt.

"Grandfather told me as he rode beneath the cover of the pines, mysteriously, before him, and as light from Otelagh shone down brightly upon him from where had first been lent shadow, the fingers of the pine's arms pointed out across the great meadow to offer the memory he had not forgotten in all the seasons that had passed over him.

"It was from where he sat upon the back of his horse, motionless, without breath, where the pines did not grow and golden grass reached high into the sky beside the cold waters that came from Wy-East, he looked out over the opened plain before him.

"Not far in the distance he said he saw resting upon flattened beds, and standing along the shore of the White River, grandfather told it was from there he first saw many deer and elk joined together for as far as his eyes could see.

"It was there, in silence, and in disbelief he said he stared.

"Grandfather remembered well in his old age as he told me; "They each looked towards me without fear as I neared them with my bow readied for my first kill.

"As we peered over the mighty herd with great hope, the voice of Great Spirit told of the sacrifice the deer and elk had accepted.

"It was through Great Creator's words, and in the promise of our need to survive the long winter, he told each of the deer and elk their spirits would live on and would forever walk in green meadows if they were not to run.

"The Great Creator asked of them each to accept his choice of those to be spared from their placement upon our wanting tables."

"Grandfather said he and his father rode through the great herds and were pointed to those few they took from the many.

"As the Great Spirit had promised, without waiting, the village had meat for winter. Their shelves were quickly filled when game would not again walk before them upon the frozen trails of winter.

"We were pleased," grandfather told me, "and as we cried out to the Great Spirit for what he had offered our people to place upon our tables, we cleaned the hides from the meat and made ready for the long journey to return to the villages of our people.

"We looked towards the heavens as we began our journey across the flat plains to where we would first rest in the village of the Wascopum, and with great hurry, dark cloud took light from Sun and suddenly fell to cover the lands.

"Otelagh was hidden behind thick mask in all the valleys.

"Our hunt was completed before the first snow fell upon those trails we had first come, and we each returned to Wahclella without loss to any of our brothers upon the long and tiring trail."

"This was many seasons ago, and in all those hunts your great grandfather was to become engaged, this lone hunt had stayed always welcomed within his heart.

"He told me that winter was unforgiving, and had brought darkness to cover the lands for many days as they did not see again the promise of Sun until the new season came.

"For many, many moons, darkness fell heavy across the lands and took sight of our village from many of our brothers eyes.

"They struggled across the frozen and barren land they once knew.

"Deep snow covered the lands. Trees and rock did not offer clue to where they stood.

"Days turned into night many times as they each passed slowly into another. Storms came to the lands as cloud brought rain and snow to fall heavily upon them.

"Thunder roared from the breaths of the spirits across all our lands. From the high peaks his voice could be heard shattered upon the land.

"There was no land spared from the wrath of that winter's long rage.

"The ground froze and again thawed many times, and as cloud drew again dark, great tears fell streaming from upon the Great Spirit's cheeks as they drew down from the corners of his eyes.

"The soils of the high peaks weakened as the ground thawed, and water thundered down their failing slopes.

"Many peaks fell hurriedly to the valley from where they had safely rested above the valley floors.

"Trees too fell harshly as their roots were wrested from the soils, and they were heard to cry out with much pain.

"We did not see the light of Otelagh shine down upon us for many long days as we sat waiting, unknowing if we were to be buried beneath the waste of those peaks that still stood strong above our village.

"The calls of our brothers to the Great Spirit fell challenged as Wind blew strong and took sound from his ears as they cried out.

"Lost to their sight were the lodges they searched that would offer warmth from the cold and food from the table.

"They were not again seen until the clouds emerged into the heavens. Then, as those of our brothers who went to search came upon them, it was then they saw their souls become attached to their spirits as they rose up to sit from beneath the deep snow as the storms of winter began to thaw.

"My son, I am now an old man that can only live out the hunt through my memories. But as I can still look towards those that will soon begin to gather, I can see gleaming within their eyes the wanting to join their spirits with the Moolack and Mowitch that await their place before their pointed bow.

"To journey into the High Spirit's meadow must be first accepted by those that join the hunt with great honor.

"Once your own son's journey to the hunting grounds allows him to sit proudly upon his horse overlooking the great herds, then he too will know of the pride he will carry with him always as his own spirit will rise up and join with all those he had come to look over that will offer his people food for winter.

"There will be one day you too will only be afforded the right to sit before the warmth of the fire as I do today, and it will be from there, you will watch the young braves of your village ride off to share in the great honor.

"As the fathers begin to take their sons to ride off to the great meadows, you will hear their promise to all our people. You will hear promise once they return, all our sons shall reappear as men to where they had first begun their long journey as boys.

"This is the promise you must instill into the hearts of those that are chosen to the honor of the hunt.

"Our people are kept safe by those men who have sworn promise to keep safe our villages for many seasons, and when Red Cloud again rises before us with no end, and it takes Sun from above us, those boys that are soon to become men must be ready for what may be shouldered against all our people.

"We must welcome those who will come to our villages and speak of peace, but we must too be ready for those that come with the purse offered them by the bad spirit.

"It is in that promise our peoples shall survive to sit with others when Red Cloud flees from each of our kingdoms!

"My son, at night, as I sat before the fire of our village, when only the call of Coyote and the Great Owl were heard, my thoughts were drawn to one of the many counsels held at Wyam.

"I had listened to the story brought before us from the Shoshone, and today it lives in my memory as it was first told.

"As I slept each night, from the day of our council when we had first been told of what would come, I began to see visions of many Suyapee each day crossing upon the trails of our lands.

"Through the visions of my dreams I had not yet been told of why they would come. I only knew what they had asked of those of our brothers that sat at the side of their fires as that story had before come.

"Those that chose to sit in council with many our brothers offered many gifts to their peoples, but they too demanded to know what trails would lead to where the land Otelagh sleeps at night meets those of the Big Waters?

"For many seasons we have seen Suyapee come from the sea, and as they come to make trade, our peoples have been attacked by the greed bound within their hearts.

"This is not good, and as I do not understand, fear has begun to enter my soul and bring dark cloud to form before my thoughts as it had once formed upon the waters of En che Wauna many seasons ago when my father first walked these trails in Wah.

"I see it is good Hyas Tyee had called upon me to begin journey from where our people are gathered, to join my spirit with Tkope

Moolack so I may too soon see beyond today to better understand what is to come of our tomorrows."

I placed my hand on my son's shoulder, and he and I knew I must now go to where Hyas Tyee has called.

It brings great sorrow to my heart that One Who Runs Fast Like Horse and I will no longer sit and look out over the waters of En che Wauna and talk.

But it is the same today as it has been for all our days for each of our people, as my life will soon begin from where the Great Spirit will allow my spirit to depart my soul and join those of my people whom await me in the heavens of our skies.

Without pause, I turned and began to walk towards where the Three Brother of Cedar were tied along the shore of En che Wauna.

As I knelt to touch En che Wauna's soul as she flowed freely before my feet, my body became like a young man and strength filled my chest and offered my thoughts to hold faith closely to my heart so I would gain further upon the last of my journeys.

En che Wauna and myself had at that moment become as one spirit.

Her powerful waters infused strength to become bonded within me. We each were alike one another, promised to all the lands, and to all the plants and animals beneath the heaven through the heart and soul of the Great Spirit.

I praised Hyas Tahmahnawis for all I had been gifted, and my heart was then filled with great joy.

From afar, I heard my name called to begin crossing En che Wauna where I would again walk into the canyon where the story of life was first offered before my eyes and spoken towards my ears.

The great canyon where life's lessons first touched my soul as it joined that of my spirit, and where I began to grow into the man that has become chief to my people of the Watlalla through the advice of council by the spirits held tightly upon the Walls of Wahclella.

So many learned seasons have past in great favor, which will linger always in the welcomed memories of my life...

Slowly I walked towards the Three Brothers where they awaited me. As I stood before them, I was filled with joy and yet I was shamed as I must turn from each of their spirits and journey far from where my hands would still bring comfort to their souls.

As I spoke of my calling by the Great Spirit, I asked each of the Cedar to forgive me as I could only choose one of the brothers to take me upon our final journey to the far shore where the Creek of the Eagle awaited me.

I thanked each of them for our many journeys together, and I explained mournfully before each of them, it was not my choice to separate either one from their brothers.

I asked them to decide between themselves to who would choose for me to be honored to sit within their hull as we crossed En che Wauna for the final journey we would share.

In wait, I stood unopposed through the sorrow of their silence.

From across the wave of En che Wauna, came Raven with much hurry, calling loudly towards our gathering with each beat of his strong wings.

Raven circled many times above where we stood, and with each pass he drew nearer to where I awaited the three brother's decision.

Suddenly, as Raven descended closer to where I stood, his wingtip slid across my shoulder, and he came to settle softly upon the side of the cedar the two brothers had each chosen to take me upon my journey to the Creek of the Eagle.

Again, I touched each of the brother's souls as I ran my fingers across their sides as I had done many seasons ago when we had first chose one another to join together in our journeys.

This moment brought both sadness and much remorse to swell within my heart as I was soon to depart from this life. Knowing of my own loss to them allowed feelings of abandonment to rush through my thoughts.

The brothers three were too a great part of our village's family.

As I reached out to lower my friend from where he lay outstretched upon the bank of the Big Waters, excitement filled my heart as Sun shone down upon us with approving eyes.

The lands seemed to dance beneath my feet as the voice of Wind sang softly upon us, and all the birds and animals came to watch from the trees and from upon the shores of our great river.

If this was my goodbye from all that lived in our kingdom, then I knew my understanding towards each of their lives had been both accepted and respected as I had spoken wisely with my own convictions towards all their life's significance to one another and to our people.

Many who had come to sit in counsel at the fires of our village had heard me speak and had felt of my heart as I told of my grandfather and the dream he had been chosen to witness beneath the long arms of Great Cedar long ago.

We took ourselves upon the waves of En che Wauna once again to join our spirits with those of the lands of the Valley of the Eagle, and as I sat in the hull of my friend, I called out to my son and asked that he come to the shore of the Eagle as Otelagh rose above our village the fifth morning.

I asked that he would again return the canoe beside those of his brothers to where they would await him.

I had made promise to the three brothers before we culled their roots from the soil that I would not separate either brother from the others.

It was then, with loud voice, I heard each of them promise they would offer the people of our village safe journeys upon all the waters of our kingdom as it would bonds their spirit with our people as we have and would be significant to one another's survival upon the waters of our kingdom.

The brothers each promised to honor all those of our village with safe journeys. From their hearts they would share of that honor before all the spirits of our lands so they too may share in the greatest of joy in knowing in that freedom we have brought to their souls.

As we journey to all corners of our kingdom of Wah, the brothers will then know of all the lands, of all the animals who depend on their limbs to make nest, and of the importance of how when the full moon rises above in the heaven their shadow's offer safety to those that hide when Pish Pish hunt.

Realizing this was to be my final venture from the shoreline where our village lies, I looked towards Che che Optin. I peered high up to the peak of the great rock where I could hear the cries of sorrow falling upon my ears from where princess Wehatpolitan and her child chose to offer their souls to the earth and not again rest in the longhouse of her father.

With great sorrow, I once more wailed to the Great Creator to keep Wehatpolitan's memory alive so we may each learn of the lesson she chose for others to remember so they too would not take faith, honor, or trust from the hearts of their brothers or sisters, or sons or daughters through the deceit of their own uncertain spirit.

In that same sorrow I have also for many days begun to discover myself eager to go from this life to the lives of which spirits share where Otelagh and Moon shine bright with promise, and seasons never change.

To go where greed and selfishness of the soul do not exist.

To go where the offering of one's soul brings promise to another's spirit, and leads to their trust before all their village's peoples.

With purpose, Wind chose to blow hard against my face and challenged me not to return to my journey with a renewed and clearer mind as they challenged my thoughts to travel upon trails I was not again meant to journey.

Through my leadership I was not taught by the elders to walk from what brings my soul discomfort, but to study why the lesson that is presented before me troubles my soul.

I was first taught to conquer my fears so that I can share before all our peoples how not to allow that same fear to enter into our hearts and take from our spirits all that is good.

I sat in the hull of my canoe and looked up from the waves of En che Wauna, and as warm wind blew softly across my face the beauty and grace of the Lands of Wah rose up before me.

Each tree that clung to the heavens reminded me of stories my peoples shared as the sticks had spoken to those that chose to sit below their welcoming arms as they shared stories of season's long ago passed.

Each limb, each needle brought worth to their placement upon the soils of our kingdom.

Without difficulty, I began to hear each of their voices call out to me as I rowed hard to the shore of the Eagle.

The stick's long arms opened towards me, welcoming me again beneath their tower. They each gave me purpose and reason to follow where my heart was wanting to be led.

Wind swept peacefully across the waves of En che Wauna. Only the piercing shrill from high above me in the heaven was heard the call of Great Eagle. I knew Great Eagle cried out as we would not meet again, but we would see one another in the skies of our heaven one day soon.

Great Coyote called out to me from the far hill above the Creek to the Eagle as she too awaited me to join her for the final days we would walk together as we climbed into the lands of Tkope Moolack.

Raven followed closely as he flew low above me as he watched closely to the trails my life would now become surrendered.

They each guarded over what I could not see beneath the cresting of the highest wave, and from what may lie hidden behind tree and rock in the shadows of our lands.

My friends, Coyote and Raven have never strayed far from my side, and as they have protected me, and have led me upon safe trails, I will be forever grateful.

Their names shall be mentioned each time I speak to our Fathers whom now await me in the Great Village above.

"Father", I plead before you, may the day soon come when you accept my friends, the guardians of our peoples, Coyote and Raven, to join their spirits with our own so they too may find rest beside those of our brothers who are today gathered before your great village's fire."

As I sat looking out across En che Wauna I began to recollect all the days I had lived and prospered in these majestic lands that offered my people all we could have asked.

I raised my arms to the heavens in great joy to have been honored to walk across these lands for all the many seasons I have lived. Seasons when both hardship and joy have filled my heart and allowed my soul to understand the power our spirits can bring once we allow the union of our Hyas Tyee into our own lives.

It has been in this end of time I have begun to understand the necessity of owning to both good and bad, for they both have offered me to gain faith through the hopes for our tomorrows.

From the east a cold wind began to cruelly sweep across the driven waves of En che Wauna. Instantly, my soul began to question why now has my journey been challenged? I had just moments ago felt assured I would certainly join those many of our people's fathers that had taken this same journey across the fast waters of En che Wauna without worry, but now, it is not the same.

The chiefs of our people each had taken upon this journey, though they were different in the course of their lessons, in those first breaths we took as we began to follow the calling of Hyas Tyee, we were then certainly bonded through our own prayers and by this award offered to each.

When my chest first raised from within me to grasp the crisp air, I sensed my strength renewed. The power of all my brothers union to one another gave me hope to see the Sun of all our people's tomorrows.

To each of the spirits of our kingdoms I had once stood before and listened to their message, and of those I had not yet journeyed, have now become brothers for all days to the soils of the Earth.

May we journey always together beneath the skies of our heavens as we look down upon the lands we have so loved...

My travel across En che Wauna was as quick as is the fox to the hare.

My ride upon my friend Cedar was like I had been placed upon the backs of Great Salmon as they fought the fast wave in their journey home to the waters of their villages.

I came upon the shore of the Eagle without effort, and it is from here, where my final journey now lies challenged before me that will prove of my spirit and of my courage through the acceptance of Tkope Moolack towards the future of my people.

All I knew that was good from the High Spirit's hands came to rest within my heart, for they offer me support in the understanding to the significance this trial was meant to bring first to my soul, then to my spirit, and finally to my people.

As I turned to face my village this final day, with tears swollen to my eyes, I knew, soon, this day would only become a single memory of many that I would cherish for all days.

With much sorrow, I then knew this would be the final moment for me to turn and look back upon the lands I have honored all the days of my life. Not only did this instance take me back to the lands of this Kingdom of Wah, but to the many seasons I journeyed beneath the lessons gifted from the lessons of our greatest of spirits.

Though my thoughts realized these were the final moments of my life's journey, I too felt great happiness as I began to climb up the trail of the Creek to the Eagle as an old and tired man of many years.

These are the same trails where I began to climb from the knolls of my youth into the peaks of my manhood as the screams of the Eagle cried out above me as I journeyed far into the long valley.

That glorious day when I was sent to join my heart with my mind as I began my test before the High Spirit, challenged the true essence of my spirit given the understanding I must adhere and accept towards the many steps leading to becoming a leader of peoples, all peoples, and not just of those from my village.

Once I was accepted to further my mettle before the trials that awaited me, I, with great heart and clear mind, strived to prove before the High Spirit of my worthiness in becoming a leader to my village.

I yearned to lead my peoples into understanding how to live life each day through the philosophies my great fathers spoke.

By the wisdom exhibited through the lectures the High Spirits shared before me as I stood before them, and as I listened to each of their lessons without offering question to why they believed only in the ways they had lain before me, they began to accept my spirit worthy as I too accepted my responsibilities in bringing both distinction and honor to our people in knowing the truths we must all live each day.

My heart swells with knowing of the honor of my joining the Great Spirit of Tkope Moolack upon the slopes of Wy-East by our Hyas Tumtum Tyees' choosing.

Though this is to be my final trek through the lands that have brought much joy to my heart, the Great Creator has shown, once I have completed my task, I will be welcomed to sit beside all those of my people's fathers as I still will look down upon our people and towards the lands that will for all days bare my heart upon them.

The strength of my spirit must allow me to rise up upon the slopes of Wy-East as the sun rises five times in the heaven. But even as Sun rose into the heavens two days ago, I felt my feet were becoming heavy and my heart slowed by all the seasons that have brought prosperity and great happiness to my soul.

I, today, have faith I will be strong and confident to crest the tall peak of Wy-East, and there, I will stand proudly upon the steep slope beside the Great Spirit, Tkope Moolack.

I will then know, through all the seasons I have lived, and as I gave up my earthly self to journey far into our great kingdom to speak before our people's fires of truth, honor, faith, trust, and of the innocence we were chosen to adhere, will allow my being to rise up to live in those tomorrows my heart now so yearns.

I am told White Elk and I will stand together and peer down upon the lands. We will search together for answer to what will offer life to flourish for all days as the storm of Red Cloud is now rising upon our lives.

Those tomorrows that can never be hidden behind the mask of evil, are now held challenged and undoubtedly in much question as they are bound by the greed of many hearts, and through blind eyes that can only foresee to what is offered today upon their tables.

My days are near their end, and as I must soon go to where I cannot speak to my son and continue to lead his mind to follow in the Great Creator's beliefs, I pray my son is ready to lead our peoples, the Great Tahmahnawis Tyee's peoples, out into where life breathes easy to those that first follow in the Great Spirit's advices.

As our peoples gather and unite in great numbers, they will always remain strong before the eyes of the Great Spirit. Their trails will be chosen safe from the bad spirit's ruse, and each day they go out into the lands, they will return with food for their tables and vines to make basket.

They shall not be afraid of what lies in the shadows of the forest, or from beneath the wave of En che Wauna, but they will raise high their heads and look up towards Sun and Moon, and their many journeys shall bring witness before others their spirits are strong.

Many days I have questioned if I were worthy of leading my peoples. But today, as Sun rises into the heaven and has again brought warmth to settle upon the lands, I have no question that might bring uncertainty to why he has chosen me in to further in the success of this effort where I do not today struggle to understand.

I have come to love this land even through the hardship of long winters.

I have found prosperity through the lead of our fathers, through the guidance of Coyote, and through the protection offered from Hyas Raven.

Today, as I begin my journey towards Wy-East from along the trail where had not long ago traced the hooves of both deer and elk, I hear the soft song of each bird upon the limbs of trees above.

Knowing their spirits are free as will be my soul, my heart has become settled in knowing only the Hyas Tyee's Tkope Kuitan awaits to carry me to rest beside the Great Creator's warm fire.

I have walked many times to find myself resting beside what remains of Great Cedar as he still lives through the memories of my fathers and my grandfather's stories. They both had sat with me and told of the many talks they and Great Cedar shared as they sat beneath his long arms.

Great Cedar offered protection from both rain and snow, and as his sweet scent arose upon them, their thoughts too were spent upon dreams seen through the looking glass of their tomorrows.

My understanding to the needs of the Earth swelled up within me. I believe it has been through those stories where holds the truth to the reasoning of my many journeys across the lands of our kingdom.

From each step I placed before the other across all the kingdoms of our lands, I began to first hear, and then listen to every voice of the many spirits as I came upon them.

Their stories, good and bad, had each allowed my understanding in their value into one another's lives, and quickly, my spirit too began to rise up within me as I walked promised in the shadow of the Great Creator.

It has been through those lessons in humility where life began to breath the truths of living into my soul, and only then, could my spirit too sail beneath the heaven where Sun rises each day, and Moon sets each night.

There have been many days I did not know what to say to the people of my village as trade had been good with those Suyapee who arrived at the doorway of our village.

We sat with them and smoked from the long pipe, and settled our trade with great happiness between us.

Yet there is much question asked as the sickness our peoples today writhe may come from within the purse of Suyapee that is hidden from our eyes.

When Suyapee had left our village many days ago, there were brothers and sisters taken from us by their disease, each suffering in the greatest of grief.

Long days and longer nights we could hear them cry out to the High Spirit to take the disease from their souls.

As the darkness of night fell hushed over the lands, we dared not enter the longhouse where they lay bound by their conviction for we too may have found ourselves stricken.

I do not yet understand how the spirit hidden of Suyapee can take our peoples from before the fires of our villages as we make trade and welcome them all with opened arms?

This question remains troubling to my soul!

Slowly I began to climb across the slope of the high cliff where I peered down into the clearest of waters of the Creek to the Eagle. I crossed without worry as I knew the Great Creator was promised of my ascent of Wy-East shoulders.

Soon, my heart fell treasured to the scent of flowers and to the bark of Cedar as Wind cast their sweet scent upon the warm air as Sun rose high above me.

Long ago, I walked this same trail with reason and purpose and it has not changed.

I, today, began to recall all that had come before me many seasons ago as I journeyed through the great forest as my trial of manhood began here at the Creek of the Eagle.

I began as a child, my soul sworn to my father. My spirit strong through the mettle I had inherited from each of my village's great shamans.

I emerged before my people eager to lead them one day through the teachings of the High Spirits.

I was honored as Otelagh shone down upon my shoulders and awarded my efforts with the warmth of his heart. His passion soon engaged my spirit into the man I have become today through his welcoming and educating arms.

Hummingbirds flew swiftly across the trail before me as they danced to their own drum, calling upon me to follow where they led through the flowers of the meadows.

The young of Great Owls sat upon the tree's limbs that hung along the streams I crossed, their mothers watched with keen eyes from distant trees as I passed.

It was not long before I turned from where the trees brought calm to my soul when they began to sing song from each side of the trail to one another.

The Creek to the Eagle beckoned me to join upon its trail, and as I walked, taking each step with respect for what lie beneath my feet, it saddened me greatly as I knew this would be my last trek across the boundaries of my birthplace.

As I rose up from the face of the cliff, I came upon the long arms of firs who reached out to touch my arms as I passed. There, resting upon their boughs, Great Eagles awaited the spirits of pish to rise up from the depths along the wawa of Metlako as they had many times before when I had come to dream.

I am pleased they choose to watch over me as I too wish to sit and rest in silence below where they are gathered upon the long branch.

They do not announce my arrival to the spirits of the forest. Their screams now silenced in their approval of my presence upon the course of Wind.

They have chosen not to take wing and fly beyond where I could see as they had each day when I had come upon them in past seasons.

I am pleased this day to have shared these waters beside them. These waters that flow always through the Kingdom of Wah, which have been poured down upon the lands from the tears hastened from our Great Creator's cheeks, to each of those waters which offers all that lives and breathes upon its lands life through its purest of gift.

I feel the Eagles too knew of my calling by the Hyas Tahmahnawis to appoint myself upon this final journey. As they look upon me and I them, I sense they too know my soul is proven and readied to join that of my spirit for all days.

I sense from within me, the Great Eagles too saw into my soul, and they knew my heart was no longer held in question by the character I once held within me as a young child.

It is to my promise of the creation by the hands of Hyas Tyee I now must first feel, and then think.

Though in the village of Wahclella rests my people, I must not turn from my view unto the heights of Wy-East, but I must strive forward and find no doubt or sorrow in this journey.

It is my spirit and the will of my heart I shall hold strong before the eyes of my Great Spirit and before the eyes of Tkope Moolack.

Welcomed, I sit and rest where the late season's leaves have not yet fallen upon the ground. Each tree points towards Metlako's long and beautiful fall into the bowl below her. I look intensely into the treasure of Metlako and my heart quickly became settled.

I must relive all the past lessons of my life's work as I walk into the great canyon that had first set my heart solidly into understanding the importance in honoring the treasures our Great Father and Earth Mother has awarded our peoples.

In that principle, I too must offer all reverence before them...

I stood at the shore of the Great Eagle and a voice fell upon me from the distant peaks that point the trail towards Wy-East.

I knew it was Hyas Tahmanawis Tyee, my leader, the Great Spirit I had listened many times to the lessons of life he had taught me as I stood before the Walls of Wahclella.

The Great Spirit spoke with much clarity. His words were thrust to my ears, each set hardened to my heart, and they each were quickly fastened to my soul.

"Tkope Moolack will take you upon his shoulders as you and he will look down upon the Illahee, (lands) and share what has brought both, great happiness and great shame to your peoples.

"Tkope Moolack lives and breathes knowing of the same stories you have been taught of our people's beginnings upon the high peak where Naha looks over her children.

"Stories that tell of where tree and bush, bird and frog, fish and worm, and deer and elk have all first come from the bond of water and sand of the Great Sea.

"There have been stories told of many wars fought between the spirits of Wy-East and Pahto by Great Cedar to your father. In those stories, it has been spoken he had faith many tomorrows would bring Sun to shine down uninterrupted upon each of them beneath his reign from the heaven above.

"It is time for you to go to the high peak of Wy-East, and from there, you will see what your peoples must suffer before the day arrives when they are allowed to return before the fires that shall burn uninterrupted for their return.

"You will see color held back from the waters of many streams and from the Big Waters of many kingdoms.

"You will see the great sticks taken from upon the lands and their souls cut from within them to build villages where the camas and wapato were first chosen to survive.

"Life will not be the same for your peoples.

"Through the visions of your fathers, you will now see all the suns of all the tomorrows your people will walk beneath.

"You too will one day sit above your peoples. One day, your son will lead them from what will come from Tsiatko's poach of Suyapee's purse.

"White Elk has seen those that are quick to approach the shores of En che Wauna from the sea who find their course lain before our lands with great hurry.

"He has told they wish to steal the treasures our Great Earth Mother holds deep within her soul.

"It has been told through vision of your fathers these new peoples will not stop, and it is from their purse, their dark purse, that will come the bad spirit as his smile and kind eyes offers us only confusion when we discover our peoples weakened by what we cannot see that takes our people's breaths easily from their souls.

"Tkope Moolack will share with you vision he has seen come upon us as Red Cloud returns!

"I tell you my son Raven, listen to all he says, and you will see through his eyes the trails our peoples must follow to live through the coming storms that are promised to rise up with grave threat across each of the nations our peoples have stood proud.

"Your heart will then become settled as you share with your son all we have asked, and only then will you be seen to rise up into the heaven to sit with your father...

"Great Elk Spirit has been given the gift of light to be shared from his eyes to the visions of our dreams. Hope and faith will spread from within his eyes before your peoples as they flee the Red Cloud of despair that is promised to arrive quickly upon them without warning.

"Your peoples will need to follow his guide as they walk across the lands when only darkness and the unknowing of tomorrow may fill their eyes and blind their souls with much question.

"From atop the great peaks that rise up above the waters of the sea to the lands that lie low in the desert alongside waters that flow swiftly from Pahto and Wy-East, Tkope Moolack has journeyed upon all the trails that have yet to be touched by man across our lands.

He has journeyed across waters that keep the grasses tall and trees green with new leaf that offer soft bed for deer and elk.

"Tkope Moolack has too looked through the looking glass and witnessed from where your peoples first came.

"From the moment of that first day, when your peoples were born from the wanting of Naha for children, Tkope Moolack has witnessed.

"Tkope Moolack has seen all the days before your people had come to settle in Wahclella.

"With sad eyes, he too sees the day when your people will be led to lands you do not know of their spirits.

"He too has seen with clear eyes the day when your people will again rest before the warm fires of your villages, and there you will make song to the heaven again through the passing of Wind's softest breaths.

"When Sun first rises at the dawn of day, and it promises little, your peoples souls must be sworn to hold true to your faith as it will be through the guidance Trope Mollack chooses for your peoples to walk free from Suyapee's own battle within his misled soul.

"Suyapee has proven he suffers much as he walks blindly past the gifts that live before his feet. He marches wildly and without care to the cadence of the bad spirit's drum.

"We must not surrender to the wants of others from what has kept our lands healthy and free from the disease of craving what we do not need to survive.

"Raven, prepare yourself as you will again speak to your son as Otelagh sets and Moon rises on the fifth day.

This will be sign that allows you to know the days of your seasons are ending. It is through your great sacrifice that all your peoples will survive upon these lands.

"Raven, I ask you to assure One Who Runs Fast Like Horse your peoples will one day return to your village's fires as the temperateness of their spirits shall overcome the scorn and treachery Red Cloud delivers upon their lives.

"The villages of our people shall await always for their longed return to find rest and bring song to the cast of Wind. This was promised before the first children of Indian came down onto the lands from the nest of Naha from above the heights of Walahoof's crown.

"Many seasons have passed since the days when our children were first led down from Naha's steep cliffs and were chosen then to settle along En che Wauna and within these Lands of Wah.

"Word has been promised by the Great Creator as he has been heard to speak; "Life shall cultivate promise from its own seed, and as my children walk beneath the sky of heaven, and as they offer reverence to all that breathes upon the lands, then all our people's tomorrows shall bring honor unto themselves before all those that will come and witness the quality of their souls."

"Sadly, one day, not far away, your peoples will be taken where only the bad spirit knows of those lands.

"It is there where our mothers and fathers, our sons and our daughters shall see end to their long march from their villages.

"Life will not be the same for many seasons, but as our people look up to the heavens and pray to be offered again the promise of Wah to be placed beneath their feet, their words, their hearts, their souls, and their spirits shall be heard and felt from where I sit today.

"It will not be long before they are seen again to settle beside the waters of En che Wauna, and life will be good.

"With heads raised, those that stand upon lands that do not share promise as what they have known for many seasons will be heard to call out with calm voice as they await the Great Father's direction in return to the kingdom they have known for all days.

"It will not be many suns or moons from when that journey's long march begins before your son will be called to lead your peoples to wail from upon the highest of peaks, those same high peaks that stand powerfully above the graveyards of the Mesachie Tumtum.

"Those same graveyards we know of today that have begun to swell with the many that did not have the strength of spirit to believe in those same tomorrows we today speak.

"My son Raven, this is the message you must speak to your son as many will gather before him so they may keep strong in the eyes of adversity. So they too will know of the trail that your son will lead them safely to one day return before the fires of their villages!"

I was assured he had directed me once again to share in my understanding to the gravity of the situation that would soon arise so our peoples may live to see beyond tomorrow's light.

This is the fourth night of my journey back into life's many challenges of all the past seasons I have lived. Only Great Coyote's call could be heard passing through the stillness of Wind across the lands.

I lie here, looking to the stars to carry my thoughts into where my dreams await me each night.

I cannot escape the sorrow that firmly holds my heart hostage.

I lay here upon my mat beneath an old Cedar, unrested, bound to my own convictions as I place importance to the words I must share with One Who Runs Fast Like Horse.

I prepared for the message I must share with my son so he would know of what he will soon face given this, his first trial before the eyes of Hyas Tahmahnawis and our people.

Our peoples must know of answers that will bring reason to their plight before life becomes questioned and their lives forgotten as are the Winds of yesterday.

This feat shall be a challenge beyond all others I had myself been faced...

I felt fear's slight through the visions of our creator.

I saw darkness where there should be light.

In that same darkness I could not see the trails we had followed for many seasons across our lands.

I did not see pish jumping into the heavens from the fast currents of En che Wauna to catch the fly.

I saw only emptied villages where a single flame still burns, but not a man or woman or child were left to share in that fleeting moment's warmth.

In fear, tears fell hurriedly from my eyes as they rushed to touch the soil at my feet, each longing through my memory for what we have always carried within our souls and shared through our spirit.

Longing for the gifts we have been so honored, for they shall be no more for many seasons beyond those of our people.

As quickly as the fiery spears were first thrown from the hands of Wy-East and Pahto from the heavens that pierced the soul of all the lands we are today surrounded, darkness too has now fallen hurried upon the lives of our peoples.

Coyote's call was quickly stolen from where my wanting heart now lies emptied.

In my sorrow, my faith for her return brings hope her call has only been cast out beyond our kingdom and across many new trails Wind now journeys...

The warmth of morning rises up from upon the cold ground of this past night. Sun again beams down upon me as I rise from where I slept.

Surrounding me are all the gifts the Kingdom of Wah has offered me to hold closely to my heart.

I have been fortunate to share in all these land's beauty.

To speak with all the animals, to smell the plants and flowers I have passed. This is a gift I shall not forget...

Though I cannot see our village, I am gifted to see through Tsagiglala's eyes the lands my heart craves.

Just there, across the Big River, rises up tall Firs, Maple, and Oak upon the beautiful face of Che che Optin that brings color to the land. She stands as strong and powerful as she shares in the determination of our people's spirit.

Che che Optin is a symbol of our people's strength, and of our union to the lands of the Earth.

In the beginning, when our peoples first came down from the peak of Naha's nest upon Saddle Mountain, we chose the big meadow to lay the foundation for our life's beginnings.

It is there Che che Optin rises above the fast waters of En che Wauna, proudly standing above where our village of Wahclella rests.

Our longhouses, standing amidst the green grasses of the big meadow, nestled beneath the shadow of the lost spirit of one of Wy-East's many children.

Though I cannot see our village, through the eyes of my memories, I see smoke from the morning's fires lazily rising up to meet the trails of wind as it passes across the lands into the heaven.

My soul is committed to be here where I stand, and though my heart does crave to again be with my people sitting before the fire to eat pish and moolack, I do not allow my soul to escape into the hands of the bad spirit who has promised to prey upon our souls until the final rays of Sun are cast down upon the lands.

Though I am not with my family in person, my thoughts allows me to wail before the feet of the Great Spirit and thank Him for all he offers those of our village who look up into the Valley of the Eagle.

To plead he remembers the strength of my soul through the freedom my spirit is connected alongside his own.

I have been taught by our fathers to remember always it is when we open our eyes and hearts to what lies before us we can become promised to survive where others have quickly perished.

Many peoples have walked upon ground where rock was first thrown from the fiery bowels of the earth, but yet they cannot see rising from those same soils lies root that makes bread that offers our peoples to live welcomed beyond the warmth of Sun's rays today.

It is the same for our spirit when we allow our souls to commit ourselves to walk amongst others without fear or threat.

There were many days when we may have had differences with those of distant villages.

Our people were each taught by the Great Spirit we must welcome all those that come before us. We, and they, must be committed to accept without question to all that is righteous between us and to the earth, and in that, respect shall lay the foundation toward our survival so we may all see Sun's rise tomorrow.

We must welcome those that come to sit with us and enjoy feast together before the open fire.

We must share thought so we may better understand and grow wise to the ways of the earth and of those others that walk amongst us.

We shall survive all those tomorrows that are now in question if we are to open our eyes and hearts to what is right through what is chosen by the Hyas Tahmahnawis for all the peoples of the Illahee.

We must find gratification by our Father's gifts and not find ourselves challenged by our own misguided complaints!

"Mitlite Okoke Nesika Ooahut!"
("Be This Our Way!")

I sit here as my spirit joins that of the brother of Cedar who had been chosen to glide across the Big Waters and deliver me upon the distant shore.

It is here, where the Creek to the Eagle's stream meets that of the waters of En che Wauna my spirit shall wait for my son to arrive so he will hear my voice once more.

Time is only the passing of Sun and Moon across the heavens, so I wait, not worried, patiently, and in happiness knowing my son's and my own spirit will be joined once again to these lands before I begin my journey to the heights of Wy-East.

Wind does not blow hard this day, but as cloud falls from the peaks above, suddenly, the calm of day is taken prisoner and cast out far from where its pleasing breaths were comforting to my soul.

Raven screams from above in the tree where I can not see.

Raven has been with me always. He has overlooked my every step throughout my journeys. We have sat upon the ground and looked deep into one another's eyes, and we have each come to understand our own spirits, and to their significance towards one another.

Raven has warned of danger that has lain where I could not see, and he has willingly led me from the attack of danger as he has kept me safe from before its sharpened teeth.

I stand tall upon the peak of this mountain, and far above the bank of En che Wauna. I peer out anxiously across the wave of the Big River and yearn to see my son come to share the visions the Great Spirit has allowed me to picture through the chronicles he has foreseen.

One Who Runs Fast Like Horse must know where I stand.

He must know I await him in great anticipation so we may once more speak.

In my sadness, I know many seasons will pass between us before our spirits meet again in the village of our Hyas Tyee.

Today, I must share all that is felt from my soul for the great son he has become to my family, to our people, and to myself.

My son knows of the respect I have felt for him as he has accepted each challenge he had faced with opened arms. He has walked from the shadows of question without fearing what may lie before him many days.

Today, he will know what he must do to save our peoples. He must know our voice will again be heard and not challenged by those who do not choose to accept the wise words Wind will share upon their closed ears.

Wind will cast itself down upon Suyapee from the heavens with great warning. Yet, Suyapee has been promised by the bad spirit if he turns from this warning and walks deafly out into the lands, he will become strong and reign powerfully over all the living spirits in all the lands.

Sadly, Suyapee will only bring disgrace upon themselves through their greed, and they will take from the soils of our lands the soul and spirit of our Hyas Ilahee Naha, (Great Earth Mother).

Suyapee's eyes will first grow wide as they look over what proves worthy in their lives as they journey across our kingdoms.

Then, sadly, more Suyapee will follow, and they will cull the mighty forests and leave nothing but broken dreams upon the barren and desolate lands.

Suyapee will take many pish from the waters in traps, and they shall build stone cliffs to entrap the pish from joining those waters they were first led.

Many seasons will pass, and as many, many, more moons than we, or our fathers have lived, pish will not find safe refuge from the change they will then be entrapped.

In great sadness, our peoples will only look to En che Wauna and see pish lain unmoving, stricken with disease. Impure waters shall wash over them, and the sight of pish rising to the heavens to catch the fly will be seen no more.

Through dreams, my son was seen to quickly become the greatest of all chiefs that have rose up from upon the soils of Wahclella.

One Who Runs Fast Like Horse will preserve hope and faith in the hearts and minds of our people as they will be forced to journey from the place of our villages.

The people of all our villages will be taken upon trails that lead to lands we have not heard others to have found prosper. To lands whose spirits are not known by our people.

Leading our people from the lands we know of their spirits will be the condition Suyapee demands upon the many as they will reign over us in hope this will keep our voices silent and distant from those others that will soon come.

We must each remember, our souls will not be taken from within us, and our spirits shall not fall weakened by Suyapee's imprisonment!

We are Indian!

We will survive!

What Suyapee do not understand, it shall be through the faith instilled within our spirits by the lessons we have acquired through the teachings of the Hyas Tahmahnawis, the abandoned fires of our villages will again call upon us to sit before them and cry out to the Great Spirit in praise for our return to our lands.

This alone will keep our peoples strong as we will demand ourselves to sit patiently until we are called by Hyas Illahee Naha to rejoin our souls to the lands we have been promised from the beginning.

Wind has begun to come fast upon the face of the mountain where I stand waiting. Raven calls out once again, and I know his warning tells my son is coming fast across the wave of En che Wauna to the Creek of the Eagle where I await to honor him with all I have been told by the Great Tyee.

Much happiness fills my heart as I say with much conviction to myself; "Here is my son, One Who Runs Fast Like Horse. He is strong. He is driven by the words spoken of our fathers as he has journeyed across many lands of our kingdoms."

Each day my son is heard to spread word of hope and faith to those that have walked from what is good in their hearts. Many of those have returned to the ways of our Fathers, and it is good!

I am pleased as I could not have asked for more of a son than One Who Runs Fast Like Horse."

"Father, I ask you to keep my son wise to the ways of the Earth, and when he hears your voice calling from atop the high peak where our peoples will be huddled, may you allow him to lead his peoples safely back to the fires that will soon burn in wait for their wanting return."

Wind has brought calm to my soul as I listen to water lap softly upon the shore. With great anticipation, I am eager to speak to my son to what the Great Spirit wishes for him to know before I am lifted from upon the lands of Wah upon the Tkope Kuitan's back as I go to where my father awaits.

My journey upon the back of the White Stallion to the Lands of the Dead is near.

I call out to my son in spirit, and he calls in return. My sons and my spirit again embrace. I know he and I will always walk the lands of our kingdoms as one together.

This too is good!

I can feel his worry rising from within him. Through his arms and hands, I feel he is troubled as he shakes. Only he knows where his thoughts now lie. Only he knows how to take the worry and concern from within his heart and free it from within where it troubles his soul.

I know once I speak the words spoken by the Great Spirit he will become settled.

He will then know well to the trails he must now follow.

He will discover his greatness only awaits his return to our people at Wahclella.

"My son, I tell you this as the Great Spirit has called my name to join him upon the shoulders of Wy-East where the White Elk Spirit runs. It will be from there you will next hear me call.

"It is with both great sadness and great joy I share this with you as this day's sun rises above where we stand.

"You will not hear my voice again until your spirit too rises up to grasp the tail of the White Stallion as you streak across the heaven to the village of the Hyas Tyee to one day again sit at my side.

"I will be with Tkope Moolack.

"Both Tkope Moolack and I will be together for all days as the sun rises and as the moon falls from the heaven.

"As I go to the great mountain, my spirit will then be connected to the Earth for all days.

"Remember, as you lead our peoples through the toils of their lives, I will always look down upon you with great pride for the son and the great leader you have become.

"Many seasons have past. Many have brought happiness to our people, and then there have been others when the cold of winter did not leave our lands or our hearts for many more suns than we were accustomed.

"We have shared each of these, good and bad together, and in each, we have grown together and shared in our happiness to live peacefully amongst all life that either stands before us, or walks upon the same trails as we.

"The Great Spirit has before spoken he will lead our peoples safely upon the trails we must share with those whom we have been told will soon come to our lands.

"The Hyas Tahmahnawis has spoken if we walk in peace amongst them, we will walk free from strife, and the bad spirit will fall harmless below our feet as we cross the lands of our kingdom.

"But as Red Cloud nears our villages, the High Spirit now sees beyond today's Sun, as he too has appeared to have become confused and does not understand the ways of these people.

"Many suns have coursed across the heaven, and in those days our peoples have fallen sick, and now lie helpless across his lands.

"Suyapee brings the bad spirit as his guest to our villages. Though we may not see him, or hear him, it is his poison that has now taken many of our brothers and sisters, mothers and fathers, sons and daughters from before our fires.

"It is a sad time for our people and for all life that had once walked free upon the same trails we have made journey. But as Hyas Tahmahnawis Tyee has spoken, we know now Suyapee will build great villages from the sticks of our forests.

"Many lodges will reach out to touch the heaven.

"Soon, Suyapee's only promise shall be to themselves, and they will quickly fail.

"Suyapee will lead those that know of life's salvation far from the lands of their births, and soon, those lands shall too, be seen no more.

"As Suyapee lays ruin to our villages they will take from our kingdoms all that is good, and they will take all that was first chosen for all our peoples as we first walked down from the high peak where Naha is seen to mourn those lost of her children.

"My son, I know all the village's chiefs must meet and go to where Suyapee sleep at night. It is there you must sit with them and smoke from the long pipe as you speak of good will and peace between our peoples.

"I pray they will know all our spirits are good.

"You must share with them you choose not to make war between our people.

"My fear is Suyapee will not hear your pledge once they see the worry within your eyes.

"I tell you, you must walk before them and hold high your heads in honor as the High Spirit wishes.

"Remember, he has taught us to walk in peace with others in all that we do.

"Remember too this, as our souls walk free from anger and worry, we shall forever walk out safely from before any difficulties that may befall our paths.

"Our spirits will live on into those days we have yet to see of tomorrow as our Great Father has spoken.

"My son, many seasons have passed in my life. Many have been spent in both good and bad, but in all these, life still thrives.

"Our people's spirits stay strong as we walk with faith, and we believe the deeds we perform are through the teachings the Hyas Tumtum Tyee has led us to accept as worthy of being named, Indian.

"Today, I have begun to climb to the peak of Wy-East and will soon find my feet firmly planted upon his silken robe. I cannot wait to join my spirit alongside that of Tkope Moolack.

"I must say to you this, through all adversity you will be chosen to lead our peoples, your peoples. They will be with the Good Spirit as he has led all our fathers so we may each see the light of all our tomorrows.

"You must follow the High Spirit's laws we have been led to accept from the beginning of our people's first day upon these magnificent lands.

"The time has now come for you to keep our brothers from joining the bad spirit's wards so they too may discover hope and gather faith within their souls as they traverse through what they may not understand in the ways of Suyapee.

"I know you will encounter many trials that will bring question to your heart. You will choose to walk before the Walls of Wahclella many days and question, why?

"You must first remember this, as you stand before the Great Wall and speak before the High Chiefs, you will hear the decisions spoken by those who have first brought honor to our peoples.

"Through their directives, those of our peoples that stay strong in the ways of the High Spirit shall walk out from the darkness of unknowing into the light of Otelagh as he offers each of them the gift of life once they follow in the teachings of the High Spirit's counsel.

"My son, to walk and breathe the air gifted from the heavens is all a man may ask as he journeys through life. We often do not know where our life will take us one season to the next.

"I have been very fortunate as my life was set to follow trails only the Hyas Tyee knew before the day of my birth.

"Today you have been called upon to follow in all the lessons your ancestors have shared before our people as we sat before the fires of our councils.

"As we first walked upon the Trail of Righteousness we began to learn of a higher authority as we saw life begin from within the pure waters that came first from the tears of the Great Creator and then formed into the streams and rivers of our lands.

"Today, you will lead your peoples into many new seasons that will bring both conflict and happiness before you.

"I have been called upon by the Great Spirit to walk across the great mountains that lead to the base of Wy-East.

"Wy-East, The Lands of Wah's Great Spirit who has brought peace to settle across all our lands as he stood opposed to the tantrums of Pahto for many seasons and brought both plant and animal to join their spirits once again across all the lands.

"Their gifts to the lands too brought hope in our own survival through the long winters we would find ourselves to suffer.

"From plant to animal, they each speak loudly to those that yearn to know of their right to live beside our villages.

"Much fire and rock once spewed from the throats of both Wy-East and Pahto's spirits as fiery spears were cast through the day and lit the heavens with light at night.

Great fires spread by Wind across all the lands.

"In fear, Elk and deer, coyote and bear, and all that lived once peacefully in the great forests then fled swiftly from their kingdoms.

"Many of their spirits were lost beneath the great fires that swept across the lands where they had once found favor.

"Much sadness fell upon the land, and all the spirits voices swiftly fell silent upon the trails of Wind as it swept hurriedly past where our peoples have since stood.

"As Otelagh crossed the skies each day and saw the ruin Pahto and Wy-East had accepted to lay across their kingdoms, from his eyes came great tears to fall for many suns upon all the lands.

"Many seasons passed, and life was not the same.

"Pish did not swim into En che Wauna.

"Birds were not heard to sing.

"The great herds of Moolack and Mowitch did not gather into where the great meadows once waited for our peoples to hunt.

"Then, as many seasons passed and quiet fell upon Wy-East's and Pahto's soul, slowly, new trees and bush began to trust once again, and they each began to return and rise from the soils.

"The Big Waters too had been cleansed of stick and mire from its channels.

"Pish returned to all the rivers and to all the streams as they brought color once again to flourish below the trees and bush of all the kingdoms they had touched.

"Life was seen to emerge from the throes of darkness as gloom had permitted uncertainty and hesitation to challenge what we had been taught through the lessons of our Fathers.

"For many seasons, life's happiness was just beyond our next step, beyond our outstretched arms. Hidden behind the advance of Wind's storm across our lands, life was not seen.

"You must ask my son, if this trial that challenges our people with the coming of Suyapee is not one alike the battles fought between Pahto and Wy-East?

"As you have heard much warning, soon there shall be no more Indian seen to walk through the Lands of Wah, and our voice will be silenced from upon the lands as we too shall flee the battles that are certain to surrender our villages beneath the flames of the bad spirit's fires.

"Then, my son, I must ask you, what of our lives shall be proven as just and righteous before the eyes of others that will one day walk across these lands?

"All that we have today will then lie corrupted and buried deep beneath the soils of our lands, only to be seen as blackened ruin.

"Through your faith, our peoples must keep hope within their souls, and one day, from high above upon the peak of a distant mountain, your peoples will hear the voice of the Great Spirit calling them each to follow you to their villages along the shores of En che Wauna.

"Do not give up in your faith, as it is in that faith there is always hope for better tomorrows!

"My son, the time has come that I must go to where I am called to stand upon the great Wy-East. I ask that you fear not what is presented before you as it will be through the kindness and leadership of all our past fathers that will bind our peoples together and take you far from the arms of evil if you believe.

"We will meet again, and remember always, as you journey through each day of your life, keep that day sacred. May each day that sun rises above you always bring joy and happiness, and may they each spread goodwill to all the people.

"Remember, with the burden of seeing beyond the cloak of darkness as life may fall heavily upon your shoulders, in that darkness, fear your final words will lie quieted and stilled upon your lips, and may they not be forever lost upon the trails of Wind where they will journey before others, unheard.

"Klahowya, My Son!

"Klahowya!"

As I walk from where my spirit held long to my words as I spoke out to the lesson my son must believe in the change our peoples would soon be faced, I begin to climb upon the trail that leads to Wy-East.

I have much time to reflect on my life as the trail is long before I stand beside Great White Elk.

Many suns have passed through the many seasons I have lived upon our lands.

From the day I was first judged by the Great Spirit I journeyed through the trials set before me of my vision quest.

It was not long after I returned to our village my father's final breath fell emptied across the longhouse as he lay in his favored robe upon the floor. His soul was taken from within him and lent to the spirits who now waited his journey into the Lands of the Dead to end.

The voices of my father and his father before him called out loudly to my name. They demanded for me to stand before my people and offer them guidance through the trials of their lives.

Through all the adventures and misadventures of my life, I grant credence towards each as they have allowed me to become the leader to my brothers and sisters at Wahclella.

Though I have erred many times in my understanding to the just paths that had been lain before my feet, I have been fortunate to walk out from the sharpened blade that awaits others in the shadows of darkness.

I understand now, I had allowed myself to become surrendered by my own judgment before pleading to the Great Spirit for what he chose for me to follow.

By the grace of our fathers, and by the compassion of the High Spirit, I know now of the honor I had been chosen as a leader for my people.

Before Sun set that day, I began to lead them to honor all that we encountered throughout each of the days that followed.

Each of our lives then began anew.

We became strong and wise through the advice of our Great Father.

All the people of our village and I had walked for many seasons with the Great Spirit, and we have not ventured from his lead as we have chosen to honor the heaven and the Earth.

This too brought pleasure to the Great Spirit as he has offered us much to survive each change that came hard upon the lands of Wah.

One day long ago, as I knelt before Elowah, I first felt one of life's greatest gifts presented before me.

I remember well, winter had surrendered its hold upon all the lands below the tall peaks of our kingdom, and Otelagh chose to warm my soul as he shone down upon me through the branch of Cedar that clung close to the soils of Elowah's creek.

Many of those trees had lived seasons longer than all our peoples who had first come to these lands long ago.

Strong and beautiful were each tree as they swayed and danced to the soothing breaths of Wind.

I stepped from along the trail and listened to their chorus as it rang out with joyous sound.

It was not long when my heart too began to sing. This was the first I had felt their words firmly fastened within me, and I dared not dance to the rhythm of their song.

The warmth cast out by Otelagh's heart brought scent to rise up from their bark as my senses were then aroused by what I was then witnessed.

Each of my travels when I stood beside where Great Cedar fell at the side of his mother offered my thoughts to drift off as the scent of his bark still rose up to bring memory to those stories my father shared they too had once shared together.

Given that day, the knowledge Great Cedar told reflecting how they had survived before the face of fire and flood had allowed me to gain faith in knowing I too would lead my peoples safely distant from the obstacles that would one day stand aggressively before us.

I have learned well as I have walked safely amongst all life that lives in these lands. I do not need to look far for answer to those questions that linger unmoving within our souls.

I have learned, before I am comforted from my most worrisome queries, I must stand quietly and invest myself amidst all the life I have become surrounded.

I must not only listen, but I must feel the lessons they share. It shall be through their words that will offer my soul solace from its own impending storms.

One other day my father and I agreed to journey across En che Wauna and sit beneath the graceful waters of Elowah as they fell hurried beside our feet in the heat of summer.

At first, I did not know why he chose Elowah to sit, but as we sat watching the water lap against the rock, my father pointed to the Dipper as it dove beneath Elowah's fast stream.

My father shared all I had to do is to look into the creek that flowed from where the Spirit of Elowah spoke, and I would see my lesson clearly before me as he taught the significance of cherishing trust and faith in our lives.

At the side of Elowah's creek I sat with my father, and there, just beneath the stream, came out the Dipper who was not afraid to enter beneath waters he could not see.

It was at that very moment I began to understand the trust the tiny Dipper had inherited within his soul.

This is how my father taught me of trusting what I do not see standing before me in all of life's challenges. It is in those challenges of trust that I have learned that faith brings strength into one's character.

We, as children of this land, will too walk across our lands and not fear what we cannot see. This alone will bring end to all we have allowed to take faith from within us.

Our faith will then grant ourselves the allowances that confidence aspires as it becomes invested into our lives.

Without question, once we hold no fear within us for those tomorrows we have yet to see, we will rise up and bring honor to ourselves knowing those days will begin with the light of Otelagh shining down upon us.

As we are led through life's challenges, our people will survive through all adversity knowing from faith the truths of life shall rise up and defeat the darkness held within one's own soul.

Even though Red Cloud has shown promise it will bring storm from above us as it looms heavy within our hearts, we will know the warmth of Sun will again fall upon our lives and his great spirit will offer our peoples to rediscover our promise within these lands reborn.

I turn from where I walk upon the trail and begin my short trek from Metlako to the base of the large bowl whose waters of the tumwata (Punch Bowl Falls) thunders. I remember, it was there, in the cold waters that come from Wy-East, my brothers and I swam during the heat of day.

Often, during the days when the end of season was near, we would join together to walk to the lake at Wahtum where we first learned the Klale Lolo gathered to take the sweet huckelberry from its bush.

We had many times, as the seasons began to change, saw the huckleberry offer much from its arms upon the open slopes of many hills.

Along this same trail that keeps safeguarded the Five Spirits, we each were allowed to look back over the lands of Wah as we climbed to the highest peak above the cave that holds the spirits of Great Eagle Falls.

We were honored to have shared the beauty of the mountains and trees as they coursed across the lands as far as our eyes could allow.

We stood in awe as we looked out over the many streams that ran to the Big Waters of En che Wauna as they flowed past just below where we stood.

This has brought us great pleasure in knowing all the lands, and each of the streams and rivers of Wah, were first chosen for our peoples by the Hyas Tyee.

These are the lands treasured by the Great Spirits, Wy-East, Pahto, and Lawala Clough. They together surround our villages and bring great wealth to our peoples as mowitch and moolack run through the forests, and pish come many each season to our nets.

These too are the lands wrought by the Spirit's grandest dreams.

As the Spirits cry out in the heavens and bring rain to fall into the Valley of the Eagle and across all the Lands of Wah, they bring new life to blossom.

To the soils they offer color and strength as fern and Maple, Alder, Cedar, Cottonwood, and Great Fir rise to touch the heaven, and the sweet scent of flowers rise up above the lands as they lead our thoughts into dream.

These are the lands where only words spoken in truth are heard offered from those of our fathers that have been chosen to stand unopposed upon the Wall at Wahclella.

From upon the great wall they are seen to offer guidance without judgment. Their words spread goodwill and understanding to the lives of their peoples.

These too are the Majestic Lands of Wah where our great fathers stand above us from within the Hyas Tumtum's Village. As they look down upon us, they lead us upon safe trails through the guide of our companions, Hyas Talupus, Coyote, and to whom I have been named, Hyas Kaka, Raven.

Sun has begun to cross overhead and I have yet to reach the tumwata that is known to hold the bad spirits well hidden within its fast waters.

Skoonichuk has taken many of our peoples from along the shoreline as it had swept them downriver where they could not find shelter from the waters where the bad spirit has been known to strike.

Skoonichuk's lair reminds me of the spider that awaits the bee that knows only the sweet honey that lies waiting within the petals of flowers as they waive in the mild breeze at the entrance of the spider's most wary trap.

One day as I returned from the trail of the Eagle with my brothers, our father sat with us and told story from long ago, before even himself or his father lived, when came a hale seeowist, blind, man into the village of our people.

My father told he came alone, walking only by the feel of the soil beneath his feet and by the breaths of Wind that crossed his face that led his feet to follow the path to our village.

He trusted no man or animal would take him from his journey as he too was told to follow the directives of the High Spirits that chose him to send out the message of promise and hope to all the peoples he passed upon the long trail of his journey.

He was named Chitsh, Grandfather. Many stories have been told of his travels and to the many visions he had been honored to share before many nations he had come.

He told those who sat with him, his sight was taken as the bad spirit became angered he was chosen to walk amongst his peoples without fear and worry of the bad spirit's powers.

The bad spirit held no power over him.

Grandfather's spirit was strong.

Today, it is known this bad spirit who Grandfather spoke has now walked in amongst our villages at the side of Suyapee as his guest before many of our brother's fires.

"The bad spirit awaits those that are weak so it may take their souls and cast them upon the banks of all the rivers and streams to suffer in great agony," Grandfather was heard to speak.

"Iskum wawa okoke," (believe this,) Chitsh stated as he stood before the fire of our peoples that night.

"I may not be able to walk with sight and see what you see, but I can feel the earth through the soles of my feet.

"As I have walked many days to stand here before you this day, I am here to tell you a story that will become as true one day as are the warnings of danger spilled upon the trails we follow by Bluejay, Coyote, and Raven.

"This story was chosen for me to share by the Good Spirits from where I have come, far away.

"I have walked from a land in many ways the same as these we now stand."

Trees sway and dance as Otelagh crosses the sky above us.

From behind bush and rock peers out all the creatures that live beside us, each smiling to the warmth of morning's light as Otelagh shines down brightly to warm their souls.

Grandfather continues; "I say to you; these lands, are not owned by one people, but all the lands of the Earth were placed for all peoples to live as we all must offer respect chosen to one another and to the Hyas Creator!

"It is Otelagh that joins our souls and warms our hearts each day.

"I have come to you with open arms to save your peoples before the arrival of Red Cloud does not go far from your opened doors.

"I have been told to walk for many days until I feel the warmth of the Big Rock-Che che Op tin-Woot-Lat, upon the palms of my hands.

"I began my trek before sweet scent would fall down upon me from new leaves that grow along the waters of our river, and now, as the new season has come and passed, the cold of winter is soon to stay amongst us for many days, and much longer nights.

"From the long pipe we must smoke.

"If you choose, we will sit together in the house of your peoples as we wait until the cold of winter has been taken from the lands.

"I will tell you of the disease the bad spirit is soon to bring again to the lands that will one day take many of those living in the villages near the great sea.

"For many days, as I have journeyed to your village, I have heard the cries of many of your brothers above me attached to Wind as they were taken of their spirit the Great Creator had first offered them, and in their loss, were not allowed to take their final journey to the Great Father's village above.

"With much sadness, I tell you, I have heard many voices calling out from those who are in search for their mother's calming words.

"So many children will be stricken with the disease cast from the bad spirit's purse.

"I have come to lead you from where evil is soon to lie heavy within the souls of those unwilling to walk from their villages and sit beside their brothers in the east before Red Cloud arrives and rises from upon the waters of En che Wauna as it kills our people with its unsettling complaint.

"Yaka Mitlite Sick Tumtum Kopa Mahsh kopa illahee nesika tenas kahkwa hyah elip nesika kunamokst mahsh konoway yaka wind!"

"It is sad to bury our young so quickly before we too die!"

"I have been told to tell you by the good spirits to walk far from the big waters where Otelagh rests at night, and to not go to trade beside those that stay in villages who will be heard crying out for their children.

"It is with much sadness that our children shall be taken from us as they bring both joy and happiness to our hearts.

"With much sadness and grief, many children are promised to become lost to our people, and our spirits shall fall upon deserted isles where our souls shall not again find safety from their plight.

"We too have been promised in the throes of our despair to be seen wallowing upon the ground like dogs through the anguish of our deepest sorrow...

"Dark cloud will covet our hearts for many suns. From within that darkness we must rediscover our spirit and walk out from where Tsiatko has challenged and mocked of our faith.

"We must remember, when those dark days come to our villages, and when we cannot see or feel our way upon the Great Spirit's trails, it is then we must climb from the bad spirit's deepest pit and grasp tightly to the hands of Sun as he awaits those who yet dream of their tomorrows."

Grandfather's vision has stayed with me always, and I have seen those many swept from our lands by the bad spirit's disease.

I have rested and have begun to enter into the heart of the forest once again.

Slowly, as I think back to all the stories my father has shared, I begin to trace upon the footsteps of my father as he and I had many seasons past journeyed upon these same trails.

One day, as we walked together, we came upon an old rock, weathered and cracked with age.

I remember my first thought was this rock appeared as many as a lammich's, old woman's face after long seasons working under the raze of Sun.

Circling this ancient rock were many trees who gave protection to where it had chose to sleep.

Lush fern, as long as a man's arm grew at the base of this old rock, a soft bed for it to sleep.

Budding bush offered cover so it may sleep without worry of what might come upon it and sweep it from upon the lands it has chosen for its lodge.

That day, was much like today, and today, that memory has allowed my father and I to join together in spirit once again.

I miss his guiding hand and his wise words of encouragement.

I miss my father sharing the stories of our peoples and of this land we have come today to call Wah.

From high above the tops of trees I hear the Hyas Eagle's cry. I sense she too feels the absence of my father walking upon the trails we had many days before long shared.

My heart is suddenly filled with both happiness and sadness. Though my father sits in the village of the Hyas Tumtum and far from where I sit thinking of him and I, today, he sits with my mother as they both look down upon me and smile.

I have been blessed by the Hyas Tyee to have witnessed many visions as they have brought great joy to my people, but in these days, the visions I have had drawn before me have now brought question of why change has now drawn darkness to fall across our lands from behind the screen of Red Cloud?

I have been honored to lead many of my people into the arms of their fathers as the Great Spirit has called upon them to rise up into the heaven.

But still, today, here, now, as I stand alone, I feel as if I am only the smallest of seed fallen from the opened cone of those same great trees I today stand beneath.

Many seasons have passed as my father and the Hyas Tahmahnawis awaited for Sun to share warmth upon my soul so my spirit would rise up and grow strong in the ways of our fathers.

But today, with much sadness, I find I am helpless.

My life today is in question if I will be strong and wise as the old Firs that stand proudly surrounding me?

I feel as if I am the first Pish to swim fast from its stream to the deep waters of En che Wauna where only danger awaits me from behind the cover of the bad spirit's awaiting spear.

Though my village rests across En che Wauna, and I am not far, I must ask; "Why now, today, do I feel helpless and without direction?"

Again, I ask; "Is this kingdom not created from the same soils as are the lands beneath the soils of my village?

"Have I not heard the call of Great Coyote and the caw of Raven above me as I have journeyed through all the lands of our kingdom?

"Have I not heard the message of my Great Father and his father as I have journeyed through all the Lands of Wah and of those of our brothers?"

I too must ask myself; "Am I worthy of resting one day before the feet of my father while sharing the warmth of the eternal fire so I may not wander in the course of Wind throughout all the lands I have not stepped?"

As Wind joins upon the strongest of limbs of the forest's mightiest trees, above me, I see their long branches clasped together as if they were one. Swaying in unison to the soft murmurs of Wind's unbending lure. They, together, share of Wind's most passionate song.

As they bow to one another, I see now they are only kneeling in greeting to one another as they offer one another their arms so they may begin to dance upon their earthly stage.

It is as though they are sharing their lives through the tolls of wind's softest of breaths as they dance below the smiles of Otelagh and those shared of Moon.

This dance must be the dance of life we each must learn to share...

There is no honor higher than to lead our peoples safely through each season and know our spirits are welcomed wherever we walk, wherever we search for root and berry, wherever we choose to fish, and wherever we wish to hunt.

I have stood before the judgment of my fathers. I have heard them speak. I have felt their words hardened within my soul.

Our Fathers are my chiefs, my leaders.

They are the men that have brought hope to invest itself within my soul when I had lacked faith I would ever lead my people safely upon the trails they had first led.

I, Raven, have become a messenger from the High Spirits to our peoples. As I have held that honor close to my heart each day, I have chosen to lead them far from where danger may have awaited them.

I have taught my peoples to walk proudly through all troubles we may have become afflicted. Once we walked free of the troubles of our past, our own spirits have yet to kneel again before those hardships we were once faced.

Tkope Moolack came down from the high peaks to stand upon the bank of En che Wauna where he had chosen for us to envision his splendor after many seasons our people had not lain witness to his mighty spirit.

We do not know if he saw our hearts had been troubled.

Tkope Moolack knows now of our good spirit. He would not trust our character if he were to stand unprotected along the bank of En che Wauna as we saw him looking towards where we stood.

He is not afraid of those of our village as our people see with two eyes to the goodness of all those that walk before us and to all life which breathes the same air as we.

Tkope Moolack knows we speak only of the truth to what we have seen.

We speak as visionaries to those who sit and smoke from the long pipe as they listen to the truths spoken by the Hyas Tumtum Tyee through our most candidness of words.

We bring honor to each moment of our lives. For in that fleeting moment we may not find honor, our final breaths may be taken, and then we may walk alone for all days.

We know the Hyas Tumtum is always with us, and in that knowing, we must walk with him, and see through his eyes, and feel of his heart, and then we will be one always with him.

Knowing the High Spirit is with us each day as he overlooks all we do in our lives, we know we must remain strong in those lessons he has wished for us to follow.

He is always watching that we follow in the commands our lands teach, and in those lessons, we know each species upon this Earth will bring honor upon the Earth as their young shall make journey amongst our peoples for all days.

We must remember Hyas Tyee can take from us our breaths as easily as he can create light and bring warmth to our lives from high above in the heaven.

Many days long ago, when I climbed to where rests the Spirit of Larch, I sat and looked out over the lands Otelagh had created through the bond of Wy-East, Pahto, and of the spirit of Lawala Clough.

From the distance, where I could not see, I had heard my Great Father calling me to serve those that choose to follow me and believe in the words I spoke, as those words, were too, first spoken by my great father.

The wisdom spelled from those few words offered us sanction upon the Illahee of the Creator as we walked in memory to his greatest of feats.

Those words, those thoughts, shall always keep our peoples safe and strong in the eyes of the bad spirits when they rise up against us.

Our Great Father has expressed the bad spirits shall then be struck hard upon the brow of their heads as was Pahto many seasons ago, and we will then be free of their trespass within the sanctuary of our souls.

Sun has come and gone many times since I had visited the high peaks above En che Wauna, and as I stood in a great meadow not far from where I can see, Hyas Tyee called out to me with warning that I must listen to Great Coyote as she too calls out to share of her story.

Louder and louder, my Father spoke to me, and each time I came to rest, I would listen for Hyas Coyote's call.

Otelagh had not journeyed far across the heavens as I sat and peered out over the peaks of the mountains. Coming from the lands of the Clatskanie and the Clatsop, in the distance below me I again saw Hyas Coyote, with head raised high to the heaven, speaking to the spirits of the lands as she stood.

From the thick of the forest she appeared into the open meadow, unafraid to what may lie hidden in the deepest of shadows.

I sat there, unmoving, hoping Coyote would not run.

She came closer, not looking towards where I sat. Each step brought her soul and my own closer to one another's again.

My heart began to beat as loudly as the Great Drum of our village within my chest.

Softly, I called out to her.

Her eyes were drawn questionably towards me as she did not at first recognize me as I did not move. But as I again called out, she knew of my voice and came hurried to sit at my side.

With tail swaying in her excitement, she too, as I, had proven we each had missed an old friend.

When I hear Great Coyote in the dark of night as she journeys across the valleys and mountains and cries out to Moon, I am reminded she has come to live amongst our peoples with honor from the Great Creator.

We, all our peoples, have been awarded a great gift in Hyas Coyote through our Saghalie Tyee's most celebrated of passions. If it were not for the night above Wyam, when Coyote first came to feed from my hand as she had done with my father, and the night when she would share the Sun and Moon drawn before me upon the ground by her paw, I may have not known of her Great Spirit as I do today.

Coyote's spirit is strong.

Coyote's soul is strong.

Coyote lives and breathes where we cannot see.

Coyote lives in a spirit world that many do not understand. Only those that have knelt before the Hallowed Walls of Wahclella and have heard the High Spirits speak have known of that world where only Great Spirits have been destined to journey.

Our Great Fathers have agreed for many seasons to speak to those that yearn to know of life. Our Fathers have not failed those that have knelt before them.

It is there, from where the Sacred Waters of Wahclella fall was heard shared the greatest of message towards our people; "If your peoples devote your lives to sustain the purity of your minds, then, you shall ascertain the privilege of preserving salvation toward your souls."

Each day, each moment, life lays challenge to our minds. We must only look deep into our hearts to walk free from the disease of the bad spirit.

We must stay strong and believe in all those tomorrows that lie beyond the horizon where Otelagh has yet to rise. In that belief, life as we know it will return, and we will survive to stand up from our mats as the new sun rises.

We too shall be afforded the right to lie down upon our mats as Sun sets without worry swollen within each of our thoughts.

We shall live another day through the teachings of the Great Spirit who claims all life upon this land has been created through his own hands from the light first cast upon life's beginnings.

Moon has begun to rise high into the heavens, and as Sun rises tomorrow, I know I will be excited to be honored to stand upon Wy-East and look into Tkope Moollack's eyes and speak of days long ago when our spirits first came down into these lands from high above Naha's nest upon the peak of Walowahoof.

Hyas Tahmahnawis has told me Tkope Moolack and I would speak of what he has seen through visions that will soon bring change to the lands. In those visions, if his are alike those I have seen, we will together search deep into our hearts and find reason and answer to the change our peoples must make to live beyond the next season.

Looking up to the heights of Wy-East, I have come to realize the faith I have had instilled within me has been created from those events our fathers first lived.

There have been days when I have listened to the advice of our past fathers without question. Though they led me upon trails that would have offered nothing but peril and death to those that did not follow and believe in their words, my faith had not escaped me.

There was a day when I traversed along a steep cliff where I could not see what lay beneath me, and this journey easily proved of my mettle before the eyes of my father.

I had not to that day climbed into the hidden canyon where a rushing river fell hurriedly towards the Big Waters of En che Wauna.

As I stood at the peak of the cliff and looked down beneath where I stood, all I could see were the sharpened points of sticks waiting to pierce the souls of those who had little faith they would not fall.

Through my faith, as my Great Spirit had led me safely to where I stood, I was led from peril and appeared unharmed upon the distant shore.

Each time my life has been placed into peril, through my faith, I have not feared what I had been presented.

I have acquired confidence through the words the Great Spirit speaks.

Through his guidance, he has permitted me to live and lead others upon those same trails where death's mask awaits those whom fear the unseen.

These past days are no different as I climb towards Wy-East. My faith has allowed me to climb without effort.

Even though I have grown old and my legs have become tired, my faith has not deserted me upon the hardest of trails.

I know I have been called by the High Spirit to stand before his judgment.

My soul has been freed from doubt. If it were not for faith, in my doubt, I would be perceived to be held in the greatest of shame as my people would not know if I were leading them upon safe trails.

I shall not be influenced by the powers the bad spirit may wish to influence upon my own spirit. I am today, a leader of my people, though I today walk from my village and from the side of my son, into the lands of the Great Spirit.

They shall not fear the absence of my being as my spirit too speaks to them as the Hyas Tyee has spoken to me from upon all the trails our lives have been chosen to follow.

This night, as I lie here upon the soft grass and fern beside the White Pine, thinking of my son who has journeyed to the Creek of the Eagle to return Cedar to his brothers brings great sorrow to envelope my soul.

I lay here, unmoving, yet I cannot rest knowing he will not see me waiting for him as in all the days before today.

This will be the moment when my son will first come to look over where I was last known to stand, and as I will not be there to greet him, his heart may become lost to the order of purpose towards his responsibilities to all that await him in the village of our people.

Though my son is strong, I still worry he may not understand why I have accepted the wish of the High Spirit and have chosen to walk far from where he now rests.

Though I cannot see across the Big Water, with closed eyes, I see my son sitting in the village at Che che Optin before the fire, looking up towards the heights of Wy-East where now my spirit is soon to rest.

I sense he knows I am leaving the world his memories today seek.

Memories where he and I had many seasons sat together and learned of one another and to the ways of Mother Earth.

But through the Dreams of the Deer Spirit, he may look up to where our fathers await those spirits that have rested upon Memaloose for many long days and nights.

I hear my son ask: "Why has my father been chosen to journey from our village to where I can no longer sit at his side?"

He too asks; "Why does my father accept to be taken from our people?"

Only within himself may my son discover the answer, as it was not my choice in the beginning to distance myself from his side.

My life was destined.

My choices decided before they were agreed.

My life was not my own.

I had but one life to give.

One soul.

One heart.

Each bonded by the requests of the Hyas Tyee to bring order from chaos to our people.

I was chosen to bring peace from the arguments towards war between all our brothers to the Earth.

This was my legacy before I was offered to my mother and father at the moment I was chosen the gift of life.

Through the eyes of Sun, as he has challenged me to succeed in the many tests he has laid out before me, my attitude towards what I did not at first understand has granted me safe passage through all the trials presented before me.

Tomorrow, my life may become complete as I kneel upon Wy-East and bow deeply towards the heaven.

My final journey shall take me into many valleys, and across many peaks as I climb through these lands to Wy-East.

My journey, promised upon the soils of the many sons and daughters of Wy-East who I have not yet met.

This journey, this trek, may be my final journey upon this Earth, and I shall bear honor to all life I pass with the reverence and compassion they deserve.

Each day I have looked towards Wy-East, I have seen he honors his lands with great forests that sweep freely across the high peaks and valleys that surround him.

As the sun has risen before me and has warmed my soul to the new day, I walk excitedly towards the peak where the call of Tkope Moolack comes.

Listening to Tkope Moolack's bugling bekons me to climb effortlessly towards where he awaits me high above upon the open slope of the great meadows.

If I choose to look back onto the kingdom of Wah before I reach the side of Great White Elk, I fear my spirit may become weak through the wanting of the bad spirit for all that I have become.

I know as Great Elk's call is heard through each of the valleys that lie below the peak of Wy-East, it is not solely his spirit that wills the trail I follow to unfold before my people's thoughts.

But, it is through their knowing in the teachings the Great Chiefs of our people taught me that all life which lives peacefully in these greatest of lands beckons me to go where Hyas Tkope Moolack had been chosen to find safety from the hunter's arrow where Wy-East's great spirit rises.

From those spirits who had once lain hidden behind the long shadows, they each have been taken from before me and I am not challenged by what fear I may have once held close to my soul.

Without caution, without worry, I discover myself joining in the same beliefs as had Grandfather.

He too had walked with great faith he would reach his destination though he could not see what lay before him, or what may have threatened to take his soul from behind the long shadows.

Tkope Moolack has asked Hyas Coyote to lead me safely upon the trail we walk. As we climb higher, step, by step, we near the high ridge that leads to my journey's end.

Tkope Moolack has also called out to Hyas Raven to spread his wings over me and protect me from what I cannot see.

I fear nothing as I walk beneath the long arms of trees, and from behind large rocks where once Hyas Pishpish would have awaited to strike down upon me.

Through the faith my life has gathered from my journeys upon this Earth, I know I will soon rise up before Tkope Moolack and be honored to walk behind his footsteps as I follow his lead.

To bear witness to the order of life through Tkopoe Moolack's eyes, and to feel the pulse of the Earth through his compassionate heart is all I could have ever dreamt to have been honored through my following our father's footsteps throughout my life.

I believe my gift to our peoples was offered through my efforts in bringing harmony between animal, plant, and man.

Those that have survived the many battles between the good and bad Spirits who have dwelled upon the flanks of Wy-East, know as both spirits may one day begin to awaken after many seasons of sleep, there is the uncertainty of surviving the rising of their battle and storm.

My thoughts have created anxiety within me, and I cannot wait to walk out from where I rest with Raven and Coyote.

I wish them to lead me quickly to the side of Great White Elk where he awaits me.

If it were not for my friends Raven and Coyote, I know I would have walked amongst all the lands many days alone.

Even though Sun was spread down upon the trails I followed, I would not have known the truths that would set my spirit free upon them.

Though I have looked up to the high peak many times, and have thought how Wy-East must welcome those that come to rest upon his lands, today, these lands as I dreamt, are sharing with plentiful fern and soft grasses swaying gently to the breaths of Wind across the long meadows.

Each bush, each tree, each flower, are paving my way along their path to where Tkope Moolack awaits.

Raven rises up upon the breaths of heaven upon strong wings, and as he soars above where Coyote and I stare towards him, he surveys the lands and calls out to Coyote.

Without hesitation, Coyote turns and looks towards me, then she pushes hard her nose against me.

I think, it is time we further upon our journey.

As Raven sweeps down towards us, we only then continue our climb towards where grass soon meets the snows of winter's long past storms.

Lying upon the ground surrounding me are a great stand of trees which had once stood magnificently poised to touch the heaven. Now their remains lie littered and broken, hiding the trail where Coyote had first chosen for me to follow.

My thoughts brought sadness as there were now no footsteps to be found that would prove I had come to the slopes of Wy-East where Tkope Moolack awaited me if my son were to search.

Coyote raises her nose to the air and looks towards me. With head bowed, she comes to my side and lays down before me.

Coyote lies before me, sadness and hurt resonates from the deepest chambers of her heart. Slowly, her paw softly reaches out to touch my foot.

Large tears wash down from both her eyes, each settling in a pool before my feet.

This moment brings much sadness to my heart as I question why her much spirited soul had been stolen as she lies grieving?

I reach down to console Coyote as I caress her soft coat, but she does not raise her eyes to look towards me, but as her ears point towards the high peak, she begins to peer intently for something I cannot see.

A noise, a voice, a scent, something has certainly disturbed her.

Still, she lies at my feet in great mourning, and for what, I do not yet understand

There, upon the highest branch rests Raven, watching.

I have not before this day brought question to what I today have feigned to see.

My eyes do not recognize what they cannot first grasp as their message drifts freely from within me.

My soul is certain great spirits run free through the trees of this forest as they are those I have been told that guard the heights of Wy-East from those others they do not yet know.

The shadows of their spirits each run swiftly towards me, and without pause, they are joined within my own.

My being has been touched, yet I cannot distinguish to whom had first brought calm to my soul?

The knowledge of all their spirits bring harmony to the essence of Wind's most harshest and demanding of breaths.

To those who have yet to understand the lessons of our fathers, I pray!

My spirit has too become renewed through the powers of their gifts. The same as it has been from the beginning to those of our people who have one day sat alone to their thoughts upon the mountaintop and brought truth from their dreams.

The truest of their spirit from that day walks upon the lands of the Earth for all days before the eyes and hearts of others. I am, today, one to all those born to the challenges of Wind, and to the soils of the Earth I am promised to return.

We are today, now soon to be one!

As my eyes close to the days of my life, I begin to dream Raven returns above where Coyote and I sit.

I see Raven as he circles the sky above and cries out to all those below. Rising up from within the deep cover of snow, the Hyas Tumtum of Tkope Moolack stands.

Tkope Moolack's great antlers shine brightly in the warmth of Sun. They reach out, as if they call out for me to grasp them tightly and pull myself up from below the steep slope so we may surrender our souls together upon the peak of Wy-East.

I look down towards the Valley of the Eagle and across to the Lands of Wah of my birth, and I am reminded, these are the lands I was promised by the Hyas Spirits Sun and Moon, and their daughter, the mother of our Earth, Naha.

I have longed for many seasons to make journey to stand where I now stand, and today, my vision has become complete!

Coyote and Raven has led me safely above the Kingdom of Wah where I am now able to touch the revered lands of Tkope Moolack.

Where no Indian has dared to touch…

My journey in life would not have been complete if it were not for Coyote's and Ravens companionship as they brought comfort to my soul.

It is to them I owe my soul as it was through their spirit I have survived!

It is to them I shall always hold close in this memory!

The fearless souls of Coyote and Raven, each have placed my life before their own as they have allowed me to witness the lands of my dreams.

I stand in awe, as I am welcomed before the Great Spirit of White Elk.

Each of my journeys throughout my life has rewarded me now with this greatest of honor.

This final journey has become the most significant trial of my life as it has taken my thoughts throughout all the tests and trials I have experienced.

I have thought back to the earliest days of my childhood spent at the side of my father, and to the day I first wailed before the High Spirits upon the Wall at Wahclella so they would lead me upon safe trails and keep me safe from the grasp of the mesahchie spirit.

As I stood upon the high rock above the waters at Wahclella, I wailed before the High Spirits so they would discern my voice from all the brothers who had first stood before them in all the many seasons ago.

As I called out to them, as Munra had told, I prayed they would hear my words and feel the honesty beholding of my soul.

I had faith they would find me worthy to kneel before where they stood upon the Great Wall.

Each of the great leaders of our people stood resigned to their decision as they juried my soul, and as they felt of my spirit they chose to speak as I was only then accepted worthy.

They demanded that I step into those same footsteps where they had long walked, and that I must speak clearly to the visions they would share before me.

That day, I walked with great pride for the first moment in my life, and I only could then return before my father and of those of our village.

It was there I told my people what I had been asked.

Given each trial of my life I have been challenged, my soul has risen up from within me and has kept my spirit strong.

Through all the trails I have followed, though I have misplaced my step many times from where our fathers had first guided me to follow, given the good I had vested within my soul, my faith allowed me to stand free from the grasp of the bad spirit's will.

I have stood as one beside all the fathers of our people, and as one, we have led our villages safely from the rush of the Klale Lolo, and from the waiting teeth of Hyas Pishpish.

Many days and nights have passed behind me. There have been both good and bad experiences in all those many days.

When my faith in our father's leadership was tested, I remembered my promise before all those that first stood upon the Wall at Wahclella as I knelt before them.

I chose to learn the lessons our great leaders had chosen for me to take back to my people, and then, my spirit was enabled to walk free across all the lands.

A great honor, to walk freely amongst others, and an honor we must not believe we are required to earn by those others that wish to enslave our souls so they may take freedom from our souls...

I remember thinking one day as I watched the Hyas Eagle fly effortlessly with the breaths of the Hyas Tumtum beneath its wings, that he too, would not dare attempt to cross the heavens if he did not believe his wings would not draw upon the breaths of the High Spirit.

Without faith, he would fall helpless and broken from upon the breaths of Wind in the heaven.

My survival, my willingness to live, has been accredited through my believing and in my sharing of those teachings to those of whom I had sat and spoke with through the long nights before the fires of our villages.

Those same truths I have shared before others has allowed me strength to lead others from straying from the righteous life the High Spirit has wished for us to lead.

Those same teachings have delivered me safely from upon the trails of adversity I have been faced.

If it were not for our Hyas Father's leadership and guidance, there would be no brothers or sisters, or any of the people of our

Nation that would have returned to our village if we had walked out where light did not fall upon the shadows of darkness.

Those of our people whom were lost to our beliefs are today concealed for all days beneath damp tombs by the desires of the bad spirit.

From the sky, I hear Raven call out to Coyote and myself as he glides silently until he lands again at my side.

Coyote then too comes again to where I stand and lies before my feet.

I understand why Coyote had become withdrawn and distraught as she appeared burdened by her questioning heart.

It was not that she had lost the direction she was to lead me after the storms of my life had lifted from the depths of my soul as I had first thought.

Tkope Moolack told me she had heard the Good Spirit tell her this too would be the final journey she and Raven and I would share until they were called upon to rise up and make journey to the Great Village where they would too rest beside me once again for all days.

Raven and Coyote have become like brothers to my people's family.

To them, I shall always care...

I reached down to stroke Coyote as I knew she would soon leave my side, but when I looked down to where she had lain, her spirit had raised from within her soul and I could not go to where I could not see to join her.

Raven's spirit too had risen from where he had just stood, and as I could not see him flying across the heaven in return to the Kingdom of Wah to watch over our people, my heart felt emptied as I could not bid them farewell and thank them for all they had accepted to offer me safe passage in each of my many journeys.

Their boundless companionship through the seasons of my life had kept me from walking into the teeth of danger as I journeyed blindly into the darkness of night along many trails.

I shall look for Raven and Coyote to join me each day Sun shall rise upon the lands of our people!

I will miss their companionship.

I will, each day, look down upon them and smile.

Soon, I know they shall sit with me, and we will renew our friendship from high above in the heavens.

Patiently Tkope Moolack has awaited me to join him for several days as I have climbed from Wah to the lands where he and his herd have survived distant from the eyes of man.

We, my people, those of whom still lived by the word of Hyas Tumtum, had heard of Tkope Moolack from our fathers.

Many seasons had passed between signs that Tkope Moolack accepted our people.

Those days were many...

But as my brothers and I sat at the shore of En che Wauna, we looked across the Big Waters. Great White Elk came from behind the tall trees and looked to where we sat.

Through the vision of our hearts, he appeared before us from the far bank of En che Wauna, and it was then we knew we were as one before all the Good Spirits that walked upon the Lands of Wah.

Though I have dreamt many nights of standing beside Great White Elk as I do today, my heart feels settled and calmed before his presence.

I neither feel concerned, nor do I sense confusion for why it is I who has been allowed to stand with Hyas Tkope Moolack and look out over all the lands of our kingdom.

I am forever honored to stand where I now stand!

Tkope Moolack and I will soon rest upon our own beds in the distant fields of the heavens. But when that moment comes, we both know what will quickly march upon our people from both horizons of Sun's many lands.

Though Suyapee may take many of our people's souls, our spirits shall live on in knowing the fires of our villages shall call out for us to join them once again soon.

Then, we will sit and smoke, and life will again be renewed.

I have much faith as our people return upon the shores of En che Wauna we will bring honor to the lands.

Pish shall too rejoice to the heavens as they will leap high to catch the fly as they return in great numbers to feed our peoples.

To live and prosper where the High Spirit had first placed our peoples to live in the beginning of days shall bring happiness and prove of our courage in safekeeping the lands for our children and for their children's children long after we each are gone to sit with our fathers.

The Hyas Tahmahnawis shall stand tall with respect for us Indian as he crosses the heavens and looks down upon us, and there he will too smile as do our fathers and mothers who await those of their children to sit again beside them.

Life shall return to the old ways when Eagle screams from above and pish come many to the waters of the rivers once more throughout all the lands of our kingdom.

I look up to plead before the Great Spirit in the heaven, and as my eyes have become clouded through the despair I am now surrounded, from within the dark cover of white pine whom rest along the edge of Wy-East's snowy mat, long shadow's of muskrat and pish pish, lolo and mowitch, the Hyas Owl and Heron are each cast out before me.

I see their spirits today dance upon the trunks of trees, who long ago stood proudly upon the mountain of Wy-East, where, before today, were thought for all days to sleep.

Each of their eyes shine bright with the promise of life, smiling, as they are drawn purposely towards me.

They had awaited me for many seasons to rise up upon Wy-East as they had been promised they would teach me of accepting my destiny upon the final trail I must journey of my life.

Their souls, well hidden within the darkness of night's long shadow, had too come out into the light to begin to live through the essence of death's dark mask.

Now, as I still stand confused to the message I have become committed, Wind blows softly across my face, their shapes now carried gracefully upon distant trails.

Here, now, their spirits have become disconnected from the light of day, now drawn only upon the soils of the earth through the memories of whom they too had once brought honor.

This, I shall for all days, too, now dream.....

Steven Warnstaff

Chapter 2

To Follow In the Footsteps of My Father

Many moons have risen and fallen upon the lands the day my father, Raven, last walked out from our village to join Tkope Moolack upon Wy-East.

As I, One Who Runs Fast Like Horse stands here upon the shores of En che Wauna, looking out over her waters, reflect on those fleeting moments I have treasured in the long ago days when my father and I shared in all life promised before our people.

I know I must walk in his footsteps and further our people's dreams through his and my own visions for the good of our people. To see beyond what is presented before us today, and to one day better understand what we have yet to bring question.

My heart is emptied of emotion. I have allowed myself to dwell in the darkness of my soul's own inescapable cave. Existing only through my sorrow do my thoughts travel, they lead me upon desolate trails to where I do not know I have once journeyed.

From within me I know I must grasp tightly the tail of the fleeting horse as my heart and soul escapes me. I must turn back, not in retreat, but in attacking the turmoil within me so I may reappear unharmed from my forage into the voids of my visions.

Though today I am yet still distant in thought from my tasks, I shall promise always to be joined to this land and to the needs of my people. I shall not allow myself to become mired through my lack of vision for those tomorrows that await us all to join.

Today, as in many days before, I have awakened from my sleep and have risen from my mat only to find myself sitting at the bank of En che Wauna.

Here, as I peer up towards the Hyas Tahmahnawis of Wy-East, I sit. Hoping again to hear my father's voice call out to me to return his canoe to the shore at Hyas Eagle.

Through the eyes and ears of my storm, I see and hear him calling, only then to have wind pass before me and mock my most grievous sadness with its rush upon me.

Still, I sit here, alone, waiting, knowing he will call. In sadness, I realize only silence does hope cross upon the paths of Wind.

Emptiness has filled my heart. That emptiness owned by the soul of the bad spirit has allowed my thoughts to wander hopelessly before lands I have dared myself to enter.

I know deep within my soul my father has gone to sit with his father, but I have been taught of hope, and in that hope, I sense my father is always with me.

Knowing my father still sits and walks beside me offers my spirit great strength to live today, and to dream of all the tomorrows Sun will bring to our lands.

I shall always follow in my father's lead as we are today, only separated by the clouds of our heaven.

Many of our village had taken their brothers and sisters, mothers and fathers, to the islands where they sit surrounded by the waters of En che Wauna. There, upon the high rock they wait for pish to rise up from En che Wauna's depths and again jump quickly into their waiting nets.

They will catch and dry the great Salmon until the first snows fall from the high peaks of our mountains. As cloud drops from the heaven and warns of storm, they will come fast to find warmth within the longhouse beside those that wait earnestly for their safe return.

They will carry with them food for the village to store high up upon the shelves of our lodge as winter's long storm falls upon us without mercy.

The day our brothers and sisters return to the village is a time we share with much happiness.

We will dance and give thanks to the Hyas Tumtum as Sun and Moon rise and fall from the heaven.

As the harvest moon lies out softly upon the horizon, without noticing, it will slowly slip silently away to settle upon its bed until the season again changes and new leaf climbs from the stick's emptied branch as they fill the trails of heaven with color.

Winter is soon to punish the lands with much storm as it can be seen lying in wait upon the horizons of our lands.

Soon, we shall be held captive within the closed doors of our longhouses, and it will be many Suns before we may again go to the Big River and take pish from her waters.

I have called out to those whom are still in our village so we may sit and speak at the side of the fire this night.

We must speak of where our people's trails may lead, for those that come to our lands are promised to be in great hurry, and they shall not wait to take what they wish from our peoples or from the gifts placed upon our lands from the vision of our Great Spirit.

Winter will come and go with the changing of Wind, and as new leaves bud upon the long arms of trees upon the shoreline of En che Wauna, we shall all be pleased as great eagles will soon scream with much happiness as they announce the arrival of the first pish into the Big River's streams.

As I sat at the council with the Paloose and Nez Perce, we spoke of the white man that come to our shores in big ships and make trade for fur of Otter.

More and more Suyapee have come to our lands each season, and now they are seen to walk into our lands in search of Beaver, mink, and fox. They ask many times where the streams of En che Wauna lead, but through the advice of our great chiefs, we do not speak.

We see in their canoes many furs, and they do not bring honor to the High Spirit as they take all they find hidden within the lands of his kingdom.

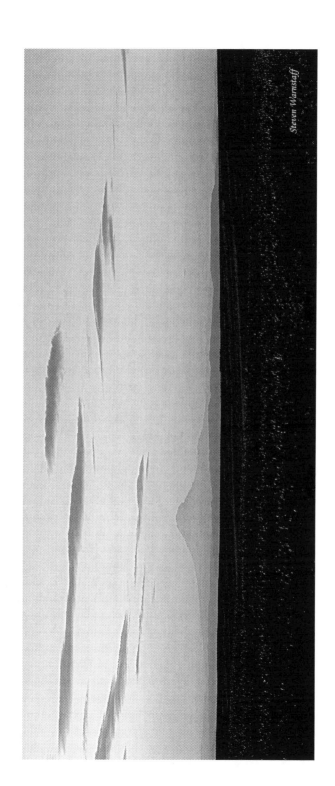

Steven Warnstaff

Chapter 3

From Wallewa Rises Question

Wind has carried the voice of truth far from the peaks of the Wallewa. Through Wind it has been told many battles have been fought between those of the Nez Perce, and of those of the Snake, the Teealka, (Enemy to be Fought).

It is not those that come from their village that lie along the big waters in the big prairie where we journey to hunt buffalo, I speak.

We sit at the fire this night at Wyam with braves and chiefs from many villages. Many peoples, many who we have met in days long ago, and others we pass many days as our villages are near as we fish and hunt in the lands of our kingdom.

A young brave that came far from the Wallewas has stood up before us and begins to tell it was not long ago, two braves of the Nez Perce and a slave taken from a battle long ago against the Snake now see no more.

He tells their spirits can be heard happily singing through Wind before the ears of their fathers each day.

"These words I shall speak were told to me to share with those that sit before the great fire. It is here where many come to know of change to our lands and to hear of those others that come to stand before us and speak only of the truth.

"I have two messages to share, and this first I will begin as I tell you of a great fight, where warriors of the Nez Perce gave chase to those of the Snake that wantonly slayed those of their brothers.

"Before the last snow came to our lands there was a great battle.

"Many Snake came to the Fast Waters that goes to join those of Little Salmon to hunt.

"This day, as Sun rose high into the heavens, Snake too came to hunt the spirit of great elk.

"To take from our lands those spirits we each day must answer, we do not accept their gift to our people until we first listen to their message.

The Snake do not care. They do not listen or feel the message cast out by our people's drums that share of the Hyas Tahmanawis of Moolack.

There were many Snake counted by two scouts as they found shelter and hid across the little river.

They dared not move as their sighting would certainly offer the Snake their long hair.

The war party of Snake soon passed, and the scouts swiftly returned to the village at Weippe Meadow and told of the battle that would soon come.

As Sun brought light from the heaven, two braves and one Snake slave took horse to the Big Clearwater to bring food and weapons for battle. They too took dog to warn of enemies that hide like snake in the long grass of the meadow.

I tell you this day, these Snake, whose spirit's rattles are too placed onto the war drums of their people, and are then cast out upon the journey's of Wind as warning to those they will soon come, their spirits are not good.

Fast like Wind, riding horse, the two Nez Perce and the slave came down from upon Kamiah Hill, as they each chose the same trail and dust rose high into the heaven, it was not long they were seen.

These three see no more...

The dog, running as the Eagle who is now promised to the breaths of Wind, runs fast to the Big Meadow where many our warriors gathered, then waiting for weapons and food to go to make war.

As dog came in much hurry, alone, we knew war had come first to our peoples.

Warning was then promised.

Enemy was near.

Great Coyote called out to all the braves of our peoples.

Many took to their horse, carrying close to their side, bow, arrows, and long knives. They too took guns not yet stored from the great hunt many suns ago.

Many rode hard, first to meet those of our enemy to see where they go.

The Snake, again promised for all days to make battle between our people. Wanting to take spirit from our peoples in the lands where the spirits speak loudest to those of our nation.

It was near where the braves and slave were sent to sit with their fathers, we first followed the footsteps of those that came to hunt.

Sun rose up to bring warmth to his peoples, and as Great Elk's bugle was sounded through all the valleys, battle did not wait.

We quickly gathered many warriors to chase the Snake from our lands.

With great surprise, our chase began from across the fast waters of the river.

Sun climbed and fell from the heavens as many Snake saw there were many braves of our people than those numbers of their village.

Word was heard spoken between the peoples of the Snake to find shelter in the big hole in ground named Sapachesap, (Drive In) from across the fast water.

It was there they hid in silence, waiting for our people to lose track.

It was in the darkness held taut within the bad spirit's soul they had been promised to have then become entrapped.

As we came to stand guard where the light of life led only into the darkness of death, wood was quickly gathered.

A great fire began to send smoke hurried into where the Snake cowered in the hole of mountain.

Great Coyote's calls could be heard across many lands, to many villages of our brothers, telling we had chased from the lands of our Spirits, these Snake who were soon to die and not see of tomorrow.

Throughout the valleys and along many rivers, word had been cast down from the high peaks the battle had ended as quickly as it had begun, and those of the Snake who had hid beneath the cover of darkness were now swept far from their father's keep.

It was told many Snake were heard to cry out to their fathers, but their pleas fell silent upon Wind as the wail of our braves who stood along the river were raised high up to the floor of the heaven.

Engaged in their victory, the screams of our brothers could be heard far away.

To those Snake who had chosen to make battle where the Great Spirits had first spoken to the peoples of our villages, to those Snake who had chosen to cull those of our people, were then only heard to cry out as their hair was taken from upon their heads and their spirits lost for all days.

Those others who had run to the Hole in the Mountain, knew only as the great fires grew hot and smoke quickly began to take air from their chests, soon, they too would be no more if they did not come out to fight and die they as proud peoples before those who waited and knew of their cowardice to stand eye to eye and fight as a brave promised to their heaven.

Many Snake slithered from within their den as have those snake we have many seasons seen lying, waiting in the long grass of the prairies to strike upon our bared legs.

There were many Snake silenced from their peoples as our sharp knives quickly took coup of our enemy.

Those Snake who did not wish to prove they too feared death waited, and it was not long their cries spent towards their father's ears fell silent for all days, and for much longer and lonelier nights as their breaths were taken forever prisoner.

They knew it would bring dishonor to their people and to their fathers if their hair was taken from upon their heads where holds close their spirit.

They knew they would not go to where their fathers awaited them to sit at their side before their fires of their village.

This was a great battle as the count of the Snake's dead were many, two hundred and sixty six, and only two braves of our people, and our slave would see no more.

It was an honor for our people that came in defense of our brothers. To them we shall remember and respect for many seasons beyond our own.

It was they who had been taken from our people before the eyes of the Hyas Tutum Tyee.

It was our brothers who chose to come fast from where it was safe to hide to warn their brothers of this battle.

This battle was too a greater defeat the Snake would remember for many more seasons as many shall now sit alone at their fires beside the empty chairs of their brothers.

For those that sat waiting in their villages and mocked of those spirits we each day stand respectfully, they too shall not soon overlook.

The fires of their village now lie dim and cold, yearning always for their people's return."

We listened intently to this braves story, and as he told the story of this battle we felt the pride of his people swell from within his soul.

This was a good day for the Nez Perce, and it has reminded me of another day when my father told me of the Snake when they stole into many villages in the darkness of night along En che Wauna and took much from what our people had made ready for the coming of winter.

They too had waited in the tall grass and took coup of many of our friends as they passed along the trails of our lands.

These people are like snakes whom do not warn others as they journey beside them before they plunge their long fangs into their legs.

They are poison to those that sit at the side of many villages fires where they pretend they come only to their village to make trade.

Many seasons ago the Tygh, whose villages lie within the meadows beside the fast waters of Wy-East, had begun to make journey to Wyam for the celebration of the return of Spring Pish.

Many of their people were killed while others were taken as slaves to be traded with those of the Shoshone and Black feet. Others were beaten like dogs, and were run hard to the Snake's village where they became slaves and whipped by their women.

Word had been passed of the Snake's attack through the warning of many village drums.

Much talk between villages spoke of war, but as many days passed, and as we each mourned those brothers and sisters taken from our lands, our people's souls became quieted through the darkness of our grief.

There were many counsels between the villages that stood below the Three Spirits, and many agreed to not make war between the Snake and their people.

But as Sun and Moon rose and fell from the heavens many times, one night, when we sat before the warmth of the night's fire, many young boys approached the fire of our village.

They stood before our counsel and spoke to those that did not stand unopposed to making the long journey to the bad spirit's lands where the Big Waters run deep in the long canyon.

They told they would return to our lands with those that came to steal and kill our friends if those that stood before them did not first choose to die.

From each village many of our boys who envisioned this hunt would offer them status as braves, turned from the wishes of the elders and rode off to join those in the hunt to recapture the honor of our peoples.

It was not long before our young boys journeyed to the lands of the Snake where the Good Spirit stood beside them and spared their lives from the sharp points of the Snake's sharp teeth as they waited beneath both rock and bush in trap.

A great battle arose upon the lands as Sun climbed high into the heavens.

Those of our people who stood proudly before the face of death gave chase to those who ran.

The breaths of many were then silenced, and as the battle offered no more Snake to be brought before the throes of death, our sons brought three of the bad spirit's people back to our lands where it was seen, as was first promised, to be hung from the high tree where those that bring wrong to our tables are punished before all our people.

Their hair was then tied upon the long arm of tree where their spirits would be taken upon the breaths of Wind and lost to their people for all days.

"I sit and speak with you not just of this great battle, but it is a message that has been sent from the Clearwater, that tells Suyapee have now too come to the lands of the Nez Perce.

When our people came from the great mountains after storm had gone from the lands, Suyapee were discovered in great misery, and were soon dead.

From the big snows of winter Suyapee could not walk to hunt the mowitch or moolack. There were no tracks to follow, not even in deep snow were the tracks of mowitch or moolack are today seen. They had both journeyed from the high peaks to rest in the meadows where they would be protected from winter's most cruelest of storm.

My brothers, Our Great Father's had once spoken to the visions that told of a new people's journey into our lands from where Sun rises long ago.

Now, as we sit before the fire this night, message has been brought to council those people have now come upon our lands.

In peace, these people who we have named Suyapee wish to make trade for horse to make journey to En che Wauna.

It is through their vision they have come to our lands to stand at the shores of the Big Waters they have been told await them to look out across the big waters where the tall boats come.

The long ago chiefs of our people, who had once spoken at the village of Wyam's great fire of this day's coming had great vision!

Throughout the many seasons our people have lived upon the shores of En che Wauna, we have listened to Wind and have known of change.

Today it is not the same as change has come without warning.

We must not fear change, but we must first look deep into its eyes and understand what good it brings into our lives.

As our fathers and those great chiefs of our people have advised, those that chose to follow in their footsteps must each agree in keeping all our peoples honorable before these Suyapee through the words spoken by our Hyas Tahmahnawis from upon the Walls at Wahclella.

I know many of you will ask if we must be alarmed as we are now surrounded?

We will hear many questions to why they have come to stand before us across the long prairie?

You will ask if we should honor their choosing to stand at the shore of the Big Waters of the Ehkolie as our brothers lead them safely through the deep trails of the Big River?

If it were not for Red Cloud and those that came from behind its veil many seasons ago we may not have question of these Suyapee.

Though it was long ago when they first came, the message they shared before our fires still burn hot in our souls, and we have become wary of their approach into our kingdoms.

I hear already worry cast upon Wind from many villages that have first heard of these men that come.

From the fires of many villages there is question; "Will Suyapee choose to leave our lands upon the big ships others have since come?"

An old woman that was taken as slave to the north many seasons ago was traded to Suyapee and she lived in their village for many suns before they told her she must make journey to again join those of her people.

As she heard talk of killing these whites who come to their lands, she spoke to her peoples and offered respect towards Suyapee as those she once lived did not step upon her as dog.

It has been told, as the braves and chiefs of the Nez Perce listened to the old woman's words, those Suyapee who followed close to their chiefs named Lewis and Clark were then spared from being cast into the darkness of their final days upon the silenced breaths of Wind's long journey.

The Nez Perce then agreed in council they would offer the warmth of their fires, the meat of mowitch, and the bread of Camas so they may live to see again Sun's rise above them in all their tomorrows.

As we had called out to many of the chiefs and braves of villages that are raised upon the shores of En che Wauna, many have come to sit and smoke in our lodge as we give thanks to the High Spirit for our lives and speak of those that come in peace to our lands.

Steam rises quickly within the lodge as water is poured upon rocks by the warder of the fire.

It is good to cleanse the soul of all that troubles our hearts, and to cleanse all that which brings darkness and question to our spirits.

This night there have been many stories told of good and bad from many corners of our lands.

From the mountains have come great snows that did not leave for many moons.

Upon the long meadows great rains fell and made lakes that stole villages from the lands as their brothers tears fell hurried from their eyes as they watched their lodges dissolve beneath big rivers.

Life was not good this season for many, and I am afraid this is sign that as Suyapee comes, bad fortune will follow their steps as they will come many before the doorways of our villages.

Great sadness was seen in our eyes as we saw in vision to the grief and sorrow of our brothers as they had nothing left of which to offer in trade as they come to our village in need for their peoples.

Through the long night we talk of our brother's needs and agree to offer them as the High Spirit has offered all our peoples all that we have that we do not need to survive the snows of winter.

I know there will be much food and hides of deer and elk to offer them warmth from the cold before they can again go to the meadows and to the mountains and return with what the Great Spirit offers to fill their purse.

I know what they feel, and I feel in their sadness as they have been forced to sit and speak of need before others.

I remind them; "My brothers, it is not weakness that we hear and see from you, but it is the knowing within our souls that as we are all brothers to this Earth and to one another, the gift of our friendship does not allow us to judge one another but offer all we have to give without indecisiveness to your need."

With these words they sit higher from the floor of the lodge, and again happiness is spread throughout all those that sit and make pure our souls before the steam of the fire.

From along En che Wauna where the lands and villages of the Cathlamet stand, a messenger comes and tells he is named Thakatu.

He who comes before us speaks slowly and with much sadness. Thakatu shares story told from those that have quickly fled their village and who survived the battle for their people's souls by the bad spirit of Tsiatko.

He slowly begins to share the story of his people, searching for words that would spell of the danger and evil his people have now faced.

"Before we departed the day of our hunt, Sun had rose and fell from the heavens many times without storm falling upon us. Many days had passed in great happiness, and trade was good between many peoples who had come to sit with us at the fires of our village.

As we returned to our village from the long hunt we witnessed many of our people's souls stolen by the bad spirit. We quickly become afraid our spirits would too soon fall unkempt as we looked out over what was left of our village.

We entered the village with great concern as we saw laying upon the ground and upon the banks of the Big River many of our people as they wailed to the High Spirit so their souls would be spared from the grasp of the bad spirit.

We do not understand why our peoples would be forced to crawl to the cool waters of the Big River and cry out to beg the Good Spirit to take from them fever."

Thakatu continued; "We looked down upon those of our village and saw our people's faces and bodies had become like blisters upon one's hands from the hot rocks of our fires.

We walked before those sick with the bad spirit's disease, and we were not sure to whom we had spoken as they did not appear as those we had left in our village as we had made journey to the high peaks to hunt.

An old woman who lay dying beside the door of her lodge told us as we began to pass her, unknowing she was still alive; "When the sun did not shine and the call of Raven was not heard from the branch, disease was cast out from Suyapee's hands to the peoples of our village as they had each touched all that was offered in our trade.

Trade was good, and Suyapee quickly began to gather the hides we had offered, and began to store the spirits of Eena and Otter into the bellies of their boats."

The old woman told as she stood before the entrance to our village with many of our people, she had seen Suyapee look over their shoulders many times with worry as they stood smiling in return.

She told us; "As Sun rested upon the horizon and darkness began to cover the lands, Suyapee's laughter fell silent upon the distant trails of Wind."

The old woman continued with slow and labored breaths; "Many days passed, and life was good! Then, as I walked out from my lodge, the moon was not seen in the heavens, and I could hear many of our people crying in great pain. I saw many crawling from their lodges to the shore of the Big River. With much sadness, I then knew the bad spirit had begun to steal life from within many of our people's now troubled souls.

From their eyes, life was soon not again seen.

Sun rose and fell many days as the mask of darkness took life from many of our people's eyes.

Many of our village were soon lying motionless where they had fallen as I walked amongst them and offered them water to take from them fever.

Many others were huddled in their lodges, each shaking as if the cold of winter had come again to settle within them. They cried out in great pain as they pleaded for the High Spirit to permit them an honorable and proud death so they may be with their fathers and mothers in the Great Spirit's village.

Soon there were few from where once had been many..."

Thakatu told the old woman's spirit was soon taken from her as she too lay there before them in great pain.

Thakatu stated he shall always remember her, as she lay there selfless, without pity, as she only mourned and cried out for those of her village.

"When we saw her eyes slowly open and life was taken from within her, we turned from her side and walked cautiously to the lodge of our great healer.

"Our great chief had too fallen hard upon his mat and was never again to walk amongst our peoples. As he lay there moaning in great pain, he screamed out to those who were left to listen. He told it was him who had first welcomed Suyapee into his lodge as brothers.

"Not long after Suyapee had left to return to their peoples, he too lay stilled upon his mat pleading with Hyas Saghalie Tahmahnawis to take him to the gates of the Hyas Tumtum's village.

"Our great chief lay there, alone, withering, and crying out with great fever.

"As he lay there alone for the first time in many seasons, wounded by the white man's disease, his final words were heard to cry out to those that stood outside the entrance to his lodge; "Suyapee had become his enemy as they chose to cast upon our people bad medicine.

"Life had then at that moment stood still for our Great Chief. It was not long after he spoke his voice was forever held in silence. His soul was quickly dwelt with the uncertainty he would see the light of tomorrow from beside the warm fire in the High Spirit's village."

We were each told by Thakatu; "Throughout the days when oue great chief lay motionless and unable to lead his peoples, there was much sadness in their village.

Thakatu spoke; "My leader's spirit began to be taken slowly from within his soul, and those of our peoples that came to sit at the door of his lodge knew he was soon to be led upon his long journey as cloud drew heavy across the lands.

'Sun and Moon had both begun to join one another as the heaven turned dark and bleak as night, and was quickly covered by cloud as they too began to mourn grievously for their lost brother.

"When Sun's light drew dim, much sorrow was shared in all the villages that still survived the bad spirit's attack.

"From the darkness coveted within the bad spirit's soul arose the uncertainty of life surviving in any of our tomorrows.

"The song of birds were stolen from upon the course of Wind, and silence fell harshly across all the lands.

"The drums that would have one day told of our village's message were too cast out upon the emptiness of Wind to all the tribes of the long valleys that would have told our chief had been taken by this disease brought to our villages by the bad spirit of Suyapee.

'Those that sat near the entrance to our great Shamans lodge who had seen neither Sun or Moon shine down upon the lands for many days, knew as silence quickly fell lonely to Wind, death had finally come peacefully to the great leader of our people.

"Those that dared enter into his lodge stood silently at his side as our village's Shamon who came down from where he lives hidden from man, soon danced.

"His steps shuddered the soils of the earth beneath his feet as he cried out and shook his most powerful stick over our great chief to bring his soul rest from the harshest of his many battles.

"In that most critical of moments, when Sun and Moon were taken prisoner from the heavens and did not bring warmth or hope to shine down upon our people

"We looked down to our great leader and saw him smiling with blind eyes as his pleads before the High Spirit had been answered.

"Our chief was taken from where sickness had lain heavy upon his soul.

"His soul sent out to meet those of his villagers who had been spared the disgrace of a dishonorable death before his father and his mother."

Thakatu told the disease of the bad spirit had also attacked many villages along the course of the Big River.

He told he had seen many peoples littered upon the ground as he came to sit with us and tell of what he had seen.

Thakatu also told us those villages too had been seen trading with the same Suyapee that come in tall boats to the shore of our villages.

It is with grave sadness, the villages did not know the face of danger as it came to stand innocently before them.

Our people's lives sacrificed through the demands of the mesachie tahmahnawis to those wishing to join with him with the promise they would one day rule over all our peoples and to all the lands we live.

Once the story was told, we looked upon one another as much tension grew within the lodge. We each knew then the urgency we would soon be faced could only offer the choice to flee or to fight those who cherish the bad spirits within them as they come upon our peoples.

The visions of our fathers have now become obvious. Without question, we each sat suffering in worry of our tomorrows.

And it was not good!

Those left in the lodge sat quietly, and I too sat alone with my thoughts screaming for answer from the High Spirit for what I must do and share with the peoples of my village.

I knew we, our peoples, could not defend our kingdoms without his support, and as I looked around the emptiness of my lodge I began to cry out to Our Father;

"Kisitilo Nesika papa klaksta mitlite kopa saghalie.
(Our Father Who Dwells on High).

Kloshe kopoa nesika tumtum mika nem.
(Good for Our Hearts Your Name.)

Kloshe mika tyee kopa konaway tillikum;
(Good you Chief of all people;)

She mika tumtum kopa illahee kahkwa kopa saghalie;
(Your heart to make our country such as Yours up above;")

Potlatch konaway sun nesika muckamuck,
(Give us all days our food,)

Pee kopet-kumtux donaway nesika Mesachie,
(And stop remembering all our sins we make to them,)

Kahkwa nesika mamook kopa klaksta spose mamook mesachie kopa nesia;
(As we suppose not their sin against us;)

Mahah siah kopa nesika konaway mesachie.
(Throw far away from us all evil)

Kloshe kahkwa.
(Amen.)"

From the mountaintop we heard the bugle of elk fall down upon the lands of En che Wauna, and we looked towards one another. In silence, we each asked if it was not Great White Elk that called out?

From the long valley we heard cry many Coyote, as they too mourned for what was soon to come to our lands.

We knew if Coyote was to join with us her tricks would confuse those Suyapee who come to our lands, and Suyapee would leave not knowing what trails to follow.

It was not long that Raven too came to sit at the door of the lodge as we came out to look for those we heard calling.

We then knew this was sign all life of the forest would come together and offer us escape upon their trails that lead through the sticks of their forests to those valleys only they alone knew.

My thoughts go to Tenas Hough and his peoples, the Makah, as their village lies on the shores of the Big Water. I fear his village may be no more as Suyapee would enter their villages many suns before our own, as our village is far from the Big Waters.

I must first send messenger to Tenas Hough and to my friend, the Shamon of the Chehalis, to the Quinault at Toholah, to the Queets and Humaluh, the Skagit and the Cathlamahs who still survive, and then to the Chiefs of the Tillamook, the Multnomah and to the Clackamas, to ask them to make journey to join before the fire of our village and sit beside all our peoples so we may make council to speak of change.

Many villages must come and gather at the lodge of our peoples so we may each tell of our vision for all the tomorrows we have been promised.

First the peoples of the Multnomah and Clackamas will sit, then those of the villages of the Clowwewalla, and Wahkikum will join those who have first come to wait.

We will sit in the darkness of the lodge so all can sit and speak without worry of others knowing of our council until we are assured the Great Spirit agrees consent towards each of our decisions.

I will take from the forest a great stick, long, hard, and I will cut from its length many sticks. Each stick will have carved the message of Suyapee and the disease they bring to our lands that takes spirit from the souls of our people.

Each Shamon shall be presented a stick calling their name to make journey to Wahclella and join those of our nations so we may sit and smoke.

From the day the messenger has begun to go upon his long journey, I ask to be marked upon the stick each Moon that does not come above our lands, and our brothers will know of the full moon when we are to gather and sing praise to the High Spirit.

From the smoke of our lodge will come much thought.

Before we emerge from within the closed ties of our lodge we must each agree to a single idea, an ideal that must lead promise before our peoples for all days.

From those words we will share before all the peoples of our kingdoms, and to those we are to pass upon our journeys, they too will know of those changes that we each must take that will offer *all our peoples to stand united before the dark clouds that have begun to spread low above the Lands of Wah.*

In those reasonings, may the paths of our journeys keep our people's safe, and may we be free from the grasp of the bad spirits that prey upon our lives and dwell direly unseen, and unnoticed, until the moment they choose to strike within our souls.

Our fathers must know we are connected to the earth and to the heaven through our good spirit.

Hyas Tumtum Tyee must look over us with the highest of respect.

In fear for those of our people who will be sacrificed beneath the lands of our births by the disease of Suyapee, and for those of our brothers and sisters, and those remaining of our children who shall be seen to walk in great distress from our lands,

I too must each day pray...

Chapter 4

New Peoples To Our Lands

Winter had come hard upon our peoples and has now journeyed far from our lands to be thrown from where we have been chosen to draw upon our breaths.

Deer and elk again number many along En che Wauna's shores from where they had lain hidden during the longest of winter's storms.

We have waited anxiously for the first pish to bring color to the river, and as the Great Eagle flies high above En che Wauna,

I know they are near.

It will not be long and our villages will be engaged in our labors as we dry fish for winter.

Smoke of our fires will tell those that pass our village we have caught many pish to trade and to store before the long winter comes.

When Sun came to the lands and Wind called out for us to rise from our mats and go to the morning's fire, there were many that walked to the shore of En che Wauna to look out over the fast waters for the first sign of pish to come to our nets.

Suddenly, without warning, a great bear, much taller than I have seen, came from where Che che Optin rises into the heaven.

Bear had lain asleep through the long winter, unseen, and unknown to our people as he took shelter beneath the cover of those trees hard fallen from Wind's long ago storm.

Today, as Sun shines down upon the lands and tells of the new season's coming, bear has begun to take the trails where wind spreads the scent of others before him.

As bear now comes to stand angered before us, we know his belly is now empty, and he must forage for food to again become strong.

We dared not move...

Our breaths lay stilled and distanced from our chests.

This day our breaths were alike the silent voices of our people lying in wait for their final journey to the sides of their fathers.

We feared he would charge if he knew we were near...

His nose slowly raised to the rush of Wind upon him.

He turned and faced toward where we stand.

His growl became stronger and louder as he sensed danger filled the air around him.

Bear's tone quickly set fear and question to dwell deeply into our hearts as it penetrated the silence of Wind with the most ominous of warning.

We knew, as he stood questioning through old and unseeing eyes, his unknowing of where we each stood would lead him far from where he had taken of our scent.

As we stood facing him, we were greatly pleased he chose not to charge.

Otelagh had begun to climb into the distant reaches of heaven.

As Sun passed overhead, Lolo then chose to turn from where he stood before us and began to journey along the river until we could not see where he would go.

Slowly, and with great caution, we each began to trust bear had journeyed far from our village.

There was worry shared by many.

We did not know if bear would come again in night and take pish and meat from the shelves of our longhouse.

We would be far from our village where we go to catch pish on the big island, and we would not hear word of his return.

From the peak of Che che Optin we hear the cry of Eagles as they soar high above the waters of En che Wauna.

In wait, we know they look down upon the waters as they cry out to the spirits hidden beneath the wave so they will offer safe journey to great schools of pish that will soon fill their empty bellies and bring food to their young.

It is good the new season comes.

Life gathers in great numbers where we make journey.

New fern rises from the warming soils, as do the first flowers who have begun to spread sweet scent across the trails.

New leaves grow plenty upon the long limbs of trees we had thought long ago dead.

From the heaven we see many geese and duck, hawk and eagle fly fast to the lands and waters they choose as their village.

In every way we have been privileged to share in Earth Mother's gifts.

Earth Mother never leads her children to stray far from where she has chosen for them to live peacefully beneath her calming skies.

From lands we could not see when the storm of winter fell hard upon those that lived in the valleys of the tallest peaks, now call for those same elk and deer to rise up from their beds and return to where winter was not long ago held taut by the great snows that coveted over their lands.

Today, new calves run and play at the feet of their mothers.

Fawns rest fast asleep in the long grasses of greening meadows.

The warmth of Otelagh shines down offering mercy from the cold, and we each are pleased.

It is a time we must show appreciation and give praise to Great Earth Mother for all we have been honored to share.

The passions of the lands speak softly through the breaths of Wind, and soon, we too will hear Earth Mother's voice call out so we may journey to the waters of En che Wauna and catch pish to feed our people.

We will soon begin to make ready for the long journey to the lands where we will gather the root to make piah sapotil, (bread) from the fields where camas grows tall and strong, and we will gather the root of Wapato from the flooded plains along the shores of many waters.

Klale (black) berries will grow strong upon their vine near the end of season, and many of our wives will gather and walk in to the long meadows and gather the sweet berries so we will have jam to cover the bread of camas upon our tables.

Sweet Huckleberry too will grow strong in the mountains of our lands, and all the men of our village will join with the women so we may give praise to Earth Mother for the gift of the fruits lent by her hands upon the open slopes of the high peaks.

But first, as the moon is quick to rise above us, and those I have called to join our village so we may speak of these new people are soon to sit beside our fires, I must gather my brothers and make ready our lodge along the edge of the Big River.

Talk will be good.

Soon we will know to all the trails we are chosen to follow.

When the light of Sun dims from above us and the darkness of cloud rises above us, our journey shall begin.

We know one day we shall return to our lands as we have been promised, and today, that day already awaits us with opened arms.

Soon we are to be gathered by those that come with hardened step upon our peoples, but in the hearts of many, we hear the voice of Naha calling us to return, and we will come again welcomed to these Lands of Wah we have from the beginning of days been promised...

Chapter 5

Dark Clouds Fall Upon the Wallamet

The snows of winter have begun to fade from the lands, and En che Wauna rushes past the banks below where our village sits.

It is now hard to rest at night as the madness of En che Wauna's stream echoes complaint against Che che Optin.

We hope soon the snows of the high peaks will too go from the lands and journey to the sea, and then we will rest before the first pish come again to our nets.

Upon the shores of the Big Water grow tall new life from upon their fertile soils.

The warmth of the new season has granted our spirits to rise up within us as many of our people have been rewarded with newborn children arriving to their arms.

With new life abounding upon Earth Mother's kingdoms, man, animal, and plant each hold hope we each will see the rising warmth of Sun cast down upon all our children's tomorrows.

From the villages of the Clatsop we have heard Suyapee have brought war to settle between those that first came to trade for furs at the big village on the banks of En che Wauna near the Great Waters of Ehkolie.

To there, we today, do not go.

Each day Suyapee who come to stand in villages in our kingdom demand from those of our chiefs we must offer their stores more furs and clamons from our lands so they can too make trade with their people.

We see with clouded eyes, and we too listen with great sadness as we feel Earth Mother shake with the gravest of fear as the absence of good will is shared from Suyapee's most threatening hearts.

Suyapee are bound only by the greed of their spirits.

Dark clouds have risen into the heavens, and they now begin to fall down upon our people and take hope from within our spirits!

Fire burns hot in the belly of the beast we yet cannot see...

It will not be long before he comes upon trails he has promised of death and disease cast happily upon our peoples.

This is not good...

Those of our people who still make journey to the village of Suyapee must hold taut to the honor of our people's beliefs so we all may walk without worry across the lands we have lived for many seasons.

"I ask you my fathers, as our brothers stand and talk before Suyapee, I ask you to guide their words carefully so Suyapee believes we are not to make war against their people."

We all must share we believe in the Earth Mother. It is she that honors all our peoples with the treasures of the lands the Hyas Tyee and she alone has bore.

We know, as Suyapee do not listen to the message cast out by Wind, they do not understand how Earth Mother has honored our peoples for all days.

I must tell my brothers they must sit with Suyapee and pass the pipe of peace and teach them to offer honor before the nest of Naha so they too will know of our tomorrows.

Suyapee must walk with the Great Spirit as she has given all our peoples what we each have held ever close to our souls in our lives.

Suyapee and our peoples are not so different. We eat and drink. We walk the same trails. We see the same animals, and sit beneath the same trees.

Our Great Spirit speaks we must first think of today, and then will be able to know of our tomorrows.

As we find honor in all the lands and to what are bound to the soils within them, then we, Indian, and Suyapee, may walk beside one another proudly for all days.

Our peoples weep as Otelagh sets upon the shores of the Great Sea, for we do not yet know if tomorrow will rise above us again with promise.

We know one day soon all we will have left of our lives are our memories of the Lands of Wah where our village's fires are promised to call out to our peoples so we may again sit before their warmth as it is cast upon us pleasingly from their flames.

We will be as the willow tree whose long arms bend to the soils of the ground, and its heart yearns to rise up and touch Sun once again.

Our baskets will lie emptied to the bounty of our harvest. Sweet blackberry and huckleberry will lie lonely upon its vine for we will no more share in their sweet reward.

It has been spoken, as we stand upon the tall hill, we will not see the waters of En che Wauna again for many seasons.

In this, we shall all days fear...

The spirits of Pish shall swim lonely beneath where our nets once welcomed those many that came to feed our peoples.

Our stomachs will lie empty, and our cries will be cast out lonely to Wind, unchecked.

Life will not be as it is today...

In the souls of our people where lies protected our spirits, we will rise up beneath dark clouds that had long ago swept across all the lands.

We will gather together and make journey across the long trail of the desert.

Though we may feel the souls of our feet suffer by the thorns of the dried bush, we will endure the harshness of the bad spirit's hands, and in the end of Suyapee's days, we will be seen honored to come again to our lands with the wanting of Naha to comfort us with her Great Spirit.

We see with great vision of those tomorrows where she too has today lain her brow gloomily upon her chest.

It is in those days she has fallen lonely upon her bed for her own children's return within the nest of their beginnings.

It shall be from Naha's soul we too shall covet the promise of our mother.

We shall once again rise up and be spread across all the lands with great promise.

We each shall be pleased for all days and all nights.

The song of Coyote shall be heard again across all the valleys of our lands. Our spirits shall become reunited once again to the kingdoms of our births.

From the heavens, Otelagh shall reign down upon the lands. The warmth of Otelagh's brow shall bear honor to the paths of our people.

We will again bring respect to all the lands of our kingdoms.

Life as we know it today shall be renewed for all days.

Our spirits shall become tied by the wealth of our souls.

As sun rises higher into the heaven time has come so many of our village will make journey to the Hyas Tyee Tumwata and catch pish and eel with our brothers of the Clackamas.

There will be many to stand with us from the Mollala, and those from the village that rests beside the waters of the Yamhill who we have not seen for many seasons.

We will together bring honor to the first pish to jump into our nets, and we all shall be pleased.

We must make trade with the Kalapuya for the blue flower of Camas and for the tarweed seed whose flower grows tall and shines yellow as sun smiles down upon the long prairies.

As we begin to gather our nets and long spear, many come from the village of the Klemiaksac where waters from Wy-East meet those of En che Wauna.

The Klemiaksac have as had our own peoples, chosen to journey to the Hyas Tyee Tumwata to stand with those of the village of the Clackamas.

It has been heard they have spoken to have returned from the waters of the Wallamet where they have seen many brothers and sister's souls taken from their village. Sadly, it too is heard they now go to the lands where their father's voices could not be heard.

They tell the darkness of the evil spirit has fallen heavy upon those of the Wallamet.

It is told the bad spirit had made battle for the souls of those that slept at night at the foot of the Hyas Tyee Tumwata.

Many canoes are filled with their peoples along the big waters, and quiet has swarmed like bees to their hives over the lands.

Warning is passed to all those that come to the Great Falls to find honor in the catch of pish.

Many do not heed the calls of Ravens as they wait to feast on those soon dead.

Our people have been warned by each of our fathers in all the days we have prospered in these lands Raven is a Great Spirit.

Raven is who speaks loudly when danger is near, and we must listen to its message with opened ears and clear minds for what he speaks.

The one called Skookum Stick points to the lands of the Wallamet and tells there was no smoke rising from the longhouses at the shores of the Hyas Tyee Tumwata.

It is told there are not now many to sit and tell of whom the bad spirit takes from their people.

We are told from the heavens came great dark clouds, each passing across the sky without hurry.

Our brothers share as they came to the shores of the Wallamet and began to make camp for the long night, they began to make fire to keep warm.

But from the heavens, falling from the darkness and coming into the light of their fires, the small mosquito who is known to battle one another for the souls of our people.

At first those of the village at Tumwata Tyee did not know of the mosquito's march towards them as the silent cadence of the bad spirit's drums did not first bring warning.

It was not long when they too were attacked without mercy.

The new season brought much rains to fall across all the lands, it was not long before many lakes began to form where once there were none.

As our brothers of the village of Klemiaksac looked out across the lands, they told they could see above the stilled waters where came up the dark clouds that brought only sadness and death to many their people.

They told those of us who this night sit beside them; "Not even the warmth and flame of fire could force mosquito to turn in retreat.

"With great sadness, we realized it was the blood of our peoples and those that came to catch pish they had first craved thirst."

Our brothers tell they could not settle upon the shores of the Wallamet as great swarms began to gather upon their camp.

They had been forced to make journey through the long night, and as Otelagh rose above the distant horizon, they have come to sit at the fires of our village.

Through the emptiness I see held taut within their eyes, I know of great worry.

In my heart I know they too fear the bad spirit has taken much from their souls.

I sense the friends of our friends who have come to tell of what they have seen may too be called upon by the bad spirit to sit beneath the mounds of his catacombs and await his distant call into battle.

Soon I fear they too will be no more upon these lands as their souls will have been cast out from within them and lent to the journeys promised to the evil that dwells promised in the darkness of our nights.

"I pray my fathers high above, where grasses sway in gentle breeze as Hyas Tkope Kuitans run free across long meadows, and where the fires are seen each night to glow with welcome to all those that make journey to sit with their fathers for all days and for all nights, they will be spared from the bad spirit's most fearsome poach.

"I pray before you my fathers their souls will be afforded to touch the heavens and speak with their fathers once they are called to take the long journey to the land of the dead.

"Fathers, as I stand here where once you too have stood, hear my plea, take from their souls all that is bad, and spare them from the unknowingness of darkness' question and far from its much binding truss.

"Papa, kumtux kopa kwolan nika skookum wawa! "Father, hear my plea!"

To those that pass our village we must tell of the Clackamas so they too do not enter into the lands that offer but death without dignity before their own fathers.

It is a wise man that sees only darkness where once was light when there is not hope as the Mesachie Tahmahnawis begins to prey upon those that sleep helplessly at night.

Today I sit upon the bank of En che Wauna and listen for the song of Wind to pass before me across the plane of heaven.

I wish to hear joyous song, a song of prosperity bringing hope before all my people.

I thirst, not for wawa, but for life and freedom so we may escape the evil that has now begun to befall upon the many.

I have seen whole villages, men, women, and children laying upon the water's edge. Each begging, pleading for the Hyas Tyee to take from them the pain and suffering they were then bound challenged.

Great fever came to those people. They shook upon the ground before me. It was the bad spirit who had entered within their bodies and had chosen to pull from their souls, spirit.

This has created much pain to invest within my heart for I, today, feel the loss of our people.

Never will I soon forget...

The bad spirit's guise did not offer hope in the souls of those many he preyed.

My memory does not fail me.

My heart feels the pain of all those yesterdays as if it were this day...

I journeyed past many villages as I called out, and there were many whose wails were not cast out in return.

Children were stolen from the innocence they were first born.

The wickedness of the evil spirit was cast down upon their helpless souls without first thought to those who had not yet lived to see many of their tomorrows.

To those I have passed, I today grieve with great sadness. I see with clear eyes their troubled souls, and I yet hear those calling out for their mothers as their pain was unyielding.

It is to those memories I cannot flee.

Many nights I awaken knowing one day those children could be my own.

As I sit here, my life has been challenged by that fear.

My eyes are alike the Hyas Tyee Tahmahnawis as he brings water to flow from upon his splintered cheeks to the lands beneath him that offers life to survive all that it is challenged.

From those same challenges, I must certainly find hope for all our tomorrows...

Chapter 6

Journey To Cathlapotle

This season has brought good catch to our village. We are pleased to know the Great Spirit has looked over our people with generous eyes.

The days have become shorter with the failing sun in the heaven, and soon we must make journey to the village of Cathlapotle to trade for the wapato and clam offered for the points of arrows we have traded from those that come from where the Great Spirit of Seekseekqua, Mt. Jefferson, looks over her mighty kingdom.

Wy-East must be pleased Seekseekqua was chosen to rule over the lands near his own. Each day they look towards one another in knowing they have both brought honor to be placed before the feet of our Great Tyee.

From the kingdom of Wy-East to the kingdom of Mazama, those spirits who once reigned in anger and fought great battles have now settled within the bowels of the earth and have not been seen again to cast fire and rock upon the great forests.

This season is good. There is much that has been saved to trade from our journeys into both the mountains, and where the waters of En che Wauna meets those of many rivers.

Huckleberries have grown thick upon their branch, many more than in season's not so long ago we do not remember when the branch had lain empty, and their berry dried upon their bush across the barren slopes.

Tears have fallen many times from the High Spirit's cheeks as the new season brings green grasses to grow tall and strong in the valleys that reach far into the mountains.

Vine grows even stronger as they rise up from upon the meadow's floor where we go to collect their lengths to make baskets. Our labors have been hard.

We have been honored by Naha to store more than what we need to use through the long days of winter's storms, and our hard work shall soon prove of our efforts before many villages as they seek what we offer to be placed within their own stocks.

The best Eena have been taken from the streams of the mountains.

We will offer many furs to trade with the village of Cathlapotle so they too may make trade with the chief of the Clatsop.

There, where En che Wauna and the Big Waters meet, the chief makes good trade with Suyapee.

Many days we see him go upriver to trade with all the villages for the best furs and for the clamon of our peoples.

The chief is just in each of his decisions, and he brings good always to settle between Suyapee and our peoples.

We have seen many Suyapee journey upriver as they pass beyond the reach of our villages.

Many come and sit with us to smoke.

There are others that come and want to know of the waters from where we take the best furs of beaver and mink.

To this we do not speak as it is there, where Pahto sits peering down upon us each day, where he may awaken once more and bring fire and flood to pour down upon our peoples.

We have walked the same trails now for many seasons with Suyapee, and many of them have been good.

Each day word is passed through Wind that good has come to our lands as Suyapee brings honor before our people and as they too offer much to trade.

Our fears have become few.

Their fears have become fewer.

It is today good to walk across our lands without knowing of fear.

Fear is cast out before others by the heart promised of question that ends in the offering of evil.

Suyapee and Indian must not bring fear to stand between us.

This would not be good.

To walk together as one and speak truth has no evil.

To walk together and not look into another's eyes only brings question to what lies in the heart of those others we speak.

Trade brings honor between our peoples. It is in accepting that trade with respect we walk as men.

For those who choose to walk alone as do the Pishpish and Lolo, and stand distant from those whose souls walk with the Great Spirit, they shall be taken by the hand and dwell all days where only those spirits that want pestilence and disease to become fastened into the souls of others shall be known to exist.

They that choose not to be our brothers beneath Sun shall not be seen again, nor will their names be spelled again before our ears.

With joy, I must say; "To fear Suyapee I pray shall not be felt again amongst our people, but it has been spoken we have not yet been taken upon the long walk we have been told by our fathers, where our peoples have not joined those spirits whom are known to those far away lands."

We choose good to rise to the spirit of our souls. We do not choose to walk half hidden by the wanting of the spirit that only offers suffering and pain to fall hard upon all our peoples.

Evil did not come from the heart of the Hyas Creator.

Evil comes from the hearts of men who do not follow in the teachings of the Hyas Creator.

It has been heard spoken by the Hyas Tyee Tahmahnawis for many more seasons than we have been told to follow in the ways Wind speaks of our Earth; "If storm comes fast and falls hard upon the earth, and snow is quick to lie deep upon the ground, do you not know to turn and go to your village as you see dark cloud again falling from the heavens?"

We together must walk and learn of one another.

As we journey across our kingdoms, the voice of Wind shall teach both Suyapee and our people that in peace we can survive beneath the light cast out by Sun to all our people.

Otelagh's and Naha's gift to their children is knowing they will rise each day, and they shall each sleep each night, and in both, they will prosper in their tomorrows as they walk with promise before those that come to stand before them.

But, if we choose to make war, behind every tree and beneath each rock, from the waters of rivers and streams, there awaiting our souls shall be the evil of our own spirits leading us toward the dark tombs where life does not exist.

I must speak of these thoughts to my people, and hope they become inspired to all days follow their hearts so their spirit will withstand the offerings of the bad spirit.

We must honor the heavens and the earth.

We must follow in the teachings of those that have come before us as they have walked the same trails, and they have seen the same troubles.

To honor our mothers and our fathers will allow our lives to follow the paths where the bad spirit cannot hide.

We shall overcome all obstacles with patience, thought, and in knowing where we must go to find our lives held virtuous and strong before the Great Spirit.

As I have stood before Wahclella's founding walls I have become a man amongst many men. I am not one man, but many.

I have been taught the ways of the Earth, and the ways of our people by the lessons through many of our fathers.

Through these teachings I must share all I have learned before my brothers, and we will soon prove of our worthiness before all men that come to sit and speak before the fires of our villages.

To this, if not just to this lone thought, we must be promised each day.

I walk to the river to see the current of En che Wauna running fast before me.

I sit patiently and await the many pish to return from behind the few.

I look over the fast waters where rock rises from the swift current, and there, rising from beneath the water's depths to touch the clouds of heaven, a great pish to catch the small fly.

My thoughts prepare me for what may come as we are gathered on our journey. I will sit with those that come, and we will find safe haven from what lurks waiting in the sanctuary of the evil one's heart.

To those we pass, I will share these thoughts, and with prayer we will each walk for all days in the light promised of heaven.

We each must understand and accept that fear, and deceit must not be shown before any peoples. Not to Suyapee, or any of our brothers who will cross the paths of our lands.

This will keep our peoples of the Chinook Nation, and all the nations of Indian strong and in favor to sit before the table of the Hyas Tumtum Tyee.

One day, when our spirits are called to join with those in heaven, we will each know our journeys were led safely by the knowing of many, and not by the few that now do not understand why their voices are silenced upon the trails of Wind for all days.

We have placed all we take to trade in the hulls of the Three Cedar Brothers. Tied to each of the canoes our brothers have promised to lead safely upon our journeys will follow those canoes filled with baskets and berries dried from the good harvest of this season.

We too take many pish smoked with Alder. Salmon and sturgeon pounded by our women to make cake is too placed in each of the canoes.

It was not long we made ready to make journey to our brother's village at Nemalquinner.

It is in that place where the waters that come from Wy-East are not good. Bad spirit comes from the waters at the feet of Wy-East when fire burns bright and smoke takes from our eyes the Great Spirit of Wy-East as he spreads wide his arms before those living upon his kingdom.

Hidden too is the wide smile of Pahto as he looks down upon his kingdom to those that make his great meadows alive with life once more.

From the eyes and hearts of all the spirits to our lands, of those who rise up above her gleaming crown, they too know the innocence of Lawala Clough as she is hidden and protected beneath the clouds of the heaven below where they each sit and threaten of battle.

There, standing in silence above the Spirit's Lake where her tears had once fallen from upon her lonely cheeks, she chooses to stand alone.

Many seasons ago, when I was a boy, I had journeyed to Cathlapotle to make trade with my father.

Though there have been days when I was demanded to appoint myself to the troubles between our peoples and between the villages that are spread upon the shores of En che Wauna, what I had shared beside the greatness of my father has not escaped me.

Those times, each moment, every story, they have all proven to lead my soul into becoming the man whom the Spirits wished to lead our village.

I shall not forget those great days and nights my father and I shared, as it was in those days he taught me of the Heron and the Goose that flew into the heaven when we approached.

My father led me to understand better the reasoning behind the legends of each Wawa we journeyed past.

He taught me how they each have brought reason and worth to the legend of our peoples.

From the maidens of Multnomah to the spirits of Horsetail, Kuitan Wawa, and to the wise Elowah, each has brought memories of my father to return before me.

Today, I know as we pass them from our chair, we will each sit in awe of not only their beauty, but of their significance to the strengths of our being.

Their stories have always resonated within our hearts, and this day shall not allow difference in their place within these majestic lands.

Now, as the leader to my peoples, I go with my brothers in many canoes.

The Three Brothers of Cedar brings honor to my father today as I sit proudly within the one certainly to be his first choice.

The best goods I bring to trade are placed in the hulls of the remaining brothers. It was first promised upon their choosing by each Red Cedar they would not bring water to touch what is placed within their souls.

To this day, many seasons from when their souls were first sewn into the hearts of our village, they have stood strong.

The Three Brothers each have willed their placement for all days into the hearts of those of our village as they have taken us upon safe journeys to many distant shores.

It was not long after we began to make journey to the shores of Washougal, Fast Waters, when we had heard Hyas Coyote call out, and we too had seen Raven take wing above us.

Across En che Wauna from the Fast Waters awaits the fires of the Nemalquinner where we will first stop to smoke and speak with their people.

Many seasons ago the bad spirit came and took many from the village with disease that came from the waters of the Ehkolie when a big ship came to look closely at our people.

Many of the village were led from this life we today know...

From the shores of the Big Waters to the villages of En che Wauna, many of our peoples were stolen of rising into the light of their tomorrows.

But there were many of the village who did not go to where the Mesachie Tahmahnawis called out to them.

Though he had offered them his opened arms with great promises and awaited them to join with him where others could not see the bleakness and desperation of his darkened soul, today, with great happiness, they do not now lie entombed and promised to the bad spirits every will.

Their souls were strong, their spirits stronger.

They brought honor to those that today walk without fear of the bad spirit.

As Hyas Tumtum leads them to know of what trails to follow in their lives, and through honoring the High Spirit's decisions, we too will go and sit at the foot of their fires and bring honor to their names.

We will smoke from the long pipe, and we shall share in accepting each of their good spirits.

Talk will be good!

We shall be pleased to see one another again…

Our village of Wahclella is far from the shores of the Big Waters, and as our brother's village sits close to En che Wauna, it brings many Suyapee to first sit at their fires and make trade before they go back to their village with the stories we share of these lands.

Many of those Suyapee we will not see, but there are those that come to walk into the lands we do not speak.

Those lands, where our Great Spirits look down upon us, and where they each watch over us to be assured we too are promised to the land's own requests, and that they will be kept for all days promised of our highest respect.

I know our brothers will know much of Suyapee and to what they do, and where they speak their journeys have led them.

They will know how many have come and how many have gone from our lands.

As the full moon falls from the heavens until it again returns, there are many Suyapee that journey to go far into the lands of our spirits.

They take with them many furs and clamons from those of our brothers that want trade.

We know to give all the Hyas Tahmahnawis has offered our people to survive for all days is not good.

Each day Suyapee comes to make trade their demands are more than what we may offer, and their minds become foolish and weak as are the sick lying beside the waters of our rivers now burning of fever.

This is not good.

They do not understand of tomorrow.

The greed of their souls takes good from their spirit, and they shall not be welcomed before the fires of our heaven...

I am reminded each day of tomorrow as Sun falls from the heavens and as his sister Moon returns to guard over our peoples through the long nights.

Though there are days when they do not climb high where we can see, from the lands where they make journey does not bring the warmth of their souls to fall upon us.

Yet we know their spirits watch over all our peoples in each of the kingdoms we live.

We hear and see the Hyas Tumtum's wrath when he knows we have not followed in his teachings. As we place our step distant from where he demands we first walk, then he comes upon us with great vengeance, and all that we know is soon changed.

It is upon those days, storm comes with great hurry. Spears swarm across the skies as bees to the bear that steals honey from their sweet nest.

Great fires burn hot into the soul of the lands.

What was once green with new life now smolders in the bleakness of darkness where only dark cloud can be seen settled firmly upon all the lands where we had each once been promised in our journey.

My eyes have grown dim with sorrow as those same dark clouds have begun to form thick over all the lands, and our tomorrows have been seen laden by question.

From far away, I felt great agony as Naha's heart must now mourn deeply for her offspring from atop Wallahoof as she looks down upon her lost children.

From where Fast Waters go to En che Wauna we see the smoke of the Nemalquinner rising above calm waters.

It is good now to go to village across the swift current of En che Wauna.

It had not been long after we put into the currents of En che Wauna that storm has again fallen from the heavens and taken the cliffs and mounts that rise up above the long valley from before our eyes.

With hurried stroke we fly above the crashing waves.

Waters run fast and strong against us as Wind blows hard across the trails of the Big River.

We each fight bravely so we may see the light of our tomorrows!

Waves crash upon the sides of the Three Brothers, but we do not worry for each of the Brothers of Cedar have promised to fly above the crests of waves so we may each day return to rest beside those of our people.

Wind's breath blows strong, each stronger than the last.

From the viciousness of the storm's calling, we hear many voices cry out with great agony before they once again fall silenced to our ears.

Then, as Wind becomes settled and we began to believe she has left to bring fear upon other's lands, she returns much stronger. Bringing from within her dark soul more conviction than she had last shown of her promise upon us.

Through the throes of Wind's harshened breaths we hear many peoples again pleading for their mothers.

Their cries lay weight to settle upon the bows of our canoes.

I feel as if it is the evil spirit that now wills our peoples to surrender beneath the waves of his greatest warriors.

Again and again waves rise higher as Wind blows convincingly of her plot.

We are ceded to the clouds of the heaven above where the flat planes of En che Wauna's currents were just lain calmed by the whispers of Wind's most disguising lure.

We cross En che Wauna with great caution.

We are each challenged with concern.

As our group have been promised to be held taut by the strong spirits promised of The Three Brothers, this day offers yet much to its question?

We plead before the Hyas Tumtum to survive the battle for our souls…

With every stroke of our paddles come great waves to crash upon the hulls of our keepers.

I can hear from far away the calling of the bad spirit for our own spirits to give up hope and faith in our reaching the distant shore.

The bad spirit pleads loudly for us to join those he has owned for many days beneath the driven wave of his storm.

But in the absence of our fear, we do not listen…

From the heavens fall great spears to crash upon the water, and as we make fast to the shore, they come faster, closer, each one bringing warning to resonate within our souls.

Many of our own village's peoples have been taken to where we cannot see the bad spirit's army that today awaits us to join within their ranks.

"To there," I silently cry out to my brothers; "We shall not go!"

I must remember I have been chosen to be the Shamon to my village by those sitting upon the Great Wall of Wahclella.

Through all the seasons I have been honored to stand before the peoples of the Watlalla and before many others of our nation,

I have shared the wealth of knowledge the Great Spirits have allowed myself to grasp.

Throughout the days of my standing before the Great Spirit, many of our nation have come to my village to sit before the warm fire through the long night and speak of their concerns.

Many of those that sit with me ask of what trails they should follow in their decisions to what brings trouble to their souls?

Those that sit while I speak have heard my message.

I have shared before them to remember it is the Great Spirit who judges those peoples who do not follow each of his rules.

I confirm with much conviction, they can only then, themselves, accept the trails I too have been led to believe to be righteous.

I have willed my soul to be led by the Great Spirits.

Through the knowledge I have been honored to have engaged, my spirit so rises honorably before others.

My peoples, all peoples who come to stand before me and believe in the words I speak, shall live to see all the suns of their tomorrows beside the seats of their fathers.

They all go upon their journeys from the foot of our fires and are then promised throughout life to be respected and honored.

They offer only what is just from the bindings of their souls and through the heralding of integrity promised of their spirit.

It shall be from those qualities they share before others they pass which will allow them to one day sit with their fathers in the green meadows where the White Stallions graze.

This journey across the strong waters of En che Wauna has taken my thoughts to many days that have passed.

It was one of those days I remember long ago when we walked from the shore of En che Wauna to this village where we now come.

So long ago, when Sun did not shine and Moon was not seen to rise into the heavens for much of the new season, we began to journey down En che Wauna.

It was not long from the time we placed canoe into river when we began to see many vultures rising up from the cliffs where they await the smell of death to settle upon the lands.

With swift wing they came to rise into the heaven from the far valley where they roost.

Quickly they circled tightly above in the darkened cloud of sky.

As we approached the entrance of the village, there were no sounds of life that stirred our memories towards what we had once known to walk freely amongst the lands of our brothers.

Not even Wind stirred our senses to the scent of fish drying in the thickened air of Alder burning.

We walked slowly from the shore of En che Wauna as our gaze turned from each side of the village to the other, and with much question, we saw many canoes tied to the trunks of those trees near the longhouses where they slept.

No one of the village came to greet us with open arms and welcome us to join them to smoke and talk at the side of the warm fire.

We stood at the center of the village as the flame of their fire still grew tall as smoke rose far into the heaven.

There was no one of their village walking along the long shores of the river when we came to the village, and we saw no brothers or sisters coming from the peaks that rise beyond the long valley where we then awaited for them to appear.

These both brought worry and concern to where their lives may have been cast.

This took hope from our hearts they would again walk before us and sit at the side of their fires, and it was not good...

We approached with caution to the entrance of their shelters, but as we called out we heard no voices rising up from inside the closed doors.

We began to ask ourselves if Hyas Tyee Tahmahnawis was also angry with those here at Nemalquinner, as he may be angry with our own peoples as Wind came hard through the sticks of the forest.

Swiftly we each sat low to the ground so we did not fall from where we stood.

Wind's throes upon us proved of its anger. Angered beyond those many days it had before come upon our lands.

Today, it does not journey quickly from its storm upon us.

We called out to those we did not see, and from the screams Wind shared, only was returned the silence of our brother's now lost cries.

This too brought more question to where our brothers may have fled in great hurry?

We chose to sit at the fire to wait.

As darkness began to cover the lands we went back to the bank of the river and took Eulachon from our canoes to eat which had been chosen to offer their spirits to our nets in the beginning of the new season.

Talk was not much as we watched for our brothers to come from behind trees and from the top of the peaks that rose up along the shores of En che Wauna.

The trails were emptied of life.

Only the cry of Pishpish could be heard far off into the thick of night's darkness.

This was not good sign as the thoughts of days past came before our memories.

In those memories, our thoughts began to wander from what is good to what is bad in what life has offered many our peoples.

Sun had crossed the heaven and the warmth of his heart was quickly felt leaving the lands.

Shadows fell below from the tallest of trees, and the cold of night entered into the lands to wait for the return of Sun's engaging warmth.

In this, we were forced to decide either to wait until Sun again rose, or to join the waters of En che Wauna and go to the village of Namuit who live on the big island, and there, we will ask if they knew of those people of Nemalquineer.

It was not like any of our people that live along the shores of En che Wauna to have not even the old to wait in village while others go to hunt or fish.

We each looked into one another's eyes and did not speak, but there in the eyes of many was lain the answer we did not wish to seek.

The Raven did not call, nor did he first warn of danger.

The call of Coyote was not heard to cry out in all the valleys.

The emptiness of the village brought visions of brothers long lost to the wishes of the bad spirit's calling.

"Where have our brothers and sisters journeyed," I pleaded before my fathers?

I asked if the bad spirit had come in such hurry our brothers did not see or hear of their quick march upon them?

I too asked; "Why have they taken the souls of our brothers and left only the flame of their fires to wait for those that come to talk and smoke from the long pipe?"

I remember from the creek where Pashit had made journey came loud cries.

Pashit ran with much hurry to return to where we sat waiting.

In his eyes I could see worry.

From his soul I could smell fear.

Through the words he spoke, we saw why our brothers had gone quickly from their village.

Pishit had seen deep into the eyes of a young boy that was lying at the bank of the stream, not far from the fires we now sit.

Great sores had grown to cover his body.

Pishit said the boy's tongue hung from his lips as if he was to beg for water as he crossed the dry desert.

In his eyes his soul could not be seen.

The young boy's face was not one Pishit knew once of their people.

Emptied of spirit the boy's soul would from that day long travel, lost in the coarseness of Wind's storm.

He had no land to call out as his home.

His spirit was then lost to our people and to those lands he had first come.

He had been taken as slave to the armies of the Mesachie Tahmahnawis.

This too was not good!

The bad spirit had come to their peoples and had stolen the innocence of their young.

With grave sadness we knew why they did not stay.

It was not good we wait.

We feared we might be chosen next to become offerings to the bad spirit's village.

It was through that vision we knew we must go!

With much hurry we took canoe to river.

With swift strokes we brought air to rise beneath the keel of our boats, and we were quickly promised above the fast wave of En che Wauna.

"To here, we shall not go again," was heard spoken by the many as we looked off into the distance where dark cloud loomed heavy above the final flames of their fire!

We chose to go to the village of the Namuit as we made journey through the long night.

We each agreed, if we could not see if the bad spirit waited in hide to ambush our souls from beneath the soils of our lands, we would not go upon the shores rising from the waters of En che Wauna until we could see behind the tree and from beneath each bush where we would first place our step.

We chose to follow where current was not fast so we would not come to big island before sun rose up to touch the heaven.

Through the visions of our fathers I feared this was the beginning of what they had seen coming to our peoples through the looking glass of our tomorrows.

I told myself many times I must not speak to what I had then feared.

This too, I knew would not be good if all our souls are to be held strong before those that may be weakened by the hands of those spirits we cannot yet see.

By the desolation of our thoughts to the questions that remain unanswered, I called out to our fathers in silenced voice.
I pleaded to the heavens they would hear the urgency of my plea.

I prayed they would feel the pain burdened to my soul as I asked them to lead our people safely upon the waters and across the distant lands of our journey.

Quickly we passed the villages of Nerchacolee and Neerchokioo where we saw their fires glowing bright in the shadows of darkness' grave.

This night, the light of the moon offers light to be cast through the tall timbers where Suyapee's bad spirits hide at night.

This is the place Suyapee calls Vancouver where we go to make trade and to take those of our people that fall sick from the disease of the bad spirit.

The Suyapee here are good.

These Suyapee welcome our people into their village, not like those whose village stood near the Big Waters who pointed cannon toward our people the day we came to speak of trade and peace between our peoples as we offered to smoke kinootle from the long pipe.

Many of our people live at the gates of the village. Some work in the fields that grow seed sown from our mother's long hair, and others go to the forests and take stick to make planks to build shelters for the people of Suyapee's village.

There are seen fire's flame from those of our brothers who camp at Suyapee's gates, but here too we choose to pass until we know of what has become of our brothers.

We have kept to the river's fast currents and go to Namuit without break so we may sit with those who live near where the waters of Wallamat and En che Wauna meet.

I believed this to be good as the villages of the great valley where the Wapato grows plenty will know all that has come to our lands from the Big Waters where Sun now rests.

We would then know to what they had heard spoken of those who lived at the village where bad waters come from Wy-East.

The heavens began to show Sun was soon to rise from beyond the bend of the Great River, and sun's warmth would begin to spread across all the lands, and we were pleased.

We heard the calling of birds again rising from where they had found rest during the night.

Many gathered together in great flocks and circled above our canoes as we neared the shores of the great island.

Raven too circled overhead as he led our way safely to the shores where lies the village of Namuit.

Sitting on the highest ridge was my friend old Coyote.

From there, she called out to those of the village telling of our arrival from our long and difficult journey.

Sun slowly rose from the flat lands of the east and began to climb into the trails of the heaven.

All life that honored these lands began to waken.

The leaf and petals of flowers opened to welcome the warmth of Sun's heart.

Rabbits scurried across the opened fields, and in the waters beside those of En che Wauna came many Eena as they passed to gather limbs to keep strong their lodge.

Deer stood from beneath great Oak where they found rest during the long night, and they too gathered and grazed upon the long grasses upon the golden fields.

As I looked at the lands and saw life here was good, I breathed heavily and gave thanks to our Great Father as we had survived the long night and would soon sit with our brothers and smoke from the long pipe.

The journey had brought worry to overwhelm our hearts, and it was a long and hard battle to not stray from the test it had offered our mettle.

With much effort and knowing what we had been cautioned, we had today lasted to see Sun's rise once more.

Life has both good and bad invested into its being.

We have to accept both as it is in both we learn.

It is in that understanding we shall go forth unto the lands and sit with all peoples and know as we toil heavily into what is brought before us by our fathers, our peoples will too survive as we have this past night.

Though we had seen death created by the hands of the bad spirit, it was not the end of our days.

The Great Spirit who looks over our peoples has always told we would walk in all days before others though our lives would be placed into great jeopardy as change falls heavily upon the souls and spirits of our peoples.

Sun and moon would rise and fall each day.

The seasons would come and go as they have from the beginning, and many of our peoples would not find favor in those changes that would fall far from our beliefs.

Sadly, those changes would be promised to take from us our standing upon the lands we had been first chosen to protect.

With honor and respect, we Indian, would walk with heads held high and know we will always belong where others will quickly kneel upon the soils of our lands as they submit before their leaders in their deepest of failures.

One day, we will return to the lands we are to be taken, and then too will the lands return as they were before our lives were separated from one another.

It is in that promise where we hear the song of birds and the bugle of elk fall pleasingly across all the lands. It is through that same promise

Wind will carry the sweet scent of flower down from the high peaks and settle upon the lowest of the valley's floors.

Pish will again enter into the waters of En che Wauna, and they will gather at the beginning of their streams in great numbers.

The trees and bush will rise up from the soils and bring honor to the souls of those pish who have promised each new season to give life to the lands.

Life will return as it was, and it will be good to share where we today stand in awe to all the gifts we have each been honored.

We walk from the shore of En che Wauna, and as we arrived near the rising smoke of the villages fires, strong scent of pish rises into the warm air.

I turn to my friend Chistup and tell him to go back and bring with him elk to share with the village of Namuit as we share the morning meal and speak of what has come to the villages along En che Wauna.

As we look for those we know sitting at the fires of their village, there are many now not living.

Those that have chased the bad spirit from within their souls have become weakened through the long fight.

I fear it will not be long and they too will be no more upon the lands beside those of En che Wauna's shores.

In memory to those I once knew that came to join with me at the side of their fires, I wail to my fathers, pleading their names shall not soon be forgotten...

Steven Warnstaff

Chapter 7

Through the Eyes of
Tsagiglala I Too Now See

It was long ago when this story I am going to share first began, where we, our people, now stand united and watch in skepticism to those Suyapee that march quickly into the lands of the Chinook from along the waters of En che Wauna.

So many seasons have since passed from the first season my father and I journeyed together to the village of Wishram to make trade before the long winter set harshly into the lands of Wah.

As we secured what we were to take for trade within the Three Brothers of Cedar, we offered thanks to the Great Tyee as we placed our lives into En che Wauna's waters to begin our long journey to where I was told pish would soon jump into our nets as we stood upon the cliffs of Wyam.

We began the long journey under the clearest of skies and the calmest of waves. The warmth of Sun shone down upon us and kept cold from challenging our spirits as wind did not blow hard against us.

Sun had grown high into the heaven as we crossed beyond the remains of La Tahb lamotai, Table Mountain, whose remains lay stilled for all days beneath the fast waters of En che Wauna where they chose to rest.

It was there, where *Waconda Illahee Ooe-Hut*, Bridge of the
Gods, once allowed Wy-East to go to Lawala Clough across
the passage between his kingdom and the kingdom of Pahto. It
too was from there Wy-East had first vowed to ask Lawala
Clough to dance each day in his arms before the spirits of all the
kingdoms.

Pahto was not pleased as he too wished to dance with Lawala
Clough, and in his anger, sent fire and rock into the heavens and
upon the lands of Wy-East so he would return to his lands to
save all the animals and trees he had promised before Sun, his
father, and to his mother Moon, to protect.

If it were not for *Wabish Illahee*, Stone Chief, their battle may
have taken all we see today along the shores of *En che Wauna*,
and we would not again be allowed to rest at night upon these
lands where our villages today stand.

I remember all the forests we passed upon our journeys. Many
climbed from the edge of *En che Wauna's* wave to the top of
peaks who rise far into the clouds. Tall peaks, which allowed me
to imagine great herds of tkope goats running across rocky cliffs
without worry.

We passed many villages that rise from the shores of *En che
Wauna*, and as I looked towards them, smoke of their fires spread
from their huts as they made ready for pish that would soon lie
drying across long racks to be made into meal for winter.

The river was busy with those that catch sturgeon in the deep
channels of *En che Wauna*. There too were many people going
fast to the village at Wyam to wait beside their brothers for the
first salmon so they could offer thanks to the Great Creator at the
beginning of celebration.

We passed many canoes filled with net and spear, and my father called out to many as he had not seen them for many suns.

The cry of Eagles screamed down upon us with warning as my father turned the canoes so we would go near the island where his father and many great leaders lie waiting for the White Stallions of our Great Chief to come.

My father looked toward the Land of Spirits where only the breaths of Wind could reach out to touch its soils and blow gently through the arms of whispering Cottonwoods.

Blowing through Wind across the heaven came summer's clouds to fall upon the lands offering soft beds for those that led our peoples upon the trials of our lives to sleep.

These were our fathers, our leaders, the Shamons of our villages whom stand privileged before the High Spirit from the Walls of Wahclella, and now share the just trails we each must follow in our lives as we offer favor toward all people.

As we came near the big island, my father began to wail to the Great Chief as he prayed to the High Spirit so he would soon come to look upon his father whose eyes had not closed to his people or to the lands he had so long journeyed.

My father again called out to Hyas Tumtum so he would look down upon those chiefs who have been honored to wait upon the big island.

Who, each day, see all their people pass upon the driven wave of En che Wauna and look upon those that come through the eyes of their memories.

As I sat looking over to the big island, I could not see what my father had seen when he told me he had taken his father to wait beside those of the Yakama, the Chinook, and the Paiute to rest.

My father explained to me what the graves of our people were like as he walked amongst them. He said there were many great men laying in their canoes, each painted with scenes once seen through their eyes from along the shores of Big River.

Each of the great chiefs were dressed in skins and surrounded by the finest of dentalia and shell, the truest of arrow and sharpened spear were placed beside them to ward off the evil spirits who yet prey upon their souls.

He said he had seen many others who had been lain to rest many seasons ago, and they were seen both sitting and lying inside shelters painted with scenes of those lands they had come.

As I listened to my father's words, and as I closed my eyes to feel of the great chiefs spirits, I could see and feel both through my father's words visions of those great chiefs who sit and look out from their shelters to the scenes their people have painted of the lands the Shamans had so loved to have once journeyed.

My father told me the Hyas Eagles who scream above us spell warning to those that are not welcomed into the wards of this island. Only the great Shamons of our people are permitted to gather here, to make offering before those spirits who look over their people's souls, and to those that keep our fathers safe and readied to one day join the fires of our Hyas Tyee's village far above in heaven.

I am thankful I do not have to take my father in mourning to where his spirit would too wait to join with that of the Great Creator.

I am thankful he has been chosen to look over our people from the peak of Wy-East, and to one day journey to where he will await me in the Great Creator's village.

I know his spirit has been always with those of our fathers. I know his soul has not yet passed into where his spirit lies within him, for Sun and Moon have not set upon the lands and brought darkness to settle for long days upon us.

I believe my father's spirit is strong and he has now been rewarded the greatest honor beyond those that rest upon the big island.

This journey, my father and I joined together, he guided me along the shore of En che Wauna where we sat at the side of the Big River and looked out into her waters.

From beneath the waves cast out from the course of Big River, it was like rain and sun met in the heaven as En che Wauna became swollen with color.

Pish came from deep below the waves of En che Wauna's waters as they gathered and waited in the slack waters to gain strength for their final push in their long journey home.

Then suddenly, without warning, they each rushed to begin their final run towards the Great Falls where awaited those of our people with net and spear in hand to share of those spirits who choose to feed our peoples.

Calm lay favored upon the lands and to the heavens as Eagles flew above us and swiftly dove into the waters where we watched them rise up with pish of their choosing.

The Eagles too awaited the many pish that rest at the feet of the Great Chute that separates both Wishram and Wyam.

Many more canoes passed where we had chosen to rest, and my father told me it would not be long before we too would go from the river and walk into the village at Wishram.

Into the distance I could see the lands move, as if they were alive and their lungs filling with air to breathe each new breath.

Much effort is spent by those I see running to the high rocks above the Great Chute beside the village to look out across the wave of En che Wauna.

More of our brothers stand to peer out into the river's channel to see if Eagle now screams from above to share in their excitement.

I had heard stories from my grandfather and father of this place where trade is plenty and good in each end of season.

They had told me strong spirits walk upon the lands here as they call out to salmon.

They are seen for many days to come fast as they make journey to many waters across our great nations.

My father told me of his friend Coyote, and it is Coyote's spirit that still hides in the face of rock above the village.

From there, he looks down upon all those with respect that offer honor to the Great Creator as it is he that chooses for pish to come from the Big Waters to feed the many.

Sun had begun to rest low in the heaven as we took from the river, and began to make the long walk to Wishram so we could sit beside those of our brothers at the side of the great fire.

As we made journey to Wishram, along the trail we walked.

We met many people from villages near Che Che Optin who we had for many days made trade and sat at one another's fires.

We walked far along the shore of the river when quickly came a strong brave upon the trail.

My father told he was from the village of Nahpooitle, people of the Lewis River, where the waters of Pahto and Lawala Clough run fast to meet those of En che Wauna near Cathlapotle.

As he passed I saw many deep scars across his shoulders and down his strong back. He had no hair growing upon his head.

There was nothing but old closed wounds from bites that tore much of his scalp.

My father only looked towards him with quick eyes as they nodded to one another in greeting.

There were no words spoken between them.

In silence, we passed.

I asked my father why they did not speak as do others we pass?

Father told me of the story this man was known, and he is now called, Quetille Pish by his people.

My father then began to speak to me; "My son, I ask you to sit here beside me and close your eyes, hear my words, and feel the earth beneath your feet as you too shall go to where Quetille Pish had long ago journeyed.

"It was long ago, when I too began my trial to find my guardian spirit upon the trail of Eagle when Quetille Pish began his

journey into the lands where Ta-wa-L-litch, Cowlitz River, runs deep.

"His father, like my own, your grandfather, sat at the fire of their village and awaited word that his son had come out from the test before the Great Spirits he had chosen to accept.

"Long days passed.

"All but one of the youth of their village returned to their fathers, and there was no word of Quetille Pish's tracks upon the trails the spirits had first led.

"Each day passed in mourning.

Each day brought dark cloud to fall upon Quetille Pish's family.

They could only fear his spirit was bad, and his soul had been taken by the bad spirit to join ranks with his army.

"Many braves of their village journeyed along the course of the Ta-wa-L-Litch to search for his body, but they returned many times without word of their search.

"Quetille Pish's mother grieved heavily as she cried out to the Great Creator.

She prayed her son would be saved from the torture the bad spirit craves to spend upon those he keeps.

"For many days and nights she sat lonely in the longhouse, and no one of their people could bring her to come out from the shadows where she long time wept.

Those of their village too knew of her loss, as they had for all days found favor in the spirit of Quetille.

189

It was told to me by my father; "Many were heard to say it was not just Quetille Pish's soul taken as his spirit had for all days walked upon the trails the good spirits led.

"There were few that questioned if Quetille Pish's heart was good as they asked; "Why did he go to where he could not be found?"

"But those that questioned where he had gone had too failed the test of finding their guardian spirit upon their vision quest, and they had no voice in the circle of their village's council.

"Son, those that brought question to be heard proved their spirits were bad, though their people could not yet see of the truth hidden deep within their souls.

"One day, when sun fell from the heavens, the Great Creator came to the doors of their shelters and took light from their eyes.

For all days, those that still walked amongst their people now see no more."

As I sat there listening to my father, I turned to look towards where Quetille Pish had walked. He had journeyed as quietly and fast as a cat beyond were I could see of him or of the dust risen behind his tracks.

Quetille was like a shadow when sun was high above the lands.

But I knew he was near.

His spirit was strong.

I felt him look down upon me though there were no hills or mountains.

But I was not afraid.

My father continued; "My son, one day when the moon fell from the heavens and sun rose up to touch the tops of trees, was then again heard the fierce cry of Pishpish along the river of the Lewis People.

"Many braves rose from their mats and ran to where they kept safe the bow and arrow, and others took the long spear to take the bad spirit of the golden cat from within his soul.

"But as they made journey towards the forest they questioned to what stood before them?

"Quetille's body had been torn from the battle he had fought bravely against Itswoot, Black Bear.

"The braves of their village did not know what to do as the cry of Pishpish has always before this day promised she was hunting for meat.

"His brothers first thought Quetille was standing before them as bait offered by Hyas Pishpish.

"They feared Pishpish awaited to trap their souls and drag them to her lair where they would not again be seen by their people.

"Quetille called out in much pain for his brothers to come to him and help carry him back to the village where he could heal from his wounds.

"He told them he had journeyed far, and it had taken many suns and moons to return to the land where his village stood along the river where eulachon, smelt, first come to all their people.

"His brothers stood in fear, unmoving, they saw death had touched Quetille's soul as they peered deep into his eyes.

"They stood questioning of his spirit, as he still stood as the Quetille they knew, as brother of their people, as Indian.

"It was told his eyes had changed to the color of sun's final rays upon the mountaintop, and he could then see into the darkness of night's long shadows like the Golden Cat.

Quetille's guardian spirit is now certainly Pishpish.

"When Quetille saw in their eyes they were afraid, he knew then his spirit was strong.

"Both he and Pishpish had become one spirit through the fierce battle they shared against Itswoot, Black Bear.

"Their spirits were now joined for all days.

"Their souls tied as brothers to the lands of the Earth.

"Together, they would go far.

"Far beyond those lands his people have ever known.

"Quetille was now unafraid for what he had not yet seen.

"Unafraid for what may lie in wait in the long shadows of their lands.

"Pishpish and he were stronger together.

"Stronger than if each were alone upon the trails of the kingdom of the Chinook.

"Quetille is strong like bear, and his heart fierce like Pish Pish.

"My son, Quetille is not just Indian.

"Quetille is not like any man or animal spirit that has walked amongst the peoples of the Chinook before this day.

"Quetille's spirit has now changed.

"Quetille is now for all days, Quetille Pish.

"Quetille Pish is what brings bond between the spirits of man and animal to all our kingdoms."

My father and I stayed for many days to fish at Wishram.

I heard my father speak of those many Suyapee who trade with our peoples, and how more come each new moon from the Big Waters.

Much talk came from around the village's fire. All those that sat at the side of the great fire then knew that change was soon to be placed upon all our tables, but in their question, was not heard answer.

It was asked by many of those we sat; "What must we do?"

My father and I had made good trade, had many fish, and sharp points.

As we sat before the fire our final night beside those that came from villages beyond the mountains we could see, my father told me he was to take me to where the Shamans to the villages of the Chinook and Yakama are only permitted entry.

I could not sleep that night as I lay beneath the stars and dreamt where he had told me spirits dance on rock under clear skies as Sun's warmth spreads pleasingly upon those that come.

My father and I had walked far along the Big River from the village at Wishram.

We passed before many rocks where were painted the visions by the hand of many the Great Chiefs of our villages of those spirits who today walk amongst us.

My father told me he had come to this place many days to sit and wail before the Hyas Tumtum for direction and strength so his spirit would stay strong before the spirits that come to disrupt all that is good upon the lives of our people.

We walked along the trail into a long meadow where a large rock rose up into the heaven.

As we stood before it, my father told me this is where rock was first chosen to share many stories of both, the days before our peoples first came to these lands, and of all the days after we came down from Walahoof from the nest of Naha.

My father shared the stories of Hyas Coyote and to many of his tricks he had played upon those that once lived in these lands.

My father told me Hyas Coyote walked in all our lands, and he did not care to whom he would deceive.

My father told me Coyote's soul was both good and bad, as are the souls of our peoples.

But it was Coyote's spirit that stood powerfully over all those of our people that now journey across the lands as she had lived long before our peoples first came.

My father told me once Coyote looked deep into your eyes when you did not see him, and he saw good in your heart, then his tricks would offer you safe passage upon all the trails in your life.

You would walk amongst others who would only offer you respect as they listen to the words the *Hyas Tahmahnawis* had chosen for you to speak.

All the beginnings of your journeys in life will only end with proof of their importance arising before the hearts of those that are called to stand before you and who listen to your message.

But my father too said; "If Coyote looked deep into your eyes and saw bad, then Coyote would bring great storms to fall deep within your soul and offer nothing but the darkest of troubles to enter your soul, and then nhe would take what is left of good from your spirit.

"Not even your brothers or sisters could then ask the Great Creator to save you.

"They would not again hear your name spoken, or your voice cast out upon Wind's favor pleading for your return to those of your village whom have proven they are of good moral, and who bring honor to their peoples.

"The memory of your being shall be forgotten for all days.

"Your soul shall be forever lost upon the Winds of storms where they alone one day choose to fall within the deep waters of the Great Sea.

"Though your beginnings may have been good, your heart and soul were not each joined to keep your spirit strong.

"In the end of times, your memory will end where darkness' shadow looms heavy above you for all days and all nights.

"Cloud will settle upon the sea where your spirit has fallen deep into the depths of the bad spirit's wave. There, you will suffer much beyond what we know today."

As I sat at the side of my father and had begun to understand the meaning of his message, it was then he first chose to share the story of Tsagiglala and how she commanded over the lands they passed from where she had one day watched.

My father told she was the Great Spirit formed from the spirits of both Chinook and Shahaptin peoples.

My father told she has watched over all the spirits that dwelled upon these lands before our people came to share in each of its many bounties.

The time when only spirits chose to journey through the breaths of Wind.

It was one day, when we came from the nest of Naha in the beginning, we too became like her children as many lived in villages below the high cliff where she had long ago built shelter.

Many suns had passed before Coyote approached who is now named, "She Who Watches."

"It was there Coyote asked; "When you are faced with change, how will you fend for your people?"

Coyote told her change was coming soon to the lands.

Tsagiglala did not answer for she did not know of change.

She did not know how she would keep safe her people.

Life as she had known it for all days was the same for all seasons that had passed in the long ago.

Coyote stood before her, looking deep into her eyes, questioning of her soul.

Tsagiglala stood before Coyote and did not know if he would play tricks against her, and with wide eyes, she did not know if to speak.

Coyote became upset at her silence, and he thought she mocked of his question, so when Sun hid behind cloud to speak to Moon, Coyote took her into the desert where he chose to turn her into stone where she would for all days look upon the lands and down upon her peoples through all that will change.

Through all that was good, and through all that was bad.

Hidden safely amongst large rocks whose shoulders guarded tightly Tsagiglala, those rocks whose birth was even before her own in the beginning in the seasons we do not know, she would for all days sit silent and be named, "She Who Watches."

She would for all days look upon those that come to our lands with much question, and in her eyes, she would see she could no longer care for her children.

Tsagiglala would then know of Coyote's question.

She would see Suyapee's hearts blackened by greed, and their spirits weakened by their own fears.

Coyote knew Suyapee would not first care to know or to understand the worth of our character to these lands we have been honored.

Suyapee would not know of Tsagiglala difference.

To them, she would be like the elk and pish, the sheep and goat, the snake and lizard whom each are painted upon the face of rock that tells of story to these lands and of our people's long journey.

Coyote chose for her spirit to be placed upon rock where she would look out over her peoples for all days.

Coyote told her she would always rest here, where no one would come to disturb her thoughts so she may one day offer answer to his question to what she did not that day know.

In silence, with breath drawn far from her soul, Coyote told Tsagiglala, she would from this day wish to return to the memories of her people.

Her name would be known by all the spirits whyo had one day journeyed across the lands beneath her.

To those new people who had not heard of her name, would now know of her as "She Who Watches."

She could not from that day call out to her people, our people, my people, to warn us of that change only Coyote knew then would come.

Even as change may not be good, and those of which we have been warned would soon march into our villages, she would now be forced to look over the people with grieving eyes and with broken heart as they would sit at the foot of our fires and smoke from the long pipe knowing our hearts were good.

We would not first see their hearts were troubled through their own misconceptions of our beliefs, and of all those unheard questions answered through the convictions of their dark hearts.

I knew one day I might sense the fear she now holds in her heart.

My father told me she would watch from across the waters of En che Wauna where Suyapee will come many.

It will be from there she would see many battles loom heavy upon the horizons of her people.

Suyapee would many days pass before her and look deep into her eyes though they could not see her.

One day, when the earth cries out with much pain, and great plumes rise from the peak of Lawala Clough and Pahto she would quickly withdraw into her soul where she would sit with saddened eyes as her peoples walk far from these lands.

She Who Watches would from that day stand submissive to the needs of her people though her voice shall be silenced, and her spirit broken...

The lands Tsagiglala once knew would then too be no more...

Father said Tsagiglala lived before Indian first came down from the nest of Naha.

This was the time when the earth became strong as great mountains reached out to thank the heavens, and the waters of En che Wauna first formed from the tears of the Hyas Tahmahnawis as Hyas Coyote led pish from the big waters of the sea to all the streams and rivers across our nations.

Coyote too led all the animals into the valleys and upon the mountains where they are today still seen, each living in the way of the High Spirit's choice.

Each knowing one day they may be chosen to lie down before another of earth's spirits and offer life through the gift the Great Spirit had chosen for them to themselves give.

Through all the gifts the Earth Mother has offered, the Great Creator has spoken that we, Indian, shall survive each storm that comes hard against us.

Earth Mother offers the tree to make shelter, the plant to heal our wounds, and pish and animals to eat to keep our many people's strong.

We must walk with and first listen to all the animals before we speak so they too know we are each significant to one another.

We too must listen to the voices of trees as they sway to the gentle breaths of wind. In their song we will know of what is soon to settle upon our lands.

Be it to storm of winter as it quickly falls heavy upon our peoples, coming fast from the lands where the buffalo run free across the flat plains of golden grass, or, when it shares of the new season as Wind changes and breathes new life into all the trees and plants that rise up and offer new leaf beside the rivers of our nations.

Through the voice of Wind, we will know of each.

Wind speaks of all that has passed and to all that has been promised to come.

I sit saddened here at the side of Tsagiglala as I know she mourns for her people.

The memory of my father is strong, and I sense his spirit is just there above me in the sky of our heaven.

I wish he were here again, sharing the stories of our people. But today, it is I that tells of the old ways and to the new ways of our peoples to my son.

He and I will soon go again to trade at Wishram as my father and I had many days long ago gone.

Those changes we have heard from Coyote that would begin to tear our peoples and our lands apart from one nation, has with great sadness, begun.

With sad eyes, as I sit here at the foot of Tsagiglala, and as we each peer across the big water of En che Wauna, rises the storm of dust.

It is new these wagons that come from the tall hill as they follow the trails our peoples had first forged upon them many seasons ago.

As I look towards She Who Watches not believing what I have seen, from her eyes, begin tears to fall as winter rains once cast out upon our peoples from storms that bring ruin to the lands.

Wind drops heavy upon the land and begins to cry out in great suffering as tree and bush sway to each corner of their birth.

Many of our father's voices fall from the heaven and attach themselves upon the trails of Wind as they announce to all the villages along the waters of En che Wauna of the new peoples that today come to begin the change we fear and do not yet understand.

Now has come time to sit and speak in the secrecy of our lodge. To make ready our hearts for what is soon to bring change before the entrance of our village's opened and welcoming doors.

I have been taught to listen to the lessons Wind brings, and today, it is not good as our peoples from this day shall not be the same.

We will be forced as it has been told in the past through the dreams of our fathers to walk far from the big river that gives us those tomorrows to which we have promised to offer honor.

Many of these people who have placed lodge upon these lands live far from the shore of the Big Waters.

They have not seen the Suyapee who now build villages near the big waters of the sea that are not welcome to the many of our people.

Our brothers do not know of the bad medicine Suyapee bring hidden deep in their purse.

They have not seen our brothers and sisters, or their children's spirits who have been sacrificed and lie unmoving beside the diseased waters of our kingdoms.

Our brothers know of trade. That is all they care to know as it is in that trade they too survive.

They have heard of the bad spirit coming upon our lands.

"It is not our worry," I hear them speak when they listen to those they do not know of the Chinook.

But I ask; "Are we not brothers to the Earth?

"Do we not all walk the same trails and catch the same pish?

"Do we not come to sit at one another's fires to smoke and make trade?

"Why do you not care to what comes in all our tomorrows?"

I, today, have learned to fear much...

Though I have gone to the Big Waters and have seen the villages of Suyapee, and as I have gone to the village near Wapato where Suyapee builds mills to cut wood. To where he cuts the heart of our mother from the soils of the earth to grow food for their people, I now fear deeply for what I have seen...

When night comes to the village, I will sit and smoke with my brothers in the longhouse. I will ask if they too know of these many Suyapee who come more and more to these lands each day as Sun falls heavy from the trails of the heaven?

I listen to my brothers tell what they have seen, to what they have heard of those Suyapee who have come and gone from our lands.

It is said, Suyapee do not go from the Great Falls to the lands of the long prairie, but go to the villages of the Nez Perce and trap the skins of Eena that swim in the waters of their large meadows, and take shiny metal from the waters of many creeks.

Those brothers of the Sioux that hunt the great buffalo tell they have seen many more Suyapee following trails that lead to the great peaks where winter's snow shall soon lie deep.

It is in that place we have heard the Shoshone tell they do not go when winter's storms scream out with pity for those that still yearn to come.

I fear when Suyapee's brothers listen to Wind they will hear of the generous spirit of Hyas Tumtum, and they will not stop from taking from us the lands and the spirits that walk beside us each day.

Suyapee will hear of the pish that come many from the sea.

They too will know of the deer and elk that lay many in the green meadows.

They will know of the fox, and they will soon know of the sheep and bear, and to the fierceness of the cougar and bear, and of the warmth held of their furs.

What I, today fear most, Suyapee will not understand the Spirit of Coyote, or to what brings strength to the spirit of our people.

It has been the call of Coyote that was first heard in the beginning as she journeyed through the long night. Across all the lands of our kingdoms to announce she was the Spirit to whom all shall first answer.

Just as Coyote has called out each night, we have been permitted to live and prosper upon these lands as she has looked over all our peoples.

We took journey in our beginnings from the nest of Naha upon Wallahoof, and as we followed her call to the lands we live, her spirit has become strong in the villages of our people.

Coyote brings good to the spirits of those that want to understand and listen to the stories she too has drawn before the fires of our villages.

Coyote is both smart and cunning.

If you do not listen into the darkness and hear her call, then, as you sleep your spirit will become lost to your soul and you will wander through the trails of Wind without her guide, through all difficulties that promise to take your soul far from your spirit.

Those whom we see today come upon the trails into the lands of Wah and do not know of the eyes that watch over them far above upon the cliffs of En che Wauna.

Owl and lizard, deer and elk, the great sheep, and the sly pishpish all look down upon them with much question.

It is the same as She Who Watches and I today look upon them from across the Big River.

Sun crosses slowly upon the trails of heaven, Suyapee still march to the river from high above beyond the hills we now cannot see.

Their voices call out loudly to one another as they struggle to keep the wagons straight upon the rocky trail.

I hear rock fall from above as they run fast from the crush of Suyapee's wagons.

More and more Suyapee can be heard riding from the high hill upon the spotted horse it has been told they have made trade with brothers of the Shoshone and with the Nez Perce.

They come fast to the kingdom of Wah so they may journey to the lands they were told they were first promised.

I wish to ask why they come to our kingdoms and not live where their peoples today await their return?

I ask if their lands are like ours and consumed by their disease?

There are not furs for these peoples to take from the animals who live freely amongst our peoples.

I cry out in the greatest of fear; "Why do they come?"

In this, I too fear greatly Hyas Tahmahnawis' answer!

From the heaven falls cloud that takes Sun from shining upon the soils of our lands.

Red Cloud, rising quickly from the dust of their wagons brings my fears to bare before me as they climb hurriedly into the heaven to reach out to our fathers.

In this, I too fear, as the visions of our fathers they had once before shared to the story our peoples will one day suffer came first from behind Red Cloud when Suyapee emerged onto our lands many seasons ago.

I ask; "Has the end of our people now begun as it has been seen through the looking glass of our father's long ago dreams?"

I listen for the voices and chants of our brothers and of our fathers from above in the heaven where they today sit and look down upon our people, their peoples.

From the heavens is heard the murmurs of our fathers to the visions they have seen proving of the wanting defeat of our peoples through the greed and selfishness of Suyapee's heart.

By the hands of those who have heard message of the lands wealth, and by those whose hearts and souls are bound by greed, we shall soon be seen no more.

The wind is stilled from the heaven above. Our father's voices are now too hushed upon the trails of Wind as their thoughts lost within the trails of their own grief.

I ask; "What must our fathers think?"

The questions must too linger upon the edges of our father's lips though they fall silent before the ears of those others they sit.

Their fears now certainly bound within the darkened trails that lead blindly from their souls.

They must know as I, as does Tsagagalalal, dark cloud has returned to take life from the lands and leave only the question of what will be soon of all our tomorrows.

We can no longer see through the darkness where light had once lain the blessing of faith and hope to dwell deeply into our lives.

Change is upon us and to our lands, and as we must now question all that has come, we do not find comfort in those same answers we question.

This day, I know why Coyote took Tsagagalalal from atop the high hill, for she too does not understand or know of how to save her peoples from the attack of these new changes that have now come suddenly upon us.

From the corner of my eyes I too share the tears of unknowing beside She Who Watches.

We each together sit here in great sadness.

As cloud passes before the face of Sun, cold falls upon the lands as we sit watching to those that journey beside the shore of En che Wauna.

With great sadness, She Who Watches now is witness to why she has been turned to stone. She is only now afforded to feel from the hardness of her heart by the changes that now swarm upon her lands and cast worry into the hearts of her peoples.

From the hardness of stone where her heart cannot be felt, now falls great tears, today swollen behind her glowering eyes.

The ground beneath where She Who Watches has been promised to stay for all days now rises as if by the rains of winter's raging storm.

I ask; "Father, if I were to see each of those changes that have been told for many seasons to come and challenge what we believe honorable within our lives, if you were to allow me to speak to all the villages of our nation, what would you say so that I too can share those words and bring hope to our peoples before the darkness of battle separates each of our peoples?

"Father, we must not welcome ourselves to walk in the steps of the mesachie tahmahnawis as he may wish.

"For all days and all nights we may find ourselves to follow him will take our peoples further from the promise you and your fathers have sworn before us that will take us into the promised lands in the Great Spirit's village."

As I listen for the words of my father, I hear the cry of my friend Coyote with whom my soul has been tied for many seasons since she was just a young pup.

I turn to look to where I hear her call.

From saddened eyes and bowed head, she peers sorrowfully towards me, and I too, towards her, as I feel the pain rising from within her soul.

"My friend, Coyote, why do you question what comes to your lands? Change is why you remain stronger and wiser above all those that have lived and of those that today live and find promise upon the Great Spirit's lands.

"Your heart is driven by those changes that happen in your life each day, and as change comes before you, your soul remains

unmuddled by what walks in darkness' question upon the trails you follow.

"The Hyas Tahmahnawis has given you great powers!

"It has been told you have been seen many times to come from behind where there is nothing to hide.

"I too have seen you come from the heart of tree to walk amongst our people as we sat before the fire in counsel.

"It was then you brought judgment of those of our people that would journey in life through the beliefs of the bad spirit, and of those that will stand proudly upon the Walls of Wahclella."

"Coyote, I know you will walk amongst those that now come to our lands and they will not see you.

"They will be told of your powers, and they still will not believe what is spoken of your affect to these lands.

"It will be through your strengths our people will follow. We, like you, will survive to see all the suns to those promised of our tomorrows!"

"Suyapee's eyes will see darkness even as sun shines bright in the heaven.

"You will enter into the closed doors of Suyapee's village, and you will bring much question to rest uneasily upon their thoughts to what they cannot understand."

"Our people will walk where you walk.

"Our people will lie silent and unseen where you choose for your hides.

"Suyapee will hear you call out into the darkness of night as you near their villages, but yet, they will not know when you come.

"It is in your powers we will know you as Trickster. You, Coyote, the one that commands others to think what is, is not!"

"Coyote, you will be our guide through all that brings question to our lives, and you will bring promise to our peoples so we may walk free beneath the light of heaven.

"We will listen each night for your call, and through the stillness of night's most lingering breaths, you will know of our people's answer that we believe in all you offer to our being!

"Coyote, we have been friends for many seasons.

Through the long winters and cruel summers we have endured together, we are still today as we were in all those first yesterdays above Wyam.

"Through the sign of Moon and Sun you first drew before my feet, our bond has become inseparable.

We are each a brother and sister to this earth, and our spirits shall forever be joined to one another as we tend to the ways of these lands.

"I only fear our peoples will believe we have brought shame upon us as we choose not to fight those that come and demand we accept what they have been promised to follow by the lessons of their own spirit.

"We must not change how we walk with our Hyas Tumtum, as it is He that offers our peoples the gift of life as we journey amongst all that breathes upon the lands of his kingdom."

As I look with much sorrow towards Coyote for what she must feel, I see scribed by an old Shamon in the stone at the side of where Coyote sits, the star that never changes and never dims in the heavens of our sky.

This, I say to myself, certainly must prove of our promise that life will not end for our people.

Life will survive through each of our kingdom's many storms, be it by weather or by the hands of men who wish to take us far from our lands and force change upon each of our kingdoms.

Only those strong of will and mind will see of all those tomorrows we have been told through visions of our fathers.

I ask in silenced voice before those that sit in the heaven above if this star that shines bright each night will now, each day, each season, bring honor to our peoples even through all the adversity we have heard to become certainly challenged?

This day is bright without cloud, but it is written in stone as the light of day dims, it too tells this change we are to witness is not good.

This change is the promise of warning that our days are soon to be no more spread with the certainty of promise unless we give our souls to the wisdom of the Hyas Tahmahnawis.

The days that are to rise up before our peoples will now become challenged in not following the trails enveloped within the darkness of mesachie tahmahnawis' cave.

It is there, in the absence of good fortune I must share before our peoples.

Lonely and barren lie the minds of those who do not prove of their promise to the Great Spirit to uphold peace between all that lives and breathes upon all our lands.

I shall ask my people to make journey beside me to the peak of Larch, and as they look deep into the darkness of its untended soul, they then will be assured to know where only those that have given their lives in accepting the bad spirit's pleasures shall soon come to crave and take us from our own.

As I sat in deep thought, I turn to face those Suyapee that now have come to the lands of our fathers from the lands of their fathers.

They come, more, and more from where I cannot see.

Great clouds of dust rise up from the soils of the land.

Suyapee's call to their brothers' fill the trails of Wind, each bringing before our thoughts the gravest of concerns.

I turn from where my gaze has become saddened.

My heart lies emptied of hope.

My soul lies unmoving and challenged to again feel the faith of our promise towards Sun's welcoming rise in our tomorrows.

As I reach out to stroke the soft fur of Coyote, her soul is not now here beside me to touch.

I turn to look back towards where Coyote had last stood.

Again, her trickery subjects me in knowing of her powers.

Coyote has now chosen to be bound to rock beside star that never moves in night which has all days proven to shine bright with hope.

Here, across En che Wauna's waters where Suyapee now have come to pass, she will sit always beside She Who Watches.

They shall both now forever watch over her people together and they will mourn in silenced breaths forever.

Coyote's spirit is shared by all those of his brothers and sisters that journey across the lands of our kingdoms.

Coyote are connected to the soils of the Earth as many have returned from the dead to live as guardians to the peoples and as protectors of the lands they have each known to respect.

Coyote is smart.

Coyote can live amongst the many and they will never be seen or heard as they lie down beside those mats where man sleeps at night.

Coyote has been seen emerging from the souls in trees.

Coyote has risen from beneath deep waters to lead Pish to the river in the days of the beginning.

Coyote announced across all the lands to the beginning of our peoples as we emerged from the nest of Naha and came down into the lands where we today sit before the fires of our villages.

Coyote's friend Raven is too always near as they have journeyed as one Spirit together across the lands of our kingdoms.

But this day, I am alarmed.

Raven's cry falls silent from above in the heaven.

I ask; "Father, where has Raven journeyed to not cry out with warning for what has today come to the shores of the Big River?"

Swiftly, as the antelope runs across the grasslands and upon our deserts, from above in the heaven, I hear my father answer as he directs me to look towards the rock where Coyote has chosen her final hide.

There, nestled above the shoulder of Coyote, drawn upon the face of the high cliff, now marks the closed and bound wings of Raven.

Coyote and Raven have journeyed together from the beginnings of these lands births as they too had first come from the waters of the Great Sea.

Today, their friendship is written for all days in stone and shall last beyond the Sun's final path through the trails of the heaven.

Life's very own defeat may be awaiting its challenge in its own final battle as quickly as Sun again rises and offers nothing to be seen but disease and death to lie strewn across the lands.

Without my friends, I too am driven to believe I must rest beside them for all days until our peoples return safely upon the nest of Naha.

I go to where both Coyote and Raven rest, and it is there, at the base of the rock their spirits have joined, my wanting to be bound tightly beside them has become great.

My knees have become weakened through the anguish of my loss.

214

I, without thinking, fall to the ground of our nation, that today, begin the sharing of those dreams we have been told others have heard us cry out in the darkest of nights.

Our spirits had at that moment encountered the greatest of our pain.

It is unjust for the earth's brothers or sisters to collide with the dreams cast disheartingly from the soul of the bad spirits whom stray upon us without reason.

It is unjust for the bad spirit to prey wantingly for the innocence of our souls as we sleep.

Arms opened to the heavens, my pleas are heard spread through the travels of Wind as they course along the channels of En che Wauna.

Our ancestors who sit watching over our lands from the island of Memaloose, who wait for their chosen star to appear so they may ride safely across the heavens, too know now the visions of their dreams have with great sadness, become drawn into our people's lives as the darkest of all truths.

We must follow in the footsteps of our Great Spirit as he has led us safely all days through the journeys of our lives.

Here, beside those I have always known as friends, Coyote and Raven, who have kept me safe upon each of the trails across our land, I will wait each day, each night, through both, sun and storm.

I will wait for Coyote's and Raven's spirits to rise up once again from where they now rest and settle beside me so our spirits will one day again be touched by one another's souls as we look into one another's hearts.

I shall wait for the sun's rise from where the moon's journey had last taken my dreams to soar only in my thoughts distant memories.

I shall wait for that day when I will be chosen once more to the right of entering into the opened doors of Coyote's and Raven's souls so we may each again look into one another's eyes and know our spirits are upon that day as we have been for all days before...

Chapter 8

Hyas Tumtum Calls Out
To All Our People

Far away, in the kingdom of Pahto, where only the great Spirits of our peoples have been honored to have first lived, once stood a village built on the long prairie of sweet grasses and beneath the strongest of trees. We have named this Siwash Saghalie Tyee, Indian Heaven.

These lands were chosen from the beginning to be the village where the most powerful of spirits were born to these lands and then were willed to walk into all our kingdoms.

Their strengths were bound taut through their bond between them and of the Hyas Tumtum's soul as their hearts journeyed each day beside him, and they were one day chosen to look over our peoples, the Hyas Tumtum's children for all days.

Each day for many seasons, as Otelagh and Moon spoke to them from the heaven as they passed, these spirits grew strong in their understanding to the needs of the people and of the lands they today live.

One day, when Sun and Moon witnessed their growth in the ways of the Great Ones that had first stood upon the lands before Indian came from the nest of Naha, they too knew these new spirits would not follow the trails led by the yearning of their quarreling spirit.

Calling to those who lived throughout all the kingdoms, Suns and Moon's voices were heard spread across the lands as they made offer to all those of their kingdoms to oversee the wealth of their gifts.

Through the visions the Hyas Spirits had witnessed, we too would know all that would come to the lands before us and how we must change with those differences we would be challenged.

We would, through many seasons, then learn how to survive upon these lands that were first formed from fire, as they were thrown above upon the land from the deep chasms within their souls.

We learned to look beyond what stands before our eyes.

We understood we must too change, as does Hyas Coyote each day so she may live to witness Sun's rise in each of her own tomorrows.

As Otelagh began to climb into the heaven one morning, a loud voice called out across the waters of En che Wauna and was heard throughout the valleys and mountains of the Three Spirit's kingdoms.

From the heaven far above where we could not see, Hyas Tumtum pleaded for the Shamans of all his people to walk along the White Salmon and into the valley where they would first look up and see the white capped brow of Great Pahto.

They were told, as they walk into the kingdom of Pahto, it is asked of them each to listen to the rhythm of wind's breaths. They were told through Wind's song they would know where to join the Great Creator's messenger within the great meadow.

The Great Drums of all the villages that lie along the shores of En che Wauna began to announce they had too heard the summons to go into the lands by Hyas Saghalie Tyee.

It has been many seasons beyond those I know when it was told the Great Spirit has called upon his people to come to the Kingdom distant from where Pahto rests.

Not even my father, Raven or his father, Twokst Tahmahnawis, spoke of hearing their calling by the Saghalie Tyee to sit with him and speak of their tomorrows.

A great privilege has been placed upon me this day, I must begin to prepare myself so my people of Wahclella will be looked upon with clear eyes, and the Great Tyee will feel the spirit held powerfully within our souls.

Our people's promise before the Great Creator in our acceptance in honoring all that lives and breaths upon his lands shall bring hope our peoples will prosper today, and in all of the tomorrows the Great Creator has before spoken.

Message has been sent to all the villages it was near the Walla Walla's villages that rise up from below the Blue Mountains, where those Suyapee that lived in their village gave our brothers bad medicine and had taken spirit from many Cayuse souls.

It has been told, today, they are no more to fear.

Many of Suyapee's people have died, many more have fled to the big village along En che Wauna where the village called Vancouver called out to those that still breathed protection.

Time is near when Suyapee's soldiers will come to take those that killed the whites from their villages.

I question; "May this be the purpose we have been called to join the Hyas Saghalie Tyee where his village is hid from the eyes of Suyapee deep within the forests of Pahto's kingdom?"

From far away I hear first the drums of the Yakima and the Klickitat, and then message cast by the Walla Walla, and soon the Umatilla's message follows.

They too will be drawn to the lands of Pahto to sit with the Hyas Creator's messenger and hear him speak.

It will not be long I am sure before message will come from the high peaks beside the wawas of the Wahpoos, Snake.

Through the cadence of the Nez Perce drums, their message will be heard by the many.

Their answer will journey far upon wind from the waters promised of Salmon's long ending journey.

Those of the Cayuse and Paiute will be heard to call out as they will follow the trails where we are each to greet one another and again join together as brothers, and not those who have depended upon war between them to settle our difference.

All the peoples that have come for many seasons to Wishram and Wyam to net pish will soon meet again.

It is good our peoples will soon sit and smoke beside the fire of the Great Creator.

We will sit with our Hyas Father, and we will smoke from the pipe and talk of the ways of our people.

From the heaven our Saghalie Tyee shall tell us all what trails to follow in our journeys as he too has witnessed of the change that today approach our lands with threat to our people.

I know, as many Indian have stepped from the trail we were first told to follow, today, now, there is much trouble wanting entrance into the doorways of our villages.

We must all be ready for what will come to our lands and to our people before darkness delves into the corners of our eyes and takes light from the heavens from our lives.

The smell of fear has absorbed itself into the journeys of Wind across our lands as we hear our brothers crying to Great Spirit.

We hear argument cast out by many villages as Suyapee has begun to walk into many of the sacred lands of our people without understanding, without knowing of how, or why they are not welcome to walk across their boundaries.

Even we do not trespass into these sacred lands except the day when Hyas Tumtum calls for those of our fathers to rest.

War is not good!

But I fear in the end of times our people will have no answer that will offer Suyapee understanding to the ways of our people.

Then, brothers of many villages will again join one another and go to the villages of Suyapee with arrow and spear.

War has proven to bring only defeat to our souls.

In that defeat, our spirits are too taken from within us as our brothers and fathers will soon walk with the bad spirit beneath the soils of our lands.

Sadly, it will be there our brothers will fall upon the fields where Naha's hair once blew free across the wide meadows and across the long prairies.

Behind each tree and beneath each bush, from atop the highest rock, and from deep within the waters where pish first come, their spirits will await the call of battle by the order of the bad spirit where within the catacombs await his armies.

Those of his braves who hide beneath the feet of others cannot wait to rise up upon them and strike them with the curse of a slow death.

In our sorrow, we will walk upon emptied trails where light is not cast before our feet.

Our spirits shall become lost from within us, our souls emptied of hope to see those tomorrows we have been promised always to share.

These trails have been spoken to be the trails that have only bad beginnings, and are cherished by the bad spirit, as they have no better endings.

Dark cloud shall settle across all our lands and our people will walk alone into the unknowingness of our tomorrows.

The lone sound cast out towards where they stand scattered amidst the darkness shall be the lonely cry of Coyote.

She too will become sorrowful by our mistake, and will lie lost upon the lands of her kingdoms without her people.

War shall not bring good to the lands or between our people.

I today fear there will be many to join in battle against those Suyapee that do not understand or want to know of our ways and why we had been chosen first to settle peacefully within Wah's mighty kingdom.

"Hear me My Father, hear me plead that our people of Wahclella will not walk where others choose, and that we will journey far from where the call of war is cast out by those that do not heed the words of their fathers.

"May those brothers too hear my plead so their spirits will walk free from the calling for their souls.

"Father, I ask that you take us all upon the journey you had shared where the Dream Spirits Speak, and may all those wishing to do battle with Suyapee know of where their souls shall lie, and where their Spirits will join those other's names that will never be heard spoken again."

Many Shamans have begun to gather with their warriors who protect them with wide eyes.

Great warriors who enable all the people to witness of their return before them as it is they that choose to stand before the head of the snake where evil has been known to hide in the darkness of night.

Canoes from many villages come hard against the fast waters of En che Wauna.

Many of our brothers whose villages do not stand near our own have come to rest upon the big meadow of our village before we begin our march into the kingdom of Pahto.

We sit at the fire of our village at Wahclella in the big meadow beneath the shadow of Woot-Lat.

Many of these chiefs I have not seen.

We have not smoked from the pipe or spoken of our peoples before this day, and it is good…

Though I knew the chief of the Clatsop would not join the chiefs of the Tillamook at the circle of our fires, the Tillamook tell me he has chosen to stay near the fort called Astoria at the shores of the Big Waters.

It is told he does not understand now why our people turn from the needs of Suyapee.

Suyapee march into our lands and take all the animals, cut the souls from the mightiest trees from the soils of our mother, and now, they wish to take all the lands from beneath our feet where we have lived for many seasons.

I am confused why the Great Creator has called out to plead we walk from our peoples and from our lands to unite far from where we can protect those left of our villages?

From where I sit, I am ashamed to know of the Clatsops chief as even I have seen Suyapee come before our people and demand to know where the lands of our spirits are strong so they may take all Naha has honored our peoples for all days through her generous gifts.

From afar, I can hear the chief call out in much question as he has been blinded by greed and through his lust as he and his people have become what Suyapee has brought before their fires.

I hear the chief of the Clatsop speak from far away as Wind brings warning of his spirit.

He speaks question to all the people of the Chinook; "Do we not understand why trade is good, and why we must believe in the beliefs of Suyapee as they offer the long gun and sharp blade to kill?"

In return to his question I scream into Wind.

I pray my message will be heard before his fires as I ask; "Even when Suyapee do not believe in the ways of Indian, do we take from our souls our spirit in all we have learned to believe in those lost within the darkness of their own cave?"

To this I must bow my head in shame to have claimed before others to have once known the heart of the chief of the Clatsop.

His name is no more spoken before the peoples of our village.

His people stand at the right hand of those that come to take even our souls from within our spirits so they may claim these lands as their own.

I fear war will soon come between our peoples.

Through the looking glass this war that rests upon all our horizons has been promised, and it will not bring good to again enter our villages!

As Sun begins to climb into the heavens, those who have come to sit with me must soon make preparation to join the trail that leads to the waters of the White Salmon where we are called to listen to the song of Wind.

Wind will share the message of the Hyas Saghalie Tyee.

To know of this honor allows me to think of how that first Pish, Ykope Pish must have felt as he came from beneath the deep waters of the sea and led the first schools into the entrance of the river White Salmon, to which in his memory is named.

I have closed my eyes many times and envisioned that night as the light of the full moon shone down magnificently upon all the lands that surrounded Tkope Pish as he first led his people to the fast waters.

I dreamt of what each tree, each bush, each animal must have thought that came to witness the beginning of what has come to always be.

I have heard Coyote call out to Raven, to join beside her. They, together will sit at the foot where En che Wauna and White Salmon meet waiting to witness the return of pish to the river.

In our beginnings, we, the Watlalla, were first to have been honored within the Lands of Wah.

As seasons passed, the Hyas Tahmahnawis has spoken to many of our fathers, and through their voice, we, who follow in their footsteps, have either to accept their words or go far from the villages where our people once had faith they would not turn from what is good.

All that we are as a people has been bore into our souls through everything our Hyas Saghalie Tyee has gifted our people.

We did not come as fortunate as we are today. We walked upon trails where light did not first shine, and as we journeyed onto those trails, many did not return before us.

This day is not unlike those that have passed with the rising of moon into the heavens.

We as children, have been told that many of our brothers had witnessed the fierce battles waged between Wy-East and Pahto for the arms of Lawala Clough.

Through those same battles cast out from the bowels of Wy-East and Pahto that had reigned down upon both their kingdoms, brought great fires to burn deep into the soul of Naha's lands.

Many trees and bush were lost to their kingdoms as they fell from where they first stood. Now, they are only as ashes swept distant of our lands through the journeys of Wind.

Forests were quickly buried deep beneath the great fields of rock heated by the breaths of the bad spirits.

Today, they lie strewn and untended, and lonely to the plant and animals upon those same lands that were once promising with flower and fern, and mowitch and moolack.

This alone proves that battle only brings scars to harden within the souls of those that are promised in the battle between what is good and bad within their souls.

Fire's stormy rage upon the earth from the heaven, and dark clouds swollen with rain have each shared in the birth of the lands we today see.

Great floods have reigned across the lands from far away when Hyas Missoula first threw spear into the frozen waters of his lake to drink.

Yet, our peoples still survive to see the light of Sun in our tomorrows.

Our honor lies in those tomorrows!

Our honor must be accredited by our vision to see Sun's rise in all of those tomorrows we will soon stand labored.

Our honor lies in all that we see as we stand upon the Great Larch and look out over all the lands of Wah, and again towards Wy-East, and beyond to those of Pahto, Lawala Clough, and to the lands where the Tkope Lemoto, White Goats, signal to Tahoma that tell life in the forests are good.

As we sit and look out over the waters of En che Wauna and witness to the return of Salmon upon that first day of the new season, we know, deep within our souls what has given us purpose to honor the wishes and teachings of the Hyas Tahmahnawis from upon the Walls of Wahclella.

These are the truths we seek to honor each day.

We must not join those promised in their battle.

It shall be as it has been seen in each of my visions.

Our peoples will not walk again free upon the lands, and Naha, with head bowed, and with tears falling from upon her splintered cheeks, shall forever mourn deeply for we, who were first born to her lands as Indian!

It is today the call of Tkope Moolack I wish to hear most from the tall mountains.

He is wise and has seen all that has come to these lands.

From the high places where his spirit is held safe from those that want, he must know our peoples are now in great danger.

I sense he is near, just behind the tree or rock where we cannot see his shadow.

He must today look upon us with great favaor, and with greater hope.

All that our people have seen and survived have now been brought forth to our memories.

Tomorrow will not be as it is today or in those yesterdays we will soon yearn.

The change Coyote had told Tsagiglala has now touched the hearts of our people.

We have begun to suffer upon the majestic lands of our greatest Spirits that once brought smiles to our faces and opened our souls to those that came to these lands to share in its every bounty.

But today, those that come from the Big Waters and from distant lands we do not know, do not give back to the Hyas Saghalie Tyee so he too can give back to the lands.

To keep fertile all that grows and breathes the pure air cast out from the bush and tree.

It is in that air that promises to offer all life to survive and prosper each day under the rays of Sun, and from those same rays, we discover we too live with the treasures offered to all those knowing of the Hyas Spirit's teachings.

This alone is what has brought suggestion of war between our peoples!

It is not good that my heart lies emptied and in question to what rises upon the lands each day.

I do not wish for battle, yet I do not wish for our people to be taken from the bounty we have known through our labors for many seasons.

I stand both confused and tempted.

Yet I do not know the answers that will bring our peoples together so we may walk again upon the trails of our fathers without fear.

In silenced voice, I cry out to our fathers to lead our peoples from this battle that now grows strong within the hearts of many.

It is not just the brothers and warriors of our villages that have known of the old ways, but now too, the young men not yet fledged by their vision quests before the Hyas Tahmahnawis have voiced their wanting to join arms with their fathers as they dance the songs of war before their village's great fires.

Through the long nights we hear the chants of our young cast out to the heavens so they may gain the strength to march hurriedly without fear before those that want nothing of our people but the lands we live, the animal spirits that feed our peoples and keep us warm during the long winters, and to take Pish from the rivers.

Suyapee is not good for they do not give back to the lands what they take from them, nor do they bring good to the table when we sit beside them as they hide behind their long guns as they speak of trust.

Suyapee do not give back to the soul of Naha for what she has privileged all peoples who know of the honor it is to live and breath beneath the heavens of her nest.

There are many of our people that have now come to walk as one nation to the lands of Pahto.

The look in each of our eyes brings much question toward those who did not hear their names called to journey to the Lands of our Spirits.

Our journey is not far before we reach the entrance of Tkope Pish. But first, we will journey to Waconda Illahee Oee-Hut, The Bridge of the Gods, to bring honor to those that fell beneath the great rush of rock and tree.

Many of our people who now lie entrenched beneath the Table Mountain were judged by the Great Creator as they did not follow in the ways of righteousness, but chose to steal from many villages, as do those of the Snake.

Here at Waconda Illahee Oee-Hut once sat an old woman who cherished her warm fire built upon the bridge that joined the soul of the lands beside those of their peoples.

The flame of the fire she tended did not grow weak and perish, for hers was strong and was cared for with the touch gifted by the hands of Naha.

Many came to take with them burning embers to start their village's fires, and all was pleased that she sat between the shores of the Big River and gave to all the people without complaint.

It has been told one day the Great Spirit, Hyas Tahmahnawis brought his two sons, Pahto and Wy-East to witness this great bridge once fallen from Table Mountain high above that blocked the waters of En che Wauna and offered the Klickitat and Yakima to journey to the Chinook villages within the Valley of the Eagle and into The Lands of Wah to make trade between our nations.

The Great Spirit told each of his sons they would choose to follow one arrow, and where that arrow came to rest would be their lands.

Pahto first chose to follow the arrow to the north, and then Hyas Tahmahnawis turned and pointed his long bow towards the south, and there Wy-East's kingdom was first born.

It is in those mystic kingdoms where today we see their magnificent heads, shone bright, wearing white robes honored of Spirits.

They are now both privileged to look down upon their kingdoms where beautiful valleys and majestic waters of lakes and streams offer life to those that rest beneath their towering shadows.

But it was not always this way...

Once Pahto and Wy-East had settled in their new lands they began to search for a bride, and as Pahto turned to the west, and Wy-East turned to the north, they both saw a beautiful maiden named Lawala Clough who stood proud above the lake where Deer Spirits are known to come quietly in the night.

Both Pahto and Wy-East first journeyed to the Bridge of the Gods, it was there, over the fast waters of En che Wauna Wy-East began to cross, and Pahto, standing before him, chose to stop him from going to where his heart too yearned to lay.

As they each stood upon the bridge they began to glare at one another as they both knew of their brother's intent.

Neither would turn from the other, so neither could offer Lawala Clough their promise to look after her for all days.

Suddenly, and without warning, as many days passed, the brothers returned to their kingdoms, but as they sat angered upon their throne, both chose to battle one another.

Great fires swept far across their lands.

The Great Spirit quickly became angered at his son's choice to make war between themselves.

Much harm befell the lands he had once created.

Many dark days passed in the histories of the lands.

Each brother again chose to journey to the Bridge in hope to go to Lawala Clough and speak of marriage, and each time they were met with the glaring eyes and temper of their brother.

The battles again fell hard within their kingdoms, and great fires again swept clean many more of the forest's mightiest sticks.

Where trees once stood now lay great fields of rock where nothing grows and animals do not wish to enter. There is nothing left standing to keep safe their souls from the Pishpish's craving hunt.

The Great Spirit once again chose to come and stand above Waconda Illahee Oee-Hut, and as his anger rose up to touch the ears of his sons, the flame of the old woman's fire soon dimmed.

Wind blew from the east, and storm came heavy across the waters of En che Wauna.

Then, with strong hands, the mighty Tahmahnawis gave a mighty push to the foundation that held strong the bond between the brother's nations.

Grave warning was then spent heavily before the ears of his sons as great cloud rose up above Waconda Illahee Oee-Hut.

The land thundered beneath the great weight of the Bridge of the Gods as it fell into the waters of En che Wauna.

Great waves swept much from the shores of En che Wauna as it hurried to the Big Waters of the Ekholie.

Quickly, En che Wauna too became enraged, and it is seen today where the Bridge of the Gods once stood, a violent river now churns.

Where no Indian can enter where the rage of the old woman and Hyas Tahmahnawis still churns vigorously in what was lost through the brother's battles upon the lands the Spirits had first bore.

Sadly, many do not believe the Great Spirit offered the old woman chance to escape as his temper was beyond reproach.

But, it has been heard when the Wind blows from the west, when standing along the shores of En che Wauna, one can hear the old woman's calling out to her children from where the nest of our people rests high above all the lands of Wah.

Many days I too have heard her calling, and I have asked if she was not Naha as she had tended to the needs of her children as she has for all days?

There are others that believe she fell beneath into the waters she so loved each day.

It was her fire that brought warmth and hope in the long winters to those that came before her, and this pleased her greatly.

All that is left is the memory of what the old woman had cherished.

She had faith through her offering that to unite all the peoples of these lands, to the peoples of all the nations, by the embers of her heart, would bring peace and harmony to all those journeying into the Kingdom of Wah from lands beyond our own.

As the bridge fell swiftly into the Great River, Pahto and Wy-East were quietly turned to stone by the hands of Hyas Tahmahnawis.

Today the Great Spirit looks down upon both his sons in great mourning.

Though the Great Spirit offered forgiveness to each of his sons, only if they took from their hearts what began the mighty battles between one another.

Both sons would from that day sit upon their chairs where their souls would always rest and remain calm.

As we march quickly past where the Bridge of our Gods once stood promised to our peoples, we see across the Big River coming many Chiefs from villages we had not sat.

They too appear to make ready for the long journey from across the Big River to join us upon the banks of Tkope Pish.

Their journey shall be long as they push hard against wind and waves before they settle upon the lands at Ithlkilak at the foot of White Salmon River.

We will wait until all the chiefs awaken to the rise of Sun from their long journey, and then we will join with one another and begin all our long journeys into those lands since cherished only through the eyes of our Spirits.

Sun is soon to rest upon the waters of the Great Sea, and we shall place our mats below where Hyas Wabish Illahee legs lie spread down from the high peak.

Hyas Wabish Illahee's feet touch the waters of En che Wauna, and he will guard us from what evil may lay in wait for us to sleep.

I look up as Sun rises to the heaven from where I slept, and this day promises to be spent with the treasures of Spirits as ribbons of color are cast brilliantly across the lands as the tears of our Hyas Tyee fall softly upon us.

We eagerly sit to eat before the last leg of our journey, and as we begin, Wind comes against us with great force.

This day will be long before we too touch the soils of the village of Ithlkilak.

There we will make camp and call out to our fathers so our hurried march into those lands will find our peoples safe from the Klale Lolo Itswoot who preys upon the hearts of those he hunts.

Mothers with cubs walk freely amongst the gardens of Pahto. They choose to walk the same trails as we when we go to take the sweet shot olallie, huckleberry, from the bush.

We must be readied to face what our peoples have feared in all the seasons we have lived.

Klale Lolo does not wait to charge and take from us our scalps.

It is wise we call out to one another's names as we walk through these lands of which are spread with food for all those that come.

Our village journeys freom Wahclella each season to where the great meadows flow across all the lands beneath the shadows cast out by Pahto's rise above the great valleys.

There are many lakes created from the deep snows of winter that are good to catch fish.

Our women go to take the berry and collect reeds to make baskets during the cold of winter to trade as we sit and warm ourselves before the fires of our longhouses.

The men sit before the great fire and bring the yew to make bow and take the shiny rock to form points for arrow and spear to trade.

Much talk is shared to the visions our leaders had been led to see, and through those visions, we each knew what tomorrow would bring upon our kingdom's lands.

There are many Indian from villages along the banks of many waters camped along the meadows of Pahto.

Bright flowers covered the land, and the grass of bear grew tall and strong.

In all the meadows were deer with fawns playing in the tall grass, and from the mountaintop stood majestic elk calling out to their herd.

Raven too came to where the smoke of our fires spread scent of pish and meat as it cooked slowly through the long days we waited.

The air was thick with the Raven's cries, and they each, daring in their dive from the tall trees, chose to steal all they could see.

During the night we heard Coyote call out to her mate, and this gave us much happiness.

We knew then the spirits of all our lands had too joined to celebrate in the gifts we were surrounded.

We were honored each day with the beauty cast from the Hyas Spirits hands.

As each sun rose into the heavens and set upon distant lands, our hearts could not speak words that shared to the spirit of these lands treasure we had been chosen.

Sun rose early and it was good to feel the crisp, cold air upon our face.

Each of our villages gathered and began to start their journeys into the lands we each lived to fish and hunt for the strong reed and grass. We would only return to where we were encamped as Sun had crossed the trails in the sky with all we had collected.

It was good to work hard before we walked in from the lands we had been pointed by our fathers.

As meal was complete, and before sun rested, those villages of the Klickitat and Tenino, of the Paiute and Yakima came to the long meadow with many horse.

Here were seen braves assembled together in wait for the High Spirit's calling upon the breaths of Wind to go to race the horse in the long meadow.

Much pleasure was heard cast out across the valley as there were many heard to wager for bows and spears, blankets, and for the best furs from the elk and bear.

Many stories were shared between those that chose to race across the long meadow.

Those with horse insisted they owned the pony with the greatest spirit.

They promised the Hyas Tahmahnawis had chosen them to fly fast as bird across the heaven.

Many came to watch.

This too was good as we each laughed as there were many braves that flew like bird off those same, spirited horse.

But not like bird in heaven, but like rock cast down from the mountaintop as they came hard upon the ground...

Many of those that fell hard sneered at those that smiled as they lay with their spirit wounded upon the hard ground.

It was not long when their own laughter grew louder and louder, and much happiness spread throughout all those that came.

Many of those braves that stood watching became brothers to one another's nations.

It was good to know we each could take from our hearts what had once kept us distant from each of our villages.

Words spoken in haste do not fall upon one another's ears as this land has from the beginning been called the Heaven of Indian.

The time we are joined as one nation is spent in peace without the memory of past judgments thrown in anger towards one another's villages.

I am one of many that now rest at the shore of Tkope Pish as we sit and speak of the day's journey that will begin as Sun again rises.

We sit with silent thoughts to what is to be spoken by the Great Spirit before us.

It is an honor to be called, but we too have worry that the message is not good as he calls upon us to quickly join upon the lands he chooses that only he knows.

My thoughts deliberate to a story my father once shared that his father shared with him as he too was one day called to walk amongst a village that sat at the foot of Pahto.

It was there when their souls were stolen from within them and cast out into the lost trails of Wind's many journeys.

The lands they were led were near those of of the Tkope Lemoto, the great spirits to all the mountains.

Here the Spirits had become quieted after many seasons of battle.

Once, long ago, great fire and smoke rose up from the lands for many seasons between Hyas Tahoma and Pahto.

Life then was not good.

All life, plant and animal that was seen to live upon the lands soon fell silent beneath the great swarms of fires and rocks thrown from each of their throats.

Hyas Tahoma and Hyas Pahto fought long days and long nights for the lands they stood over and ruled.

Meadows were then swollen with rock where once green grass and bush and tree stood proudly.

All the elk and deer, the bear and cougar, all the birds, and all that breathed the air of the heaven fell victim to their battles.

Many fled to lands beyond those they had known.

Many did not know the lands they had entered, and they swiftly perished as they could not find safe haven.

The waters of the streams and rivers became hot with temper, and pish too were placed upon the hot rock and dried under stormy skies.

The land turned dark and cried out for mercy.

But neither Tahoma, or Pahto, chose to surrender their lands.

Their battles continued through many more seasons than our people have lived in these Lands of Wah.

One day there was one Tkope Lemoto that came down from its high place where it had hid from the battles that came to the lands.

He stood upon the shoulder of the high mountain and called out to each, Tahoma and Pahto.

Tkope Lemoto told them he had grown tired of their threat as the land his own Spirit had drawn upon the kingdom was now to be shared as the lands of the people.

Sadly, they both were held hostage through their own senseless dispute.

Tkope Lemoto proved to both brothers there was land for both if they would only look beyond what they could see directly before their eyes.

He told them it was not wise to want more than what they have earned, and they must settle their disputes under the clear sky of heaven.

From that day forward, the skies began to clear from the smoke risen by flame.

The land cooled and rock hardened upon the soils of their kingdoms.

The waters and rivers that came from their high places began to offer food for pish as it reached the grass and bush where the gnat and fly waited.

Then too the animals began to return to their lands as there was food for all.

From the heavens came the bird's soft song as they too were again pleased to be promised to the lands their families had always known.

Many seasons passed peacefully between the brothers.

Life returned greater than it was in the beginning before the long and fiery battles took all that was, and it was good.

Word had spread long ago a great chief left the lands of En che Wauna and journeyed to the peaks where the Tkope Lemoto climb amongst the high rocks.

He had never since been seen, but at night those who listened as Wind fell down from the mountain, could determine it was his cry to the Great Spirit they heard.

Each night his voice resonated across the valleys until his wail to Hyas Tumtum reached the waters of En che Wauna.

When Sun rests, and Wind fails to blow it final breath, he too lays upon his mat to wait the tomorrow he so hopes to share.

Many seasons have passed from when he journeyed last to the lands of Pahto, but as we begin to rise up and gather our packs, from great distance is heard Wind's calling.

It is the voice of the Great Spirit that first called our names to join together and make journey where he awaited our arrival.

His message beckons us to walk to where he now waits.

We each hurry with great pace.

Prancing like deer. Dancing to the rhythm of the earth beneath our feet, we find we are not challenged as we climb higher into the kingdom of Pahto.

We look towards one another with understanding this journey shall be like no other we have taken.

It is like a race upon the track of long ago, and we must hurry to please those of our people that were not called.

The urgency of our journey speaks loudly within our souls.

Our peoples who wait in our villages must know as we are the Hyas Shamans of our peoples, we will not fail them as we kneel before the chair of Hyas Tahmahnawis Tyee.

As if we had wings, and they were spread to the heavens, and Wind carried us above the tops of forests, we climb higher into the lands where awaits the destiny we have yearned for all the seasons of our lives.

We follow White River where it bends and comes from the shadows of the forest. The trail lead us to the banks of the river where the Great White Salmon first led his children to the waters below Pahto's deepened snows.

We chose to rest where the meadow was soft with long grass, and as we peered down to where the waters slowed from their descent towards En che Wauna, there too, rested pish as they peered up towards where we had sat.

Pish suddenly rose up from the depths of the river, and as they leaped into the air of their heaven, their spirits rose up from within them and told they would swim to where the river ends.

It will be there, we shall begin the final days journey as Tkope Moolack awaits us.

Then we would go upon the trail led by Tkope Moolack alone.

It was then known by all, Tkope Moolack would keep our group safe from danger from what may lurk from upon the turns of the many trails we would be led until we touched the soils with our feet where we have been called.

Sun has finally spread warmth upon the lands as his journey in the heaven has risen from the tops of the forest and has shown promise there would be no storm rising from the high peaks.

It was good we would not walk beneath dark cloud and the cold of rain as we begin to journey through long meadows that have begun to offer no cover when the spirits begin to throw spear across the heaven.

The trail is long.

We have walked through many meadows.

Stands of pine are only seen to rise up at the edges of the waters who run fast beside us.

From the distance we hear the chatter of squirrels from the tops of the highest branch as they look down upon us.

Warning others there are new faces walking beneath the trees where their nests hold safe their young.

Still, we do not yet know to where we are to complete our trek into the peaks where wait the Great White Goats.

This is the trail our people shadow when we journey to the Heaven of Indian.

I remember we will soon see standing before us the mighty brow of Pahto as he will climb high above us into the heaven.

When we come to where the forest ends and the land opens to the long meadows, then we will stop and wait for Tkope Moolack to lead us further into the lands we do not know.

Many seasons have passed as I have journeyed here many times during the warmth of summer.

I have seen many lakes with pish leaping high into the heaven, each calling out to our people to rest beside their stilled waters.

From the east where the Yakama and Klickitat come I have journeyed many days across the slopes of Pahto.

It was on the slope of Pahto once long ago I found a small peak, red rock rimmed heavy upon its peak where once spewed fire and smoke to cover the lands.

My eyes yearned to see what lay inside the open vent, and without thought of fear, I climbed the steep slope until I could peer deep into its soul.

What I had seen was not good.

This was the child of Pahto.

Together, they had created the lands below their rise where they had first yearned to touch cloud above the great meadows of bright flowers and lush grass.

Smoke and steam rose up from within its bowels, deep moans rose up to be cast across the heaven.

Strong scent filled the air.

I could not breath.

I am certain it is here, beneath the burning soils of Pahto's lands the bad spirit lives.

To this place I know well, and it is not one I ask to see again. I too have made journey to the Heaven of Indian, and one day to have arrived at the shore of big water as the hyas takh, big meadows, lay waiting for me to rest upon its long grass.

Here too pish jumped to catch fly.

Pahto shone bright with much color, and as his face fell deep into the stilled waters of Takh Lakh lake, it was decided there he would sleep until Sun came again to the lands.

Deer came to graze and drink from the lake.

Elk too came and stood watch over all that moved.

Great Eagles sat in the tall branch of trees, and swiftly took wing and took from the stilled waters pish into their sharp talons.

Life was good for all that have returned to live within the lands of Pahto.

Sun fell quickly from the trails of heaven as darkness covered the lands with its mighty blanket.

I chose to sleep at the shore of lake where I made fire to cook pish that welcomed my hand beneath them as I bent low upon the shore and raised them from within the waters.

These are the lands where the calm waters reach out to touch the feet of Pahto as it offers comfort to his soul.

I too was pleased to rest beneath the bountiful stars who offered my thoughts to dream...

We have come to end of river, and here we will camp for the night and wait for Tkope Moolack to come down to meet us from where he hides safe in the far valley.

We each have settled in our camp as the darkness of night draws near. We look up to where the Stallions run, and we each can be heard to plead to the Great Spirit so he will look over us and bring us safely to the lands he has chosen for all those that come to sit and hear of his lesson.

As I lie looking to the flame of the High Spirit's fires far above in the heaven, I see there are many stallions who run fast beyond where I cannot see in the distant lands of our people.

It is not like any night I have watched, as many stallions run fast and prove to have no end.

I fear there are now many of our people promised of their souls laying unkempt by the greed of the bad spirit within Suyapee's darkened soul.

I am awakened by the call of Jay as it sits in tree and looks down upon me with questioning eyes. As I rise up from my mat he does not fly off to sit upon another tree's long branch, but he hops down with closed wings as he rests closer to where I sit.

I find myself quickly questioning of what he asks?

His soul is good as he finds trust promised within my spirit.

He is not like most other Jays as those others sit high in tree when we walk through forest and shout out danger to the animals and birds that scurry to hide from our sight.

I look to him, unmoving.

Wanting to know of his thoughts.

He still sits on limb, now with opened wings before me, proving he is strong like eagle.

Those that found rest near where I had lain through the night heard the cry of Jay, and as they looked to where I sit, they too are amazed as Jay drops to the ground at my feet.

I first think he wants food from my purse, but as I offer him nut and drop it at his side he does not reach to take it from where it lies.

Now my thoughts wander, uncertain to why he comes?

I look to each side from where I sit, and upon the far hill sits Coyote, smiling.

I ask myself if this is not a ruse taken from Coyote's grandest purse?

Coyote has been a friend for many seasons, and she and I have travelled many trails. But today, she sits distant, watching, knowing well what Jay wishes.

Coyote's smile widens, and from her belly now comes quickly her loudest and most unnerving howl towards the essence of moon.

Now I know, it must be Coyote's newest trick.

Even those who I walk, look towards me, and then turns to see Coyote's wide smile. They too now question to what the message she wishes to share before us all through the soul of Jay?

I remember long ago when my father told me of him, and I when I was a young boy, he told me to sit on ground and sit patiently and Raven would come to me to eat from my hand.

My father told me as I waited for Raven to come to where I sat, I did not move.

Raven did not yet know of my heart, and it was good, but Raven still uncertain watched me with sharpened eyes.

With much patience Raven dropped nearer the ground upon the lowest branch, and as Wind softly blew, Raven, with opened wings, came to where the scrap of food awaited his sharp beak at my feet.

As Raven took the scrap from the ground he looked up towards me, and loudly screamed!

I ran fast like horse that day, and Raven began to laugh raucously from the highest branch as he watched me disappear behind the dust of the trail.

Raven screamed only to thank me for the scrap, but I too did not know of his Spirit.

All those that stood distant and watched my father and myself too laughed, and I did not come to canoe for long time.

I remember as I returned bleakly to where our people waited, I was told as I looked towards my father, my eyes were crazed with the fear of unknowing.

I think I may not have trusted my father the many days we journeyed to the village at Wyam until I was unafraid of those Raven that cried out overhead.

I know Coyote knows all that has come and will come to the lands of all her kingdoms, and this I sense she too wants to play trick on me with Jay as my father once too played.

I remind myself I must now trust, as it was that lesson my father wished for me to learn.

I was called by those that placed meat and pish upon the open pit of the fire for the long day ahead.

As I walked to the stick where they sat, Jay too followed where I stepped.

I looked at Jay and asked; "What do you want?"

Jay's eyes did not drop from my own.

My curiosity grew each moment I waited for answer.

But yet, Jay did not speak.

Still Coyote howled to the waning moon as it disappeared into the distant trails in the heaven.

Coyote is sly. But I am not afraid of her tricks, or of her new friend, Jay!

My brothers and I sat together and ate what food was offered, and it was good. We could not have asked for more.

Still Jay stood at my feet, looking towards me as if he thought to know of me.

But as I thought this was Coyote's trick, I did not give attention to her newest ruse.

We who have come to sit together waited as we were told Tkope Moolack would soon come.

We slept through the long night as Moon shone bright with promise of tomorrow.

As the warmth of the new day rose above us flowers opened to the warm rays of Sun, and all the animals came to the meadows to rest from where they journeyed during the night.

But Tkope Moolack did not come.

Those with whom I came all asked where the great Spirit White Elk had journeyed?

Through the morning we waited.

With great patience, we waited.

Some went to the distant hill to look beyond the lands we could not see, and they returned without answer.

Others went to the opposite hill and looked to where we could not see, and they too came back without answer.

Many began to question why we were told Tkope Moolack would appear in the early hours of morning, but we had no answers.

More questions arose, but again, there was only silence spilled to the winds.

Patience did not prove well for the many...

Every step I took, Jay too came.

Still looking up towards me as if we too were to be friends.

Again, I asked him; "What do you want?"

Again, Jay did not speak.

I walked to where I slept through the night and sat upon the trunk of tree, Jay came and sat again at my feet.

His trust was calming to my soul, and I too trusted him and hoped my soul would too offer him solace.

Possibly, we were to become friends?

Suddenly as I turned to look towards Coyote, she disappeared into the heart of tree.

She has again turned into the Spirit world where she first began her long journeys throughout all the lands of our kingdoms.

I had not looked for Raven as he too goes with Coyote as friends.

But I have not seen him all this journey, and this gives me pause to think of what message Raven and Coyote today share?

I ask to myself if they were called by the High Spirit to join us upon the trail and go to where they too had not gone before?

But I feel as Coyote has now gone to her world of Spirits, Tkope Moolack may be near.

I sit patiently, only looking towards Jay.

He and I have each welcomed one another into our domains as we have not parted from the first moment of Sun's rise.

Jay and I sit, each not wanting for each other to go from one another.

I find Jay welcoming as he has trust.

I too find him trusting of me as he does not take wing and go to limbs in tree.

I reach down to him, slowly.

My hand opened to his feet, hoping he will come to my hand so we can look closely into one another's eyes and see into one another's souls.

Jay jumps softly as he comes to my hand, climbing onto my shoulder where I turn and look into his eyes.

I see his soul is good.

Still Jay does not speak.

Words do not matter when the heart is pure and the soul warm for all those that come to sit beside you.

Jay and I are now joined together, our spirits strong, our respect beholding for one another's gift.

The Shamans that too wait with me for Tkope Moolack look towards Jay and I, and they begin to talk of our friendship and trust.

It is that trust we all must accredit within ourselves so when we sit with the High Spirit we are not moved by emotion, but only speak of the truths we hold promised within our souls.

Wind begins to rise up across the lands, its breaths soothing under the warmth of Sun.

Jay spreads its wings as he sits upon my shoulder, and as a small breeze awakens the limbs of trees, he turns to face Wind and glides to where Coyote had been last seen to sit upon the hill.

I follow him closely to see what he does, but still he turns to face me, as if he needs me to understand what he does, without question.

All those that sit and noticed Jay and I had turned and began to speak between themselves.

Not looking towards where Jay and I now sit, separate from one another, they did not see Jay fly from my shoulder.

Again I turn towards Jay only to see he too has disappeared into the heart of tree.

Now I am certain his spirit is strong as he too goes with Coyote.

Our souls have become bonded for all days, alike Coyote's and mine for all the days from the first night we chose to sit and bond above Wyam.

It is Good!

I walk to the grand Cedar where Coyote and Jay have gone, and as I sit beneath its long arms I reach out to touch its soul.

My eyes begin to close as the sweet scent of cedar's bark drifts down and fills the air around me.

I cannot fight its powers, and quickly, I am alone to dream.

Soft clouds like green moss and fern that lie along the waters of mighty rivers begin to form into the heavens.

Warm Chinook Wind blows softly to offer peace to yield itself within my soul.

Its breaths surrendering only to the scent of flowers as their sweet scent surrounds me.

All the animals gather beside me and speak stories of what they have seen.

Birds rest upon Cedar's mighty branches.

They sing songs promised of faith and of hope.

Each praying their tomorrows will alike our own, again bring children to their nests.

They each have been told of the battles Wy-East and Pahto had suffered before there was peace spread across their lands.

But, now, they have all witnessed the evil of the white man's ways and speak of grave warning that much is to change, and they too will not be the same as it will too change for Indian.

Those that come to sit with me under tree tell they had chosen long ago, when white man first came and trapped the innocence of Eena, to run and hide before their spirits were too taken and their souls spilled upon the ground without thought of what will be left in all the suns of their tomorrows.

The scenes they paint upon the trails of my thoughts offer me nothing but contempt for those that come to take all from the kingdoms of our spirits.

For many seasons we have all walked together, knowing we each shall never own all that is and all that will ever be upon the lands of our kingdoms.

When we see bird with nest, I ask; "Do we cut the tree to take wood for fire?"

It is the same for the white man when he takes all the Eena and leaves us with no more to keep warm in the throes of winter's coldest storm.

It is not what the Great Spirits teach before those that wail before the Walls of Wahclella.

Still, cloud that rise up into the heavens have not turned to storm, but threat looms heavy upon the horizon.

It is not long when those same clouds have begun to darken and drop from the heaven and threaten storms that may not soon end.

It is not good!

From the distance the roar of thunder fills the air.

Closer and closer to where I dream, their echo comes.

Though I sleep I know of their warning, just as the white man comes many to our lands.

There is no place to hide, no defense we can build that will keep them from spilling harm unto the lands.

We have traded much.

We have given up more.

We have begun to become what we fear!

This is not good!

The white man steals water, and the pish do not swim.

The white man steals the soul of our mother as they cut deep into her soil so they can grow plants we have not asked to be placed upon our tables to feed our people.

Our people, Indian, have taken only what Earth Mother offers to our cache each season, no more do we ask!

Again thunder falls from the heaven and panics all that live upon the lands of our kingdoms.

Warning has come too late as we Indian have stood alone and watched the white man sacrifice even the blood from our hearts.

Now little is left of our souls.

Our spirits have been left untended, and we are now weak and suffer much.

This too is not good!

The thundering of hooves awakens me.

Startled, I quickly stand from beneath the cedar.

I look to my brothers who too stand in awe to what they see standing before them.

It is White Elk...

He has come!

The light of day has passed two times from when we first stood at the side of Tkope Moolack at the end of Tkope Chuck, White River.

We have seen much of the battles of Pahto as great meadows of molten rock have lain hardened upon the ground and were strewn hastily along the trail we step.

With Tkope Moolack at our lead we have journeyed past the kingdom of Pahto and have now lain witness to the Great Tahoma as he rises to touch the edge of the heavens above.

The lands are spread magnificently before us each day, and our hearts and eyes are pleased.

A testament to the powers of those Spirits that watch over us, care for us, and offer happiness and hope to swell within our souls so our own spirits will rise up and touch those we meet upon each of our life's many journeys.

From the east we see many chiefs come of the Klickitat and Yakima, of the Umatilla and Walla Walla, too come the mighty Nez Perce and Shoshone to sit with us and speak with the Great Spirit.

All the nations of our lands are now present.

It is good we sit this night and smoke the long pipe as we share the bounties of the land as we eat.

This day has brought tired legs to each.

A long journey.

A long climb to touch the stars of the heaven…

As darkness nears we all go to where we sleep beside the warmth of the fires.

In the darkness of night those of my brothers that journeyed alongside me all sit and talk, but no one asks to where Coyote and Jay had gone.

They do not know they went into tree, and had journeyed into the Spirit world where they will wait until they are called to join us once again.

Coyote is never far from my side. She appears and disappears many days, but she comes to sit beside me when I call out to her so we may share the bond of our friendship.

As I lay asleep beneath the branch of cedar, I dreamt Raven did not come as he was chosen to watch over our peoples.

From high above Raven can see all that moves below in all our kingdoms through his keen and focused eyes.

It was not told to me then as I dreamed if Raven would come to join Coyote and Jay, but hurried through the whispers cast by Wind, I could faintly hear his caw.

It is good to see he comes, as he too has become a close friend with whom I have made journey beside many times.

We rose up on the third day and looked up to the lands of Tkope Lemoto high above where we sat.

We each agreed it was time to prepare for the final day of our journey.

White Elk looked towards us and began to lead upon the trail to the peaks of the White Goat.

It is there, where awaits the Great Spirit.

The Old Spirit that has lived many seasons and has witnessed each change cast upon the lands beneath him.

As Wind blows at night I have heard his pleas cast to the ears of Hyas Tumtum from our village at Wahclella.

I know he has seen much, both good and bad.

I have felt his sorrow, and I have felt his joy through his song placed upon the trails of Wind as they are shared across all the lands of our kingdoms.

It was here, where the White Goat climbs each day to look down upon the lands where the first battles between all the brothers of the Cascades began.

Long ago, it was not good to breath where we now climb. We cross many streams where great rivers had once begun their long journeys to the Big Waters.

Fish swim fast before our feet as we cross above them.

Once great forests climbed into the clouds where they touched the feet of Hyas Tumtum. Now, as we climb into where pillars of rock hold fast to the slopes of the highest of peaks, we must be near where we will sit with the Great Spirit and hear him speak.

White Elk stops!

White Elk slowly turns his mighty crown towards the call of Wind, and he listens to its message.

As we sat and looked towards Tkope Moolack it was not long before he looked back to where we awaited to follow his lead.

Time passed slowly as we looked towards the far peaks, but nothing moved.

The clouds of the heaven stood high above the lands and were not swept from where they too remained unmoving.

Ravens gathered to the limbs of trees before us, and many deer and elk too came to rest in the long meadow.

Slowly, Tkope Moolack too knelt upon the ground as had his brothers, and it would be here we knew we must wait.

We waited for the unknown.

We waited for what or whom we could not see.

From our hearts we knew this day would be like no other.

I sensed we, the peoples of many nations, would soon know how we as Indian will from this day forward walk together as brothers.

Our differences would become meaningless and forgotten through the purpose our lives would from today lead.

From afar I see Tkope Lemoto eating in the high meadow, and as we each sat to wait, they began walking hurriedly, shielding one tall, strong ram towards where we rest.

They are many.

They scurry freely across the narrowest of trails across the scree.

Their hooves do not loosen rock to fall upon us from high above the cliff.

I look to all my brothers as we await the voice of the High Spirit to speak;

As the many white goat have gone into a valley beneath the tall hill where we cannot see, only one, the lone Tkope Lemoto who was guarded behind others then came.

Our hearts can be heard pounding from within our chests as we watch the eldest of the Tkope Lemoto come toward where we are gathered.

From my heart is sent message that I must stand and walk to the lead of all my brothers before I am to again sit.

I feel upon my back a wet nose, pushing me, each time further from where I first began.

When I turn to look behind me I see there is nothing that brings the chill of winter to be placed upon me.

I feel Jay clasped to my fingers in my hand, but my hand lies emptied to his keep.

I too hear the caw of Raven from above, but as I look high to the heaven, he does not fly.

A voice from above tells me to look towards Tkope Moolack that rests alone beside the White Pine.

It is time.

Sun now warms the land as it rises above the crowns of distant peaks.

My brothers and I each stand to turn and peer towards Tkope Moolack, and as we watch in disbelief, White Elk rises as a pillar from upon the ground as his great horns reach far into the heaven above where we cannot now see.

We each believe it will be from there the High Spirit will appear and speak of our journey.

From the emptiness of air, trickster Coyote appears, walking like man upon two legs towards our group.

Smiling.

Knowing we do not yet understand…

We each think she is now certainly preying upon our eyes as she appears to be laying question within our hearts as we attempt to make sense of what message we are now witnessing from within our souls.

Quickly she changes into the form of an old and withered man.

Many suns and winter's long storm have fallen upon him without prejudice as he cannot stand straight like tree to touch the heavens.

The seasons have not been good to him as his youth has for many days become lost to his keep.

We look towards one another and ask; "Could this man be who we have heard talk before the fires of our villages to the legend of the man who walked from the villages of his people to rest for all days in the mountains of those spirits we hear call out through the languished breaths of Wind?"

We stand bewildered…

From where we could not see, not from limb of tree or from the heaven comes Jay to sit upon rock.

His wings spread wide like Eagle, proving his spirit too is strong.

Swiftly, as we look towards the old man that has changed from Coyote, Jay changes into long stick the old man now gleans in his calloused and weathered hands for support.

With hurry, Raven circles many times above, each turn sharper than the last until he lands upon the shoulder of the old man, where he peers deep into his soul.

I think of the honor they must both share, as Raven disappears and becomes the eyes of the old man so he can today too see.

We, in disbelief, do not yet understand what we have been lent to consider.

This is the kingdom of our Spirits.

It is from those Spirits who first came to these lands and created life that has rose up from the waters of the great sea and had first made journey into the kingdoms we have come.

We shall each be forever honored to stand where we today stand!

Sun had stood stilled to the heavens as we watched the powers of our spirits turn from animal and bird into man.

Our thoughts this day were alike the dreams we shared in our yesterdays to what our spirits might share before us.

Wind blows hard from the high peaks, and as it again settles, the old man voice resonates through all the valleys and meadows from where we each have come.

We first hear him state; "My children, I have called upon you to journey for many days to the lands of the White Goat to hear me speak.

"It is good you make journey to sit here in these lands to listen to my words so you will know of all those Suns that have passed behind the shadows of Moon, and to all those tomorrows when Sun shall rise above those living of our peoples.

"I too, long ago, was called to come to these lands to learn of the old ways of Indian.

"To sit and hear of our peoples of long ago.

'To know why they were chosen in honor into these lands so the ways of our fathers and mothers in the beginning would not become fastened to the ways of Wind so the memories of our presence shall not become lost for all days.

"When I first came, I was told to climb to the peak of Old Tahoma and to look down upon the bountiful lands where our villages stood proud amongst all the valleys.

"You have seen today each of the Great Spirits to appear before you, first Coyote, Jay, and then Raven.

"I have been given much in my old age, as I have died to live again through their strongest of spirits.

"I tell you this, as I was sitting upon the peak of Tahoma when the Great Spirit first spoke, he took from my eyes, sight.

"I could not see from where I had come, or to where I might be chosen to go.

"Faith quickly became fear, and there I sat thinking my soul would be lost to my spirit as I too would fly unfeathered within Wind's many travels and not be heard again of my voice before all my peoples.

"The Great Spirit told me to be wary of what I ask as I pleaded with him to return my sight so I may too honor those lands below.

"In that fear he saw I was weak, but through my knowing and trust of his mighty powers, he told me I would become strong.

"The Great Spirit told me as I was only a mortal man, I would first learn of trust and faith before he would choose to bring light again to my eyes.

"From that day I have learned to see all that I am surrounded through my belief in the faith he speaks.

"Today the Great Creator has brought sight again to my eyes, and I am pleased.

"I sat for many days upon the peak of Tahoma, shaken from the cold of his snows, and afraid to climb down from upon his steep and frozen slopes.

"Day after day I became more weary.

"My heart lay sullen in my greatest of defeats.

"I asked myself many times if I would choose to die or live?

"One day, as light fell upon my face and brought warmth to fill my soul, I knew what I must do.

"I told myself, I must grasp within my being and thrust my heart to trust the Great Spirit would lead me down from the heights of Tahoma's most steepest of frozen slopes.

"I learned quickly when one cannot feel, and when one cannot find faith in trust, then life as we know it will be no more.

"Why I tell you this will prove that you are all now that young man sitting atop Tahoma's peak, each afraid, sullen, and defeated by your own question of the days that have come before your peoples since Red Cloud first covered the lands with dark smoke.

"For those that have heard of the warrior who had no home that came to these lands long ago, my name is Smowhalla.

"I am from the Wanapum peoples who live near the Big Waters of the Snake, Wahpoos.

"This is my story.

"I was first named by my people to the peoples of the Earth as Kuk-Kia. I am the One Arising From the Dust of Earth Mother.

"As I have now begun to bring back to our peoples the Washani of old, our peoples will become strong and will be again as one people beneath the heavens of Otelagh and Moon upon the soils of Earth Mother.

"I am the keeper of the Earth.

"All lands, those of the Paiute and Apache, of the Sioux and Crow, to the lands of the Nez Perce, and of the lands of the Chinook, I am promised to my keep.

"It is through vision of the Highest Spirit I stand here and speak to you.

"I am told to share with words there is no purpose for Suyapee to come to our lands and take from our peoples all that we have kept honored within our souls but his greed.

"We have welcomed all others that have come in peace to sit beside our people at the fires of our villages. But even as we have welcomed Suyapee and have offered meal and chose trade, they are heard to demand they want more and more from the lands we know.

"It is not easy to understand why Suyapee come and demand all from the spirits that have made the lands of our kingdoms powerful and brimmed with new life each season.

"Through saddened eyes we see their numbers are many, and we feel they hide their truest of spirit deep within the darkness of their souls where hope does not shed light for our tomorrows.

"As they come upon us with smiles and opened hands, we find ourselves fearful Red Cloud will soon return and conceal these lands beneath its cruelest of face.

"From within that unknowingness of darkness' shadows, life shall quickly become swallowed, and all that we know and had once seen to live freely upon our lands will be no more.

"My grandfather told as he looked down from his high place even Owl who sits in tree at night could not see when Suyapee first came from the Big Water as Red Cloud fell cruelly across all the lands.

"Grandfather told Owl's voice was then silenced, and he did not hunt where he could not see.

"For many days and nights Owl sat upon the high branch above the village, and it is thought by many, Owl had first given witness to the true soul and to the spirit of Suyapee.

"When Suyapee first fled our lands, and Cloud raised from the waters, a loud cry extended from the branch where Owl was seen to sit.

"Soon his call was shared by many of his brothers and sisters across all the valleys of all the lands.

"As light from Sun was last cast across the lands, warning had been spread to all our nations telling our lands would soon be not ours to make journey.

"From both water and from along the shores of En che Wauna, we will fear what now hides in the shadows of the forest's many sticks.

"Each night as our brothers sat at council before the fire of their village, Owl rested above where they sat, guarding fearfully the sanctity of their village.

'As Owl looked down upon them, they saw nothing but worry flickering brightly from within his old and knowledgeable eyes.

"You too must question as they; "What did he see?"

"As I have looked down upon our kingdoms I have seen the lands have begun to become unsettled more and more as each new sun rises above the lands.

"Each season when the leaves of trees have begun to give color and shape and bring promise to the lands, there are many Suyapee who have come and have chosen to build villages along the shores of En che Wauna from the Big Waters.

"As I have peered down to the Big Waters from upon these mountains, I too have seen large boats appear along the clearest of horizon.

"First one, and then another, and again, sadly, another.

"Today, as you walk along trails where our great grandfathers had only first stepped, you find throughout the lands of Naha, your peoples are not today alone.

"With great burden, our hearts are today stilled.

"In our worry, we sit with our brothers unmoving at the side of the flickering flame of our lives.

"Our souls are promised in unrest, and we find them lying lifeless with much question.

"Through vision, as our fathers once spoke as they had looked through the looking glass of our tomorrows, we each envision the flame's flicker soon smothered.

"With grave sorrow, we raise our eyes to the heaven where our fathers sit beside the eternal flame of our people.

"It is to there, where our voices rise up and are heard to cry out for the Great Spirits to save our peoples from this change we cannot now influence to go where life had begun as we walk across our lands in fear.

"Earth Mother has told me our people will again be discovered bound to the laws of the lands Suyapee choose for us to stand, to sit, and to rest.

"I tell you this message must be cast before all our peoples so they too will want to worship Earth Mother before the watchful eyes of Great Spirit.

"I tell you the Great Spirit will take harm from before all our peoples as he oversees the many kingdoms of those that walk with him and dance to the seven drums, to the songs of seven singers, and to the ring of many bells that call out to the spirit of Earth Mother.

"We, the great Indian, must again follow the ways of our fathers and their fathers before them, and as we dance and sing to the ways of the Washani of old, then we will become strong and unafraid before those that now come many to our lands.

"Once the earth was all water and God lived alone.

"He was lonesome and he had no place to put his foot, so he scratched the sand from the bottom and made the land, and he made rocks, and he made trees, and he made a man, and the man was winged and could go anywhere.

"The man was lonesome and God made a woman. They ate fish from the water and God made the deer and other animals, and he sent the man to hunt and told the woman to cook the meat and dress the skins.

"Many more men and women grew up and they lived on the banks of the Great River whose waters were full of salmon. There were so many people that the stronger ones sometimes oppressed the weak and drove them from the best fisheries.

They fought and nearly all were killed.

"God was very angry, and he took away their wings and commanded that the lands and fisheries should be common to all who lived upon them.

The lands were never to be marked or divided.

"God said he was the Father and the Earth was the Mother of mankind; that nature was the law; that the animals and fish and plants obeyed nature and that man only was sinful.

273

This is the old law.

"After a while, when God is ready, he will drive away all the people except those who have obeyed the laws.

"Those who cut up lands or sign papers for lands will be defrauded of their rights and will be punished by God's anger.

"Suyapee asks for us to plough the ground? Ask them shall you take a knife and tear your mother's bosom? Then when I die, she will not take me to her bosom to rest.

"Suyapee ask our peoples to dig for stone. Ask them, shall I dig under her skin for her bones? Then when I die I cannot enter her body to be born again.

"Suyapee asks our peoples to cut grass and make hay and sell it and be rich like white man, but how dare we cut off our mother's hair?

"It is a bad law and our peoples cannot obey it. I want our people to stay with me wherever I go. All the dead men will come to life again; their spirits will come to their bodies again. We must wait here in the home of our fathers and be ready to meet them in the bosom of our mother.

"Earth Mother has been heard to tell it is to those that follow through with their dreams that she promises to offer the gifts of all your tomorrows.

"It was long ago, before the white man came, a medicine man and great prophet told of the whites and how they would come to our lands as friends.

"He told soon they would take from our peoples all that we had known through all the days we have walked with the Great Spirit.

"From their bad spirit's purse they would spread across the lands disease."

That disease he spoke we now see today sited upon the bodies of all those that now lay dying and dead upon the banks of En che Wauna and in many of running waters across our lands.

"There will be many more of our peoples souls thrown emptied of life upon the banks of many rivers.

"Villages will lie emptied, and the call of our brother's voice will then lie silent upon the courses Wind chooses.

"As we look upon the lost spirits of our peoples with saddened eyes, the voices of those still living will too fall silent as the final tear from our people's eyes shall fall unnoticed as we walk upon the trails that had one day been lent to the promise of beginnings, but now, only bring certainty to our endings.

"When we pass before what remains of our peoples, we will not again take those from their villages to our own to care.

"As they cry out when there is no one left of their own villages, those that had survived the wasteful taking by the bad spirit will stand alone in their misery and grieve greatly in their despair.

"We will then be separated of our good spirits across the kingdoms of our brothers, and we will not be joined again as one people, but our powers will be taken from us as we will then become many peoples with no nation.

"Many villages will not welcome the brother or sister of the villages that rest beside their own, and many will become afraid to those they cannot decide as those that had been friends for many seasons as the mesachie tumtum has taken spirit from their eyes.

"Sadly, many of our brother's souls will be cast emptied upon the High Spirit's most lonesome of trails...

"We must again join with the spirits of animal. We must be as one with all that lives upon the lands, and we must search our souls through dreams as we reach out and seek the wisdom shared from all life blessed upon this, all our Illahee.

"We will dance upon the earthen floors of our villages upon our knees in honor to the Great Spirit.

"We will only take from the soils of our lands what Earth Mother has given our kingdoms from the beginning of their creation, as they came from the waters and from the first sands that had washed up upon the shores from the great sea.

"It was thought Suyapee would come to live amongst our peoples in peace, yet, others live by the words spread by those that come upon our red face who are promised to fear what they do not know of our peoples.

"It is those that now come with musket and powder that bring others to open the great spirit of the earth with long knives.

"From beneath the ground that gives life, our Earth Mother's soul shall soon lie separated and stilled of her Spirit.

"Our Great Earth Mother's spirit shall be swept from the lands as wind gathers from the heavens.

"Our lands will quickly become like the emptiness of the desert where only the snake can hide beneath the dry soils where not even green grasses grow, or great forests rise up to touch the feet of our fathers.

"The lands will certainly then forever be lost from our people's gathering for all the snows of our lives.

"We must stand in defense against the long knives.

"It brings dishonor to the Earth and to our peoples to carve from her body her heart that offers sustenance and hope for all our tomorrows.

"To take water from those that thirst brings much disgrace through the beliefs of our peoples.

"We have wished nothing more than to honor those lands we have been accepted, to live only by what Earth Mother finds needing for our peoples as we make journey into our tomorrows.

"As we sit, we too, through the message of our dreams, see those brothers who have had their spirit taken from within them rise up from beneath the earthen mounds where they had lain for many days, unmoving.

"We see clearly and without question those that had once walked beside us now have joined together and united in one village under the blanket of one great nation.

"Our peoples are the promised ones through the gift of Great Spirit.

"We will be the first and last of Mother Earth's creation to peer through the Looking Glass.

"As we look into tomorrow we can imagine the sun of our tomorrows for the remaining of our seasons if we stand defiantly without war first cast between our people.

"Before those Suyapee who choose not to understand the need to walk the same trails as we who have first come, we must pray!

"We have been promised to again walk the old trails of our fathers where we will discover deer and elk lying amongst green pastures.

"As we stand and peer out over the waters of En che Wauna we will again witness fish leaping to the lengths of the heaven as we follow in the ways of Washani.

"Our peoples will be rewarded for walking with Earth Mother, and we will all be pleased...

"We are told we must sing and dance through the long night, and as Sun comes once again into the heaven, we must make journey to the villages of the whites and tell them of Earth Mother's message.

"We will ask to sit together and smoke from the long pipe, and in the eyes of Suyapee we will see they are afraid.

"Suyapee will look into the eyes of our brothers whom they had long ago taken from our villages.

Suyapee's spirits will then certainly lie confused and bring much question to where they must go to hide from the strengths of our spirits.

"As Suyapee kneel before the feet of their own spirit father to again discover strength from where now lies only weakness within their souls, the same dark cloud that had once rose up behind their arrival to our lands will be chosen as swift justice upon those whom still look toward us with pause.

"To those people, I wait sincerely to see the fear challenging the good that remains in their souls as they look upon us Indian with yet more question.

"With loud voice, warning shall be delivered to those that oppose our beliefs and to those who do not want to understand the medicine of our people.

"They will be seen no more to walk beside us upon the trails of our prosperity!

"Our brothers too believe that man first rose up from Mother Earth, and once they have been chosen to pass into the Spirit World, they will return to the soils from where they had first been created, and only then will they be seen to live.

"We must remember that life comes from death, not death after life.

"It is through our believing in the soul of Earth Mother that will allow our peoples to live after we have walked beside her and have led all our brothers to learn of her.

"As we walk behind where her footprints have first stepped, and after we have been lain upon the sacred grounds of our graveyards, only then will our spirits rise up to be alongside all those that first rode upon the White Stallions and sat at the sides of their fathers.

"It is spoken that we, Indian, are the chosen ones to live on into the tomorrows of our dreams as we find honor in respecting all life that runs free upon all the lands.

"It has been told as quickly as the sun rises we will live freely beneath the village of our Great Spirit above.

"Alongside clear waters and fast streams we will again see pish gather in great numbers before our eyes from where Suyapee had long ago taken from the purity of many waters the innocence of their spirits.

"We shall once again walk without fear of the whites holding hostage to all the lands.

"We will again rest settled where our villages had once stood unopposed by any but the spirits of the high peaks as storm of wind swept down harshly upon them.

"The only tears to fall will be from the Hyas Tahmahnawis' eyes as he too rejoices our return to the lands of our kingdoms as they fill the great waters with clarity and with great depth where the spirit of pish will again become gathered unchained.

"We are told we shall again enter into the open meadows of the high peaks where we will take from upon its bush the sweet huckleberry.

"As we ride into the great forests, sticks shall dance favorably beside each of the many trails we follow.

"These same trees shall lead us to where we will again walk in amongst great numbers of Moolack and Mowitch.

"We will sit high upon our horse as have our fathers before us. The great herds will lie down before us and honor our people with their meat for the long winters.

"Our lands will be cleansed of the Suyapee who do not believe in the ways of Washani. Their disease shall be ridden from our lands, and our lives will be spared of our own disgrace before others who step upon the kingdoms where Indian has first lived.

"Listen to Wind, and in its message you will know of the Washani we are told we must follow."

"As the long pipe was passed between all that sit and listen, I began to speak of the Hyas Tahmahnawis Tyee whom our peoples have listened closely from the beginning.

"We have journeyed safely across the lands he has drawn before us through the teachings he has led us to understand to be the truths in our lives.

"We are to honor the land we live.

"We are to honor the spirits of animals that walk amongst us.

"We are to take nothing from the Earth Mother that we do not need.

"Earth Mother has given us much to be pleased from beside the trails of our kingdoms.

"From the soils that are the Earth Mother's womb, life has been reborn for many suns beyond those of our own.

"We have not asked for more than the High Spirit has gifted our peoples.

"As we strive to keep our lands and waters rich and bountiful with new life, we hold within our calloused hands the dreams of all our tomorrows...

"Our peoples must not forget where we first came.

"All that our peoples have remaining of our lives are the memories cast up from upon the very soils of our lands.

"The few pish that shall yet honor our waters shall be heard calling each of our names upon the passing of Wind.

"Our villages great fires shall be promising to once again enlighten those that come to stand in their own silenced wake.

"Through the statues of our fathers soon cut from the hearts of ageless sticks whom once gazed approvingly over our peoples as we made journey beneath their rise unto the breadths of the heaven, will be proven unquestioning of our people's longevity and worthiness to the lands we honor.

"From upon the painted cliffs high above En che Wauna, where today deer, elk, and sheep await to look down questioning of those tomorrow whom shall pass upon the waters of En che Wauna, they shall too share privilege considered of our people's presence upon these lands.

"Our people's memory shall live on through each season as Otelagh's hands will remain opened and bring warmth to fall from the heaven and create new life to flourish across all the kingdoms.

"May the strength of our souls bring breadth unto our spirits, and may we, in honor to our fathers, forever journey upon long and destined trails with the purity of our spirit unchallenged from within the mortality of our souls...

"Welcome to these lands where the spirits of men have joined the Great Spirit of Earth Mother.

"May you always walk beside your fathers, and know they too, shall forever walk beside you...

"In the last of our days as we sit and look out over the waters of En che Wauna, all we will be afforded is what our great fathers and their fathers had been persecuted in long ago days.

"We, who will survive, will be forced to sit above where our villages once stood, and we will only be able to dream of what our lands once were before Suyapee came and changed things.

"We must ask in silenced breaths to those that walk amongst our peoples;"

"Does your Great Chief in Washington believe he is the great creator from where all things first came?"

"Then, upon passing, we shall be seen to yet offer Suyapee again our opened hands and it shall be heard spoken the word of welcome…

"Kloshe tumtum mika chako."
"This Is the Way of Our Peoples…

"Now go you to your peoples and tell them what you have seen.

"Tell them what you have heard.

"May our people be survived by our children, and by their children long after their own through the many seasons of our morrows.

"As you have seen, I am of many spirits.

"I am both man and animal of the Earth.

"My spirit is strong.

'Now go I to the Earth where my bones will be with Creator for all days.

"Tell your people, our people, what you have seen today.

"Paint upon the rock where all can see the picture of today so they too can see the light of Sun enter within their eyes where many stood blinded to the truths we must find honor.

"Paint upon the rock the picture of our Spirits so our people can feel the warmth cast out from their souls.

"Paint upon the rock that proves of faith and hope so they too can see through the Looking Glass and know of our tomorrows.

"Tell them!

"Tell Them!

"Make them believe their spirits are strong by what you have seen this day!

"Go you to your peoples, and may all your tomorrows be well spent as we dance and sing to the seven drums, to the bells that bring rhythm and reason to our hearts, and to sing to the Creator for she is and will be all we will ever know.

"Go you to your peoples, and one day, when Pish first come to river, I too will come to you once more.

"Make not the eyes of Tsagiglala become blinded to our ways through your absence of faith!

"Kloshe Tumtum Mika Chako..."

As he spoke his last word Raven came out from Kuk-Kia's eyes and took sight from him for the final time.

Jay too changed from stick and fell from his hands to the rock and swiftly took wing and flew with Raven high above from where they had first come.

Then, as cloud came to the heaven and great Wind blew, with great sadness, Coyote came out from Smowhalla's Spirit and leaned her head to the heaven as she began to cry out across all the lands of our kingdoms in grave mourning.

Coyote's heart had too changed through the speech Smowhalla offered to all that came.

We were each now bonded to the ways of Earth Mother and to all the spirits she offers our peoples to keep us strong through the dark days that have been promised to bring our people's souls disparity.

As all the spirits departed from where the soul of Smowhalla stood, a cloud of dust rose up from upon the Earth and climbed into the heaven.

Kuk-Kia was seen no more as his spirit had then journeyed to where his life had first begun....

His soul had now passed again into spirit so others may too have faith in the hope they will be honored to see the sun of all their tomorrows...

Chapter 9

Does Not Suyapee Too Dream

Word had been spread across all the kingdoms of the Washani of old as we had been asked.

Far into the night can be heard the dance of seven drums of the Washat in many longhouses drawing close their spirits with the Creator.

The clanging of bells presents the heartbeat of all life to live on into all our tomorrows, and the wail of our people rise up to the heaven as they dance and sing in honor to the Great Spirit for all he has offered our peoples from the beginning.

Many days have passed, many good, some bad.

But today, word has come from those of the Cayuse they have given Suyapee those that took spirit from soul of Suyapee at Walla Walla.

Five were taken to village along the Big Waters of Wallamet named Oregon City, to be judged for the sins of the people.

The Cayuse's voices were not allowed to be heard as they were guilty before they came, being they were Indian and not believing in the ways of the whites.

As the Cayuse stood before those that judged, they told bad medicine had been spread through Whitman's hands as many he touched fell to the ground in great agony.

For many days, those of our brothers were taken from our people through the poisons offered them from Suyapee's hidden purse.

Sun did not rise again into their eyes.

As those that judged listened only to those whose loud talk offered only the threat of hanging to those bravest of our brothers.

They cried out for our brothers blood to be drained from their souls, and their hair taken from upon their scalps so they could not go to sit with their fathers.

Their voices were heard beyond the walls of the court to offer no mercy to our brother's spirits.

It was not long before judgement was announced to all who killed, and they were told, they each would be hung before the people of the white man's village by their necks for the murders of the Whitman.

The Whites were pleased they would not see again Indian in their courts, and soon, they hoped, not in the lands our Great Creator had first promised for us all to keep!

Tiloukailt was a friend from many seasons ago.

We sat at Wyam and spoke of the love of our country.

We spoke of how the deer and antelope ran with the promise of Wind's storm beneath their feet.

It was good, and today it is sad to know he is gone from our peoples.

Tiloukailt will not be forgotten.

His name shall always be spoken at the great fire of many villages.

He did no wrong in taking the evil from within those that killed our people as they came to the white's village for help and education, to learn of the white man's ways, and of their religion.

The whites had bad spirit in their hearts as they too first killed our people!

It was told a man of great religion came to Tiloukailt and sprinkled water upon his head and asked; "Why, if you are innocent, did you allow yourself to be placed into the hands of the whites?"

Tiloukailt replied to him; "Did not you missionaries tell us that Christ died to save His people? So die we, to save our people!"

As I listen to those words past spoken by Tiloukailt, I must too ask myself; "If Suyapee believes in a man he has not seen, and if Suyapee believes that He, Jesus, will deliver us from all evil if we believe in Him, then in Suyapee's faith, does he not too dream?"

From The Beginning, as we have been taught from the Bible, there has in history been fought great battles for both land and religion.

Battles were fought for the beliefs many chose to be held challenged, and to those that did not walk amongst them and believe of their way, were then forced to follow the footsteps of others.

Those whom thought, they alone, were the chosen ones that could do no wrong before the eyes of their God, did not many return to their peoples and rest upon their mats again.

It was not long when mankind's selfishness wore on those that did not follow in their ways, and mankind's conceit arose before the many each day.

This is no different than today, as we too find ourselves yet peering into the mirror of their eyes.

We have been seen from that first day which first promised promise for all our peoples, to have misplaced the gift where humanity would have once walked in peace and in love for all we have been given by the Great Creator.

To know we had once been gifted the privilege to walk freely without worry or fear upon the soils of the Earth, must leave all our people's hearts and souls emptied.

Our hearts have become burdened and lain in question to what our lives may have once stood?

It is written, as Sun first rose upon the lands and above the seas the second day, there was promise of light and warmth spread upon those that would soon walk upon the lands.

To each of God's children, their yearning to survive their first days beneath the Sun of day and beneath the Moon of night would not bring great challenge.

But, as God chose for man and woman to join one another in the garden, and the bad spirit arose before them with promises he could not keep, and as both man and woman took from the tree, fruit, that was to stay upon its branch so all others could see, the light of day dimmed from the heavens, and the darkness of night became harried for all nights within their dreams.

The trees of our forests rose high into the heaven, each sworn to hold high the sky. Each tree passing along their crowns the promise of Sun and Moon, bringing either day or night from above us in the heaven where God peers down upon each of His children.

From the heavens, as moon rose over the lands, stars were promised to shine upon the trails our lives must then be led.

Through our faith, our promise would be not to walk aimlessly and without direction as we journeyed through the trials of our lives.

In the Bible is suggested, Wise Men went to where the Angel shines bright in the night's sky. From great distances, and from many kingdoms, came the many as they followed the bright light risen to the heavens.

We must ask as we too came from a kingdom where pestilence and death only awaited us by the sworn word of the evil ruler or by the sharp point of the spear as it was cast by his armies; "Have we not too followed where the star shines bright and in that promise of the Great Creator has awaited our peoples to flourish upon these lands?"

As night turns again into day, when light touches the peaks of mountains and warms the desert sands, day again brings life's promise before all as it takes away doubt to our survival upon the lands.

From plants and trees shall come fruit and nut that will bring sustenance for all the living creatures that walk and breathe across the lands of the Earth.

There has never been written that I, alone own the lone tree that bears the sweet fruit.

As many come to plead as they too thirst for the tree's fruit, and as I am surrounded by the many of distant villages, I ask; "How can I refuse the people what God first chose as gifts extended from His most merciful hand so we each too may taste the gift of the fruit's sweet nectar?"

Was it not written that Jesus offered food and drink to the many when little was first placed upon the plates of few?

It has been written, all God has created was founded for mankind, and that we only rule over the birds and animals, all the creatures.

We do not rule over all mankind as God alone brings punishment upon those that walk amongst others who challenge the balance between right and wrong.

God alone judges those whom wish only to make war from where peace first resonated amongst the people.

To those that choose to offer hate from their hearts rather than to respect the love of our spirits that strives to rise each day from our souls, it is written that God shall condemn those that do not believe in Him or of His Son, Jesus.

In end of their days, their lives shall be taken from the soils of this Earth and their names shall not again be spoken.

It is written that God had chosen His Son to be sacrificed so others may live, but, I ask you; "Can we not from this day, each walk together in peace and bring light to shine down upon our lives through the Great Creator's eyes as we journey upon the trails He had chosen for us to first follow?"

We must not be taken away from what is right before the eyes of the Great Creator as those others walk amongst our peoples where we are gathered.

This is not the way of our people!

This must not be the way of Indian!

Though Suyapee have walked in amongst our kingdoms from great distance, it was not the promise of the Angel's bright light they followed.

Suyapee followed the trails of Indian, and as they chose to close their eyes to our people, only the darkness of their souls spread out across the lands.

Disease and death soon followed, and still we did not choose to hear the message of the bad spirit.

We honored the laws written in the Book of the Great Creator, though we had not yet met.

We knew we must forgive!

We knew we must have hope!

We knew we must allow faith to yet yield strength within our hearts so our souls will be saved in the end of our days!

"It brings me great sadness to tell you, my people, we must go to where Suyapee chooses.

The days shall be many as Sun and Moon pass through the heavens many times, but it will be through the eyes of our dreams we will return.

May we walk together as proud people, and may we return to our lands as prouder people that know we have followed the words of the Great Creator.

All that He had once offered us Indian, will be for all days.

May we hear through wind the soothing song of Naha, and may her song bring joy to our hearts as we wait again to join our souls with her own.

May the smoke of our fires rise high to the heavens from where our villages once stood, and may they again lead us to sit beside those stones that have brought marriage between our people and to all the lands.

May we Indian, be only those again seen as the many Suyapee who come to our lands with closed eyes and dark hearts will not share in the end of their days!

May their spirits not rise from their souls to again walk across the lands, and may their souls be swept destined upon Wind's harshest breaths.

Be their souls not seen or their voices heard calling out again as they fall emptied and silented beneath the harried depths of the great Sea.

Chapter 10

"I Ask You, Remember Us, Indian"

"Welcome to our lodge!

"I stand here before you this night to speak of all those of our fathers who have accepted challenge into the trials of becoming chiefs.

As they, in the end of their days, were called to sit once more before the Walls of Wahclella to listen to advice spoken of those privileged before them, and as the light of Sun shone down upon them, their lives were placed before all our peoples for all days, either in memory, or upon the sacred Walls of Wahclella.

"Many of our village's chiefs were chosen from my family, but they as I, are joined with you as one family below the Great Spirit's opened hands.

"I am no better a man than those of you that sit with me tonight.

"There are those of you that may have been led to take the journey into the Valley of the Eagle if it were not for my father's voice heard above all others by the Great Spirits.

"Those of you that have grown from our youth beside one another had too completed the arduous trial before the Tumwata's of Eagle.

"It is a great honor to sit with each of you, as we, all of you, have chosen to follow me, as I too am bound to follow in the words spoken by our Hyas Tumtum.

"We have come far…

"We have journeyed upon many trails as we followed them through the seasons of our lives.

"We have survived each season, and we will be accepted by the many as we cross their paths.

"We are Indian.

"We are the chosen ones to listen to Wind and know the message she sings.

"We are the ones that walk through the lands without fear as we have Coyote, Raven, Jay, and White Elk watching over us each day.

"We will live to always see tomorrow's day.

"This has been promised to our peoples for all days!

"From the beginning, when our people first came to these Lands of Wah, we were not many.

"Our minds were strong, and our faith stronger.

"Patience and prayer allowed our people to anticipate they would discover a land untouched where they would begin again to make our villages so we could each lay upon our mats and rest.

"A long journey came to end when our people stood along the shore of En che Wauna and the first pish leaped high into the heaven to catch the small fly as it willingly fell into our wanting nets.

"Life was good as it is this day.

"We could not have asked for more.

"I called out to you and your sons to sit with me and smoke again from the long pipe. We will soon call out to our wives and daughters to join us in the longhouse and bring honor to Earth Mother for all she has awarded this great kingdom.

"We will sing and dance to the Great Spirit, and as Sun again rises, we will go with great sadness from the lands we shall always love.

'We will not lay our heads low to the ground as we walk from our lands, but we will sing to Earth Mother and offer her praise for who she is and for what she has offered our people, her children.

"From her most bountiful heart, we must take what is offered, and we must walk proudly as her children.

"We will not surrender our souls, and we will not surrender our spirits to the greed of these peoples who march upon us with the gravest of intention.

"Suyapee have now come many to our lands.

"We cannot one day go upon those trails we have journeyed for many seasons without seeing in their eyes the fear of hate.

"Though they wish our people would stand before them so they may take from us spirit, we will have no war...!

"It has been told through the visions of our fathers our people will one day return to the fires of our villages that await our return.

"Life will not from tomorrow be the same.

"The land Suyapee chooses for our peoples are not good.

"The shores of En che Wauna are many sun's distant, and fish do not jump where we will be swept.

"The sticks of the forests are not healthy. Few rise from the soils of the lands to touch the feet of the Hyas Tyee.

"Great Cedar do not rise up to touch the heaven, so remember them each through the memory of your dreams.

"As we march from our lands, reach out to touch those Cedar we pass, and speak softly to their souls as they too will mourn our peoples as we will for many days mourn them.

"They will await our return, and then, we will again sit beneath them and share story, and cherish their sweet scent cast out into the journeys of Wind.

"Only deer and elk will be seen to run free across the lands. But it will be those same deer and elk that will look upon us with great sadness as our hearts will be drawn from within us for many suns.

"Our spirits will lie unmoving as our voices will become silented before the long arm of Suyapee's armies.

"Tsagiglala will not look over our peoples as Coyote once told, for we will not be where she can see.

"She will know where we go.

"She will feel our souls.

"She will hold our spirit close to her heart.

"She will wait for many seasons before she and we will again one day look into one another's eyes and know we have returned to one another.

"Coyote and Raven will follow our people for all days, and their spirits will look over us.

'It will be through their spirit we will be called, and then, we will march unchecked to the lands where Naha mourns for her children.

"I tell you, do not fear what we cannot see today.

"Fear only for the lands of our births, as they will not be the same tomorrow as they are today.

"Sticks of our forests will not be seen standing proud upon the lands.

"The waters of En che Wauna will go to the sea without hurry, and many pish will not return to their villages.

"Do not feel sorry for our people...

"Feel only the sadness Suyapee will hold in his heart as he does not listen to the words of the Hyas Tyee or hear message in Wind.

"Feel only the urgency of the message offered from the soul of Naha, and soon, we will see Suyapee begin walking across these lands without sight for their tomorrows.

"Our people will survive and come again proudly to our lands.

"On that day, as Sun rises, we will step silently and without trace upon the shore of En che Wauna, and as we go to where our village's fires have awaited our return, we will call out to Naha and announce; "Your children have today returned."

"My grandfather sat with me many suns ago along En che Wauna where we waited for pish to come to the waters, and there, as we sat, he spoke to me of what was right for our people.

"He told me his father spoke with him, and his father spoke to his son as I am speaking to you today. He told me what he asked of me that day would be with me for all days.

"He told me all he had been asked had allowed him to become a leader for our people, and that he had not led them down trails where they would not return through the questions he was first presented.

"All our chiefs had journeyed many places in their lives, and they each had asked many new questions as seasons became many as they presented many obstacles before their paths. But it has been in those lessons our fathers first shared that first brought faith towards their decisions.

"Our chiefs followed in the beliefs the High Spirits had first offered them to understand and accept as they knelt before the Walls of Wahclella.

"Today, through their leadership, our people are yet seen to survive through all the adversities of the many yesterdays that had presented themselves before us.

"This day I have shared my message before the Suyapee who came to smoke and talk.

"I asked them to carry within their purse this message to those that want our peoples to go far from the lands we know.

"I offered them from my own hand the finest furs of Eena from my shelf, and as I pleaded before them, I asked them to take to their people the message I will share with you this night.

"I ask you, when you first look from the peak of Great Larch, across the waters of En che Wauna, and into the lands of Lawala Clough, Pahto, and Tahoma, and to the lands of Wy-East and Seekseekqua, what do you see?

"When you look to the heaven and see bird, why does her song bring comfort to your heart?

"When you sit beneath the Great Cedar as deer and elk come to lie in the green meadow, why does your soul become settled?

"When you catch pish from the Great River, why does their offering allow your heart to become aroused, and as you taste the flavor of the first pish caught in the new season, why does it offer hope for all those tomorrows when you wait for their spirits to jump again into your net?

"When you look to the peak of the tall mountain, and stands Coyote grieving to the fullness of Moon's lonely shadow, ask, what she too has lost?

"When Raven flies to your feet and looks deep into your eyes, ask, what does he see of my soul?

"When Owl calls out into darkness of night, ask too, what does she know?

"When trees bow to the songs of Wind, ask them, do you wish to offer me your arms so we can each dance?

"When tears fall from the Great Creator's cheeks, ask him if he is pleased when the first flower's scent rises up to welcome the new season?

"When you kneel before the Walls of Wahclella and seek the truths from her waters, ask, what must I first do?

"When you look upon Multnomah and hear song cast out by the soft voice of Wind, ask if this is not the love song cast out to all that remember the fallen maiden's sacrifice to save her people?

"When you hear woodpecker tapping upon his drum, ask him, what message does he wish to share of his song?

"When you see the goose flying in formation as the new season comes, ask them, are they not happy to return to where seed grows many upon the hair of our mother?

"When you go to the mountains to take berry from the bush, ask not why the Great Creator shares with all her children, but ask, how can her Spirit not share with all her children who have chosen to settle always within the gift of her cradle?

"When you walk across rock sharpened by battle where once meadows of green grass offered soft bed for the night, ask, what has wars between brothers rightfully won?

"I ask you, when clouds form softly unto the heaven, why too does your heart offer great hope to what will be in the tomorrows of your dreams?

"I ask you, when color comes to the heaven as Sun travels to kingdoms we too do not know, do you not wish to again feel Sun's warmth drawn within you when morning comes?

"When Jay comes to feed from your hand, ask him, what does he know of your spirit that brings trust to bond your souls for all days?

"I ask you, once Great White Elk has come from behind tree to stand before you, can you now not see his white robe always from great distance knowing he watches over you all days in your journeys into the heights of your spirit?

"I ask you, when you have answered all that you have been asked, is your heart full?

"Or, is your heart still emptied through the absence of your knowing if what you have answered is the truth spoken of your spirit?

"I ask you?

"I ask you to remember this, to live each day knowing that tomorrow may never shine as bright as today if you are found wandered upon all the lands of our kingdoms as are the fallen meteors of our heaven.

"You must be taken by your invitation upon the Great Earth as you each discover the sacredness of the grounds you encounter.

"You must not be led astray from the gravity of their burnished and most honorable paths.

"I ask you, do not let pass our vision!

"I ask you, as you emerge before our people, choose your stance gracefully so they willingly accept the truths spoken by all our fathers, and through those words, they shall become influenced by what you profoundly speak before their yearning hearts.

"I ask you, let all those that come to stand before you hear you speak; "We Shall Honor the Earth and the Heavens.

"We Shall Honor Mankind!

"We Shall Honor the Spirits Bore to Each of the Trails in Their Journeys!

"If your spirit stands proudly before those that come to listen, then one day you may be promised to be seen crossing the heavens as do the Hyas Eagles.

"Your Spirit on that day shall then be seen proudly pointed toward the Great Creator's chosen star, and it will glisten brightly so your trail before the doors of heaven is not chosen in darkness where you would be promised to walk blindly and offered nothing but bad endings to follow unto each of your mere beginnings.

"As you rise above into the heavens of the Creator, and as you follow in the truths he speaks, that day, you too shall be accepted by all your brothers to Have Seen the Sun of Tomorrow's Day!"

"As you are welcomed into the gate of the Great Creator you will hear him say; "Kloshe Tumtum Mika Chako.

"WELCOME...
"Klahowya...

"I ask you, where have gone the sticks of our forests, or those spirits who once walked free across all the lands?

"I ask you, where have gone the trails that once led to the Lands of Wah where the Creek of the Great Eagle awaits those of their fathers whom are chosen to accept the challenges of life's lessons placed before their souls?

"I ask you, what of your spirit?

"I ask you, when you stand before the Great Walls of Wahclella, do you hear of our Father's greatest speech?

"I ask you, do you want to hear the voices of your spirits as they lead you upon those trails they too had once thought to journey?

"I ask you, do you want to hear Coyote's Spirit call out as she pleads to join her spirit with your own as she travels far into the unknowing darkness of long nights?

"I ask you, when you look towards your children when they sleep, do you not wish for them to see the rise of Sun in all of their tomorrows without worry or complaint?

"I ask you, do you wish to see through the eyes of Tsagiglala and hold hope for all our tomorrows. Where all the spirits across all the lands will once again be set free from pestilence and enabled to breath freely under the same heaven as it was in the beginning?

"I ask you, are we not allowed to find warmth under the same Sun, to walk before all our brothers and know our souls are connected to this Earth without question arising from the storm within our mortal souls that we each belong?

"I ask you, as you listen to Wind, and as her breaths course harshly upon you from the trails of our heaven, and when you are caught standing without cover, what do you fear when her cries call out determined across the lands with great urgency to the state of her children?

"I ask you, what did you hear that defines the foundation to her message?

"I ask you, what must you do?

"I ask you, will you not kneel before the feet of the Great Spirit, and will you then know through the morality of your spirit your life is worthy of rising to the heaven upon the back of the Great Spirit's White Stallion as it delivers your soul to one day sit before the chair of your father and warm yourself at the side of the fire that never dims?

"I ask you, what have you seen through the lens of the looking glass of all your tomorrows?

"I ask you, where has your spirit led you in all the seasons of your past, and where do you hear your spirit calling for your soul to join those Spirits that yet await you today?

"I ask you to answer to only yourself, and may the truth be spoken from your soul.

"Be the Great Spirit With You Always...!
"Mitlite okoke Hyas Tumtum kopa nika kwonesum...!

"Welcome, My Brothers...
"Klahowya, Kopa Nika OW...

"Welcome to the lands of our peoples.
"Kloshe tumtum mika chaco kopa okoke illahee of nesika tillikums.

"I Ask You, Remember Our Peoples...
"Nika Wawa Nika, Mitlite kopa tumtum Nesika Tilikums...

"Klahowya

"Welcome My Brothers..."

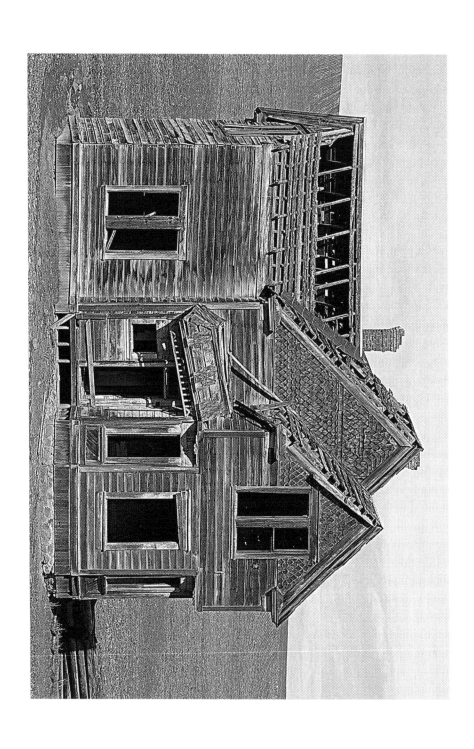

Epilogue

The failures of mankind began with our lack of understanding and acceptance for difference.

From our hearts, where greed has become entangled with self, in accepting our tragedies, we have allowed ourselves to repress all hope towards our futures.

We reluctantly discover ourselves to live under the same sun and moon of our heaven with the understanding that we are governed through our efforts to preserve the gift of life we each have been awarded under those same entities.

Mankind was first chosen to this Earth to journey through life together and not become separated by our individual wanting. If we understood why to look beyond our own prejudices, then we, as peoples to this Earth, would become unified under the laws of morality, and where righteousness could only stand alone upon the highest of our podiums.

Humanity is not a gift we can afford not to accept.

Humanity is a gift we must strive to protect, to honor, and to respect as we journey into the unknowns of our tomorrows.

We must each believe every person is our own equal, no more, and no less.

The qualities of our lives must not depend upon the strengths of our arms, but through acceptance of difference as our lives progress into the futures of all our tomorrows.

Through difference we learn, through learning, mankind shall survive...

Steve Warnstaff

Acknowledgements

Dallas Winishut—Warm Springs Reservation Educator

Valerie Switzler—Warm Springs Reservation Educator

Horsethief Lake State Park, Washington State

James Day—Horsethief Lake State Park, Washington
Tsalalagal Tour Leader

Mike Theisen—Blacksmith, Fort Vancouver

Drummers & Dreamers---Click Relander, The Caxton Printers,
LTD. Caldwell, Idaho, 1986

Hear Me My Chiefs—L. V. McWhorter, The Caxton Printers,
LTD. Caldwell, Idaho, 1992

Robert Davis—Photographer, Educator, The Dalles, Oregon

Printed in the United States
By Bookmasters